BLACK LIGHT: WORTHY

STELLA MOORE

©2021 by Black Collar Press and the authors.
All rights reserved.

No part of the book may be reproduced or transmitted in any form or by any means, electronic or mechanical, including photocopying, recording, or by any information storage and retrieval system, without permission in writing from the publisher.

Black Light: Worthy
by Stella Moore

Published by Black Collar Press
Don't miss a release! Sign-up for our newsletter here!

EBook ISBN: **978-1-947559-58-5**
Print ISBN: **978-1-947559-59-2**

Cover Art by Eris Adderly, http://erisadderly.com/

This book is a work of fiction. Names, characters, places, and incidents either are products of the author's imagination or are used fictitiously. Any resemblance to actual persons, living or dead, events, or locales is entirely coincidental.

BLURB

Handling bossy, demanding millionaires is just a regular Tuesday for Katherine Callahan, one of the most in-demand financial planners on the East Coast. Austin Barrick may be baseball's biggest star, but she figures there's not much difference between him and the rest of her clients.

That is, until he walks into her office, flashes his million-dollar smile, and asks her to dinner. Before they even leave her office, Kit discovers a thrilling dominance beneath Austin's easygoing charm, and finds herself thrust into a dark, fascinating world of pleasure and pain.

But in a society that values beauty above all else, she's learned one simple, brutal truth: Fat girls don't deserve happily ever after. Can Austin's sweet, steady dominance help her embrace a life she's only dreamed of? Or will she let a culture of shame keep her in the shadows?

CHAPTER 1

AUSTIN

Favoring his right knee, Austin Barrick limped his way through the crowded locker room and lowered himself onto a bench with a grunt. It was the only verbal acknowledgment of the pain shooting up his leg he allowed himself.

He was getting too fucking old for this.

At thirty-two, most people were just getting into the swing of things, career-wise. But he was racing head-on towards retirement and he knew it. What was worse, the rest of the team knew it, too. It was impossible to miss the sideways glances of the rookies and the sympathetic smiles of the more seasoned players.

A pair of naked, hairy legs appeared in his peripheral vision as he worked at a knot in his neck. "You okay there, Barrick?"

Tony Fucking Torres. The Washington Hawks' newest shining star. Brand new recruit from the University of Michigan, and still young enough for a smattering of pimples along his otherwise perfect jawline.

And, although nobody had come right out and said it yet, Austin's replacement.

Without looking up, Austin waved a hand, dismissing his young protegé. "I'm fine. Just a headache from listening to you hens clucking all damn day."

Grumbling and laughter filled the locker room, but the legs didn't move. "You sure you're okay, man? I thought I saw you limping."

Finally lifting his head, Austin peeled his lip back in a sneer. "Sorry to disappoint you, kid, but you ain't getting rid of me that easy."

Ignoring the twinge of guilt at the hurt on the younger man's face, Austin made his way to the shower, forcing himself not to limp, which meant his knee was screaming at him by the time he'd showered and dressed for his meeting with the new financial planner his agent had pushed on him. Apparently, this chick was the cream of the crop when it came to investments and shit, and it had taken some serious fast-talking to get her to even accept a meeting with him.

She was obviously not a baseball fan if she wasn't falling all over herself for a chance at Austin Barrick's finances.

Most of the team had dispersed by the time he made it to the parking lot, so he allowed himself a slight limp on his way to the monstrous SUV that had been his first big purchase when he'd signed with Chicago ten years ago. He could afford a dozen just like it every year with his current contract with the Hawks, but he was loath to part with his first.

The money chick's office was nearly an hour drive with traffic, and his mood hadn't improved any by the time he found a spot at the far end of the parking lot and limped his way to the shiny glass building. "At least there's a fucking elevator," he mumbled to himself as he punched the button for the tenth floor.

The elevator in question zipped up to the requested floor

almost silently, and the doors opened to reveal a wall of windows with *Katherine Callahan, CFP* printed on the spotless glass entrance.

A severe-looking older woman with her silver hair clipped back in a bun from which not even a single hair dared to escape, glanced up from her computer when he opened the door. "Do you have an appointment?"

"Yeah. Barrick."

The woman's gaze flicked downward, and her unpainted lips came together in a time-honored expression of disapproval. "You are fifteen minutes late, Mr. Barrick."

"Sorry about that," he glanced at the name plate on the sleek metal desk, "Donna." Despite his irritation at not just being late but being called on it, he flashed her a grin. "Traffic, parking, all that jazz."

"Ms. Callahan has a very tight schedule."

Gritting his teeth behind the smile, he nodded. "Understood. Won't happen again."

With a noncommittal hum, Donna stood and rounded the desk. "Follow me." Sturdy, practical heels clicking on the tile, she led him down a short hallway to a corner office and gave a quick, brisk knock on the closed door.

"Mr. Barrick is here for your four o'clock," she announced, opening the door to a huge, sparsely decorated office.

Austin followed her inside, expecting a similar version of the gatekeeper. But the woman behind the desk nearly had his tongue rolling out of his mouth when she stood to greet him.

Hair so dark it was nearly black fell in sleek waves over her shoulders, brushing against the swell of breasts she'd tried to hide behind the perfectly cut business suit. Lush, full curves instantly filled his imagination with visions of her bent over the polished wood of her desk, welts covering her gorgeously round ass as he gripped her hips and pounded into her.

Giving himself a mental shake, he stepped forward and

stretched out a hand. "You can call me Austin. Katherine, right?"

Pale pink lips turned up in a polite, professional smile and almond-shaped eyes met his as she accepted the handshake, but there was no warmth in the brown depths. "Pleased to meet you, Mr. Barrick." She held out her unoccupied hand and the efficient Donna placed a thick, white folder in her palm. "Thank you, Donna. Would you bring us some ice water, please?"

Jesus, the woman was as cold as the refreshments she'd just requested. "Thanks, Katie." It was petty and rude, but the snotty way she'd called him *Mr. Barrick* had gotten under his skin.

If she'd been ice before, her voice turned glacial at the nickname. "Katherine or Ms. Callahan, please."

What did it say about him that the clipped, cold tones just made him all the more eager to see her splayed out on her desk for him? He imagined miss prim and proper Katherine Callahan would be utterly embarrassed by the images running rampant through his imagination. Then again, maybe a little humiliation was just what she needed. In his experience, it went a long way toward helping stubborn little subbies learn their place.

Even if she wasn't a submissive—and wouldn't that be a damn shame—he couldn't seem to keep his brain from conjuring up an image of what she would look like with an embarrassed flush covering her entire luscious body. His foul mood vanished as his imagination went into overdrive.

"Katherine," he conceded, pushing aside his bad mood and turning up the charm with an apologetic smile.

"Thank you." Taking her seat, she opened the file Donna had handed her. When she gestured to the guest chair, he sat with a silent prayer of gratitude for the opportunity to stretch out his knee.

"I had your agent send over your current portfolio," she began, her eyes glancing down to scan the contents of the file he had a sneaking suspicion she already knew by heart. It was a power play, meant to let him know she didn't consider him any more important than any other client. And he couldn't help but respect the hell out of it. No doubt she had more than one client who needed to be knocked down a peg or two on a regular basis.

"And?" he prompted when she paused.

"It's not bad." Flipping the file closed, she looked up, her lips curving up in a fierce, damn near predatory smile. "I can do a hell of a lot better."

"You don't need to sell yourself to me. Mary said you're the best, so you're the best."

"I appreciate the vote of confidence. Would you like me to explain what I have in mind?"

"Sure." Not that he'd understand a single word of it. He just liked listening to her talk. She had a voice like good whiskey—smooth with a hint of a bite.

"To start with, you're a little stock-heavy at the moment. Which was a good move at the beginning of your career, when you could reasonably expect a steady income for a while. You've had decent growth the past few years, so now I'd like to look at preserving your current capital."

The implication pricked at his pride—and his temper. "I'm not retiring."

She raised a single, perfectly sculpted eyebrow in his direction. "I didn't say you were. But you will be, and relatively soon, all things considered."

Leaning forward in his chair, he jabbed a finger at her from across the desk. "I've got a good five years left in me, at least." Maybe. If his goddamn knee would cooperate.

"Which, in the world of financial planning, is relatively soon," she replied without so much as blinking. Turning to face him more fully, she folded her hands on top of the file and pinned him with that ice-queen stare. "You may be a big shot out on the field, Mr. Barrick. But in here, I'm the all-star. You can either listen to me and I can give you a nice, comfortable life once you are inevitably forced out, or you can take your money and your business elsewhere. I have neither the time nor the patience for clients who throw hissy fits in my office."

If she hadn't had a damn good point, he might have walked out then and there. But she was right, and he was wrong, and he was man enough to admit it. Leaning back again, he flashed her another smile. "Fair enough. In here, you're the boss." Points to her for not so much as blinking when he deliberately emphasized *in here*.

Instead, she just inclined her head and gave him a polite, "Thank you."

Donna chose that moment to return with a small silver tray laden with a pale blue pitcher and two matching glasses. She silently poured water into one of the glasses and placed it on a coaster in front of her boss before offering him the second glass.

"Thanks," he said, toasting her with the tumbler. Apparently, the two women were cut from the same cloth as Donna barely acknowledged him.

"Do you need anything else, Ms. Callahan?"

"No, that's all for now. Thank you, Donna." Katherine took a sip of her water as her assistant slipped silently out of the room. "All right, Mr. Barrick. Where were we?"

The desire to see if he could ruffle her won out over any desire to hear more about stocks and bonds and whatever the hell else she wanted to talk about. "You were about to agree to have dinner with me."

It worked. For the first time since he'd walked into the office, she looked flustered. Pink crept up her neck from under the collar of her stuffy business suit and her eyes widened slightly. "I'm sorry?"

"What are you apologizing for?"

The color on her neck rushed to her cheeks. "I wasn't. You —" She took a deep, deliberate breath, and he tried valiantly to ignore the way her breasts rose and fell beneath the curve-hugging blazer. "We never discussed meeting outside the office, Mr. Barrick."

"Then let's discuss it now. What are you doing tonight, Katherine?"

"Working."

"Come on. Even a woman as dedicated as you has to eat sometime, right?"

"I—well—yes. I suppose." Little wrinkles of confusion appeared along her brow, delighting him in a perverse way. Throwing her off balance was the most fun he'd had with a woman in… hell, he couldn't remember how long, in or out of the bedroom. Even the eager submissives at Black Light hadn't captivated him the way she had in the past few minutes.

"Then eat with me. We'll go wherever you want. We can talk money or whatever makes you happy that isn't turning great big piles of cash into bigger piles of cash."

A polite smile, bordering on patronizing, curved her lips. "I'm not that interesting, Mr. Barrick. I'm afraid you'll be bored to death."

"I highly doubt that. Dinner with a smart, gorgeous woman? What could possibly be boring about that?"

She pulled her bottom lip between her teeth, worrying at her perfectly applied lipstick before she caved with a quiet sigh. "All right. But just dinner, and just this once. I don't date clients, Mr. Barrick. It's—"

"Taboo?" he interrupted with an exaggerated wiggle of his eyebrows. "Sexy?"

"Highly inappropriate."

Grinning, he placed his elbows on the desk and leaned in. "Baby, you're about to find out that highly inappropriate is my favorite way to do things."

"I hate to tell you this, Mr. Barrick, but that isn't exactly a state secret."

The dry, sarcastic retort had him blinking in surprise before he snorted out a laugh. "See? Gorgeous, smart, *and* funny. You just keep adding to the deal here, Ms. Callahan. I don't see myself getting bored any time soon."

"If you say so. I have some things to wrap up here and then I'll meet you downstairs."

"Works for me. And you can figure out where you'd like to eat, too. I'm up for," he deliberately let his gaze drift from her face to her spectacular breasts and back up again, "anything."

Snagging one of her business cards from the display on her desk, he scribbled his number on the back. "Text me when you're ready and I'll meet you out front."

CHAPTER 2

KATHERINE

Staring at the scrawled numbers in front of her, Kit tried to make sense of what had just happened.

Austin Barrick, starting shortstop for D.C.'s Major League baseball team, the Washington Hawks, had just asked her out. On a date.

Or maybe not.

Definitely not. Shaking her head at her own ridiculousness, Kit flipped the card over and turned back to her computer. She made a few notes in Austin's—*Mr. Barrick's*—file to follow up on some questions she had for him, then moved on to her next client. But her gaze kept drifting back to the business card.

It couldn't be a date. Pro athletes dated supermodels and actresses, not overweight financial planners who worked too much and preferred curling up on the couch with a book and a glass of wine to partying downtown.

Definitely not a date.

Picking up the card again, she stared at the number printed on the back in his surprisingly neat handwriting. If not a date, then what? He wanted to discuss his portfolio over dinner? It seemed unlikely, since he hadn't seemed all that interested in what she'd had to say while they were sitting in her office. He didn't seem like the type to spend hours discussing how she planned to—what was it he'd said? Turn his piles of cash into bigger piles of cash. Some clients wanted to know every nitty gritty detail of their financial plans. Others were content to throw everything at her and never talk again until their quarterly update. Mr. Barrick struck her as the latter rather than the former.

Which brought her back to square one. Was this a date? Or something else altogether?

What seemed far more likely was she'd text him and he'd never respond. It wasn't even out of the realm of possibility that this was some elaborate prank and he'd be sitting around with his baseball buddies, talking shit about the dumb, fat bitch who thought she'd had a chance with Austin Barrick.

It certainly wouldn't be the first time she'd lived through some variation of that scenario.

Ignoring the rolling of her stomach, she pushed away the memories and refocused on the computer screen in front of her. Mr. Barrick had been her last official appointment of the day, but she had at least another hour of work before she'd feel comfortable calling it quits. She'd happily stay longer, but Donna refused to leave until she did, and it wasn't right to keep her faithful admin tied to the front desk any longer than necessary.

Thankfully, she was able to lose herself in the numbers and figures on her screen for a while. The Garrison account needed some attention. Her bright, irritatingly young millionaire entrepreneur wasn't seeing the growth she'd promised him, and she couldn't quite figure out why.

An hour later, she finally resurfaced, satisfied she'd done what she could for now. Raising her arms over her head, she stretched out the tense muscles in her back and her gaze landed on the business card she'd shoved to the side earlier.

There was still absolutely no way this was a date. But if it was a prank, why the hell should she let him think he'd gotten one over on her? Men like him—hot, successful, entitled—needed someone to bring them back down to reality on occasion. And as far as she was concerned, she was just the woman for the job.

She'd snatched up the card and punched the numbers into the phone on her desk before she'd thought better of it. After two rings, her finger was hovering over the End Call button, but before she could press it, a familiar deep voice answered. "Barrick."

Did he have to sound so sexy? Her mind blanked for a moment before she remembered why she was calling. Straightening her shoulders, she braced for battle. "Mr. Barrick? This is Katherine Callahan."

"Well, hey there, Ms. Callahan." Her name was a low purr, and she pressed her thighs together in a vain effort to ignore the sudden ache between them. "Have you decided where you want to eat yet?"

"No. Mr. Barrick, I..."

"That's all right. I'm sure we'll think of something."

The laughter in his voice spurred her into action. "Listen to me, Austin Barrick. If you think for one second I'm going to let you use me as the evening entertainment for you and your baseball buddies, you've got another thing coming. I'm sure you all find it hilarious to trick a woman into thinking you're interested in her, but I can assure you, I do not find it the least bit amusing."

There was a beat of silence before he replied. "What the hell are you talking about, woman?"

Red colored her vision, and she squeezed the handset so tight it was a wonder it didn't snap in half. "I'm talking about rich, entitled assholes who think it's funny to use the fat, gullible, desperate girl to get their jollies. Who think the world owes them something just because they can hit a ball with a stick and run around in circles. *That's* what the hell I'm talking about, Mr. Barrick."

"Are you finished, Katherine?"

There was a darkness in his voice that had her heart slamming into her ribcage. "Yes."

"Good. Let's get something straight. I have every intention of using you for my own entertainment, but not in the way you seem to think. I still haven't quite figured out what exactly you've cooked up in that brain of yours, but I don't think it's complimentary of either yourself or me. And the entertainment I have in mind damn sure won't be shared with any of my—what did you call them? Right." His bark of laughter lacked any trace of humor. "My baseball buddies."

During his scolding—because there was no doubt in her mind it was exactly that—heat infused her cheeks. Was he trying to tell her... no. There was no way a man like Austin Barrick was interested in her *that way*.

"Also," he continued, his voice taking on even more of an edge. "I may be a rich, entitled asshole, but I've never hurt a woman just for the hell of it. Not emotionally, anyway."

"Well, I..."

"I'm not finished," he snapped. "The next time I hear you put yourself down like that, you won't sit right the rest of the night. I don't put up with that kind of talk."

"What?" she squeaked. It was like a line out of the books she kept hidden on her Kindle, but he couldn't possibly be talking about *that*.

"I didn't stutter." The statement came from her doorway, not the phone speaker, and she dropped the handset with a shriek.

Behind him, a frantic-looking Donna peeked over his

shoulder. "I tried to stop him, but he wouldn't listen. Do you want me to call security?"

Calling for help would be the smart thing to do, judging by the thunderous look on her intruder's face, but she shook her head. "No. And you can go home, Donna. I'll be fine."

Donna's expression turned mutinous. "Kit, I am not leaving you alone with this man."

Again, that would be the smart, rational thing to do. Despite his prominence in the sports world, she didn't know a damn thing about him as a person. He wouldn't be the first pro athlete with a hidden dark side. And hadn't she caught a glimpse of that darkness in him just now?

Still, something in him pulled at her. As stupid as it may have been, she sent Donna what she hoped was a reassuring smile. "Mr. Barrick and I have dinner plans."

"Oh." Frowning, Donna looked from her to Austin and back again. "Well. If you're sure."

"I'm sure. I'll see you in the morning."

Still looking uncertain, Donna backed away and turned to head down the hall.

Taking a step forward, Austin let the door to the office swing shut behind him as he slowly stalked his way across the room. "Care to explain that phone call?"

"Not particularly," she replied with as much dignity as she could muster while facing off with the man who she was fairly certain had just threatened to spank her. Dignity was particularly hard to hold on to when she could feel her arousal soaking through her sensible panties. Did he somehow know that he'd just tapped into one of her most secret, unspoken fantasies?

"It wasn't really a request, Katherine."

"You're very bossy, you know that?"

One of his eyebrows lifted and her core quivered in

response. "I do. Stop trying to change the subject. What the hell was that all about?"

Now that the heat of the moment had passed, embarrassment was creeping in. "I apologize. It was uncalled for."

With a low, throaty growl, he reached across the desk and captured her chin between his fingers, forcing her to look straight at him. "It was absolutely uncalled for, little girl. But I would still like an explanation. Now."

Little girl. The phrase shot an arrow of heat straight to her core even as it pissed her off. Gathering her indignation around her, she jerked her chin from his grasp and sent him her best icy glare. "I don't owe you anything, Mr. Barrick."

"You didn't just talk shit about yourself, I'm pretty sure you insulted me in the process. I think I deserve to know why. Tell me about the phone call."

"Fine!" Cheeks flaming, heart pounding, she straightened in her chair and lifted her chin. "I assumed you were playing a prank on me. That I would text you to let you know I was ready for dinner and you'd already be home, sitting around with your buddies, laughing about the stupid, naïve, fat girl who thought you were serious about taking her to dinner."

Shock replaced the anger in his expression. "That's some imagination you have, Ms. Callahan."

"I'm afraid I can't take credit for an idea that wasn't mine, Mr. Barrick."

"You really think that's what I meant? What the hell do you think I'm doing here, then?"

Fighting to save even a scrap of dignity, she tilted her chin up, daring him to pass judgement on her actions. "Obviously I misjudged the situation based on previous unpleasant interactions with the opposite sex."

She saw the moment it clicked with him. The stormy blue of his eyes cleared, then clouded again with grief. "That actually happened to you?"

With a nonchalance she didn't feel, she lifted a shoulder. "It happens to women all the time. Especially…"

"Katherine," he interrupted, his voice dropping to that threatening growl she found so inexplicably alluring, "I am a big believer in consent. But I swear, if I hear the word 'fat' out of your mouth again this evening, I am going to be forced to break every rule in the book and wear your ass out, with or without your permission."

Ignoring the flare of desire his words inspired, she narrowed her eyes at him. "You can't just go around threatening to beat people, Mr. Barrick."

"I generally don't. I'm making an exception for you."

"But why?" The question burst out of her, like some living creature she was no longer able to keep in its cage. "Why me?"

"You're gorgeous and smart with a spine of steel. Why the hell wouldn't I be interested?"

Rolling her eyes, she snorted. "I didn't realize they let blind men play professional sports."

"Only as umpires," he shot back with a smirk. "Seeing as how I'm not an ump, I'm obviously not blind. And I'm also not leaving this office until you agree to go to dinner with me. For real, this time."

"You're incredibly hardheaded."

"Right back atcha, kitten."

Oh, crap. She'd always been a sucker for a sweet, cutesy nickname. "Kitten?"

"Kit, kitten. Seemed to fit." The smirk shifted to full-on grin. During their meeting, she'd noticed he turned it on whenever he wanted to charm his way out of something.

It pissed her off how well it worked.

"Mr. Barrick, I'm not sure this is a good idea given our professional relationship." It was a last-ditch effort and they both knew it.

"If it becomes an issue, I'll find a new money guru."

"They won't be as good as me."

The blue of his eyes heated, and she had to fight the urge to launch herself across her desk straight at him. "I have no doubt you are the ace, kitten."

Feeling like she might combust if she sat there a second longer, she popped out of her chair and pulled her purse from the bottom drawer of her desk. "One dinner, Mr. Barrick. That's all I'm agreeing to."

"I'll take it, for now."

She packed up her laptop and followed him out of the office, making sure to lock up behind them. When the elevator doors opened to the lobby, Austin slipped an arm around her waist as if they'd been dating for months instead of having just met that afternoon.

"Decide what you want for dinner yet, kitten?"

"I want you to stop being so familiar, Mr. Barrick."

Laughter rumbled in his chest and he turned his head to whisper in her ear. "I've already threatened to spank your ass twice tonight. I think we're well past familiar, don't you?"

"I don't care where we eat," she responded, ignoring the reference to his wildly inappropriate threats.

"What kind of food do you like? Give me something to work with, kitten."

"Do I look like the kind of woman who's at all picky about food?"

Stopping beside an older, black SUV, Austin moved his grip to her arm and spun her to face him. There was no mistaking the anger in his expression, and her bottom clenched as if it were anticipating the spanking he kept promising her.

"That sounds dangerously like putting yourself down, Katherine."

"I suppose," she managed past the sudden tightness closing off her airway.

"I've got half a mind to skip dinner altogether, take you to my place, and make good on my promise to turn that gorgeous ass of yours red."

"You wouldn't."

Regret flashed in his eyes, and he loosened his hold on her arm. "You're right. Not until you agree to it. But once you do, baby, that ass is all mine."

CHAPTER 3

KATHERINE

"Why on earth would I agree to that?"

The corners of his lips curved up. "For starters, because it turns you on."

"It absolutely does not." The heat she could feel rising to her cheeks belied her words, and she prayed he couldn't see her blush. Austin Barrick was proving to be the worst kind of temptation, all wrapped up in a sexy, funny, irresistible package.

"Liar," he shot back good-naturedly. "Just think about it. For now, where do you want to go for dinner?"

"Wherever you'd like to eat is fine with me." Another lie. She'd been looking forward to the juicy burger she'd promised herself to celebrate landing Austin Barrick as a client. Not that she would ever, in a million years, tell him that. His ego was already more than big enough.

Again, he raised an eyebrow at her, and something inside of her trembled at the implicit threat. "Is that 'wherever' as in, you really don't care? Or is that 'wherever' as in you have something specific in mind and you're going to make me play the guessing game until I figure out where that specific place is?"

She might not have been a supermodel, but Katherine Callahan had been on her fair share of dates. And not a single one of the men she'd been with had ever called her out like that, not even after months of dating.

It was embarrassing. And also hot as sin.

"Probably the second one," she admitted sheepishly.

"Then I'd prefer for you to save us both the time and just tell me what you want. I told you that you could choose, and I meant it. Now, where would you like to go for dinner, Katherine?"

Her tongue seemed to swell to twice its usual size and she could feel the blush covering her entire body. Why was it so hard to just admit what she wanted? At work, she had no problem demanding what she needed to get the job done, but out here, in the dating world, it felt damn near impossible to just tell a man she wanted a freaking cheeseburger.

"Whatever you want is fine," she repeated, trying to ignore the people trickling out of the building, sending curious glances their way.

The half-smile on his lips moved into a smirk. "Whatever I want. You're sure about that?"

"Um, yes." But something in the way he'd asked the question made her think they weren't talking about dinner anymore.

"What I want, kitten, is you. You, under me, screaming my name." He took a step forward and she backed up straight into the side of his SUV. Leaning in, he caged her in with his hands on either side of her head. "You, tied to my bed, so I can teach you how I feel about lying and self-deprecating comments. You, limp and boneless, after I make you come so many times you forget your own name. And maybe some Chinese takeout once we've gone a couple rounds."

Her heartbeat roared in her ears and for a terrifying moment, she worried she might pass out right there in the parking lot. "Burgers," she blurted out.

"There." A bright, triumphant grin split his face. "Was that so hard?"

She shoved at his chest, but he barely moved. "Are you going to stand here and gloat or take me to dinner, Mr. Barrick?"

Still grinning, he opened the passenger door and helped her into the SUV. She had about five seconds to take a couple deep breaths and get her wildly beating heart under control while he walked around to the driver's side.

Not that it did any good since her heart rate kicked back into overdrive the second he opened the door. She was really going on a date with Austin Barrick. The best shortstop Major League Baseball had seen in nearly thirty years.

As if that wasn't overwhelming enough, he'd singlehandedly fulfilled some of her wildest fantasies by going all bossy alpha male on her. She was half convinced she'd have a wet spot on her skirt by the time she got out of the car again. Which was a damn shame since this was a one-time deal. Getting romantically tangled with a client was stupid, and Kit prided herself on never being stupid.

With another flash of his annoyingly charming smile, they were backing out of the parking lot and headed somewhere. She assumed it would be a place where they served cheeseburgers. Her stomach growled at the thought. The wrap she'd ordered at lunch from the deli down the street seemed like ages ago at this point.

To his credit, Austin didn't mention her demanding tummy, if he noticed it at all. When he turned onto the highway, she groaned at the sea of taillights.

"Gotta love rush hour," he quipped, far more cheerfully than the situation seemed to warrant.

"I forgot how bad it could be around here."

Glancing over at her, the corners of his lips dipped down in a frown. "Do you not usually work in the office?"

"Oh, I do. I just usually come in early enough and stay late enough to miss the worst of it."

"Jesus, woman. How many hours do you work?"

Suddenly feeling defensive, she tilted her chin up at him. "As many as I need to."

"I see."

Something about his tone told her he did see, far more clearly than she wanted him to. "Are you going to tell me you don't push yourself as hard as you need, as much as you need? You don't get a reputation like yours without busting your ass, Mr. Barrick, regardless of how much talent you may have."

That devastating grin flashed again as they inched forward. "You follow baseball, Kit?"

Shit. She'd tipped her hand. Trying to play it cool, she shrugged and glanced away like her entire body wasn't on alert, waiting for some signal he was laughing at her. "My dad does, religiously. We went to a game every Saturday during the season when I was growing up. Baltimore will always have his heart, but if there's a game on, he'll watch it."

"I could grab a ball from my bag and sign it for him, if you want."

"Really?" Warmth spread in her chest at the unexpected offer. "He'd get a kick out of that. Thanks."

"No problem. What about your mom? She a fan, or is it more of a daddy-daughter thing?"

The stab of grief was familiar, but somehow it had never lessened over the years. "My mom passed when I was in high school. She was never really into sports, but she'd always make us snacks when a game was on."

"I'm sorry, kitten."

"It was a long time ago." And it was yesterday. Grief, she'd learned, was funny that way.

"Still sucks."

The simple acknowledgement somehow soothed her more than the words of shock and pity she'd been fending off the last sixteen years. "It does. Were your parents fans before you started playing?"

"Hell, no," he said with a deep, rumbling laugh. "The biggest disappointment of their life has been my utter lack of interest in football. But my sister made up for it by dating and marrying our high school quarterback, who had a pretty decent college career. Wrecked his shoulder his senior year though, so he never made it pro."

"How awful for him."

"Yeah. But he got the girl and two of his own little quarterbacks out of the deal. He seems happy enough, which I don't really get because I know what living with my sister is like."

Adoration colored his tone, and she couldn't help but grin. "I've heard younger siblings can be a trial."

"Older sister. And bossy, to boot. What about you? Any other little Callahans running around?"

"Just me, thankfully. I'm a spoiled only child and I wouldn't have it any other way."

"Sounds like someone doesn't like to share her toys."

How could he take such an innocent statement and make it sound so outrageously dirty? Her breath seemed to back up in her lungs, and for a moment, she was rendered speechless. "I suppose not," she managed to squeak out.

From the corner of her eye, she saw his lips twitch, giving her the distinct impression he was laughing at her. But before she could muster up any outrage, he was maneuvering his vehicle off the road and into the parking lot of an incredibly tacky fifties-esque diner.

"This is where you're taking me to dinner?"

"You asked for burgers," he reminded her. "And it's either this or we wait another two hours in traffic for something better."

"Fair enough," she conceded with amusement. Nothing about this day had gone the way she'd anticipated from the moment he'd walked into her office. Why should his choice of restaurant be any different?

"Wait there. I'll come let you out."

Charmed, more so than she wanted to be, she did as she was told and stayed put until he opened the door and held out a hand. Slipping her hand into his, she let him help her down from the SUV. They rounded the back of the vehicle where he popped open the trunk and dug a well-used ball from his bag, along with a sharpie.

"What's your dad's name?"

"Charles. Charlie, put Charlie. He'll get a kick out of it."

"To Charlie. Thanks for raising such a smokin' hot daughter."

"Austin! You can't put that on there!"

"I didn't. But it got you to stop calling me 'Mr. Barrick'." Capping the pen, he handed over the ball, which actually read *To Charlie - Baltimore sucks, root for a real team this year* followed by what she assumed was his signature. She shot him a glare and dropped the ball in her purse.

"Thanks. He'll love it."

"Any time." Taking her hand again, he led the way across the parking lot while she silently lectured herself about getting her hopes up.

It's just dinner. Nothing more. He didn't actually mean any of those things he said, he was just trying to get a rise out of you.

Well, congratulations to him, if that had been his goal, though she was determined not to let him see exactly how much he affected her. Pushing aside her inner turmoil, she focused her attention on him, frowning slightly when she noticed he was favoring his right leg.

"Are you okay? You look like you're limping."

His easy smile morphed into a scowl. "I'm fine," he bit out, his tone making it clear he wasn't happy she'd asked.

There was more bite to his response than the simple question warranted, and it spiked her own temper in response. Yanking her hand from his, she stopped in the middle of the parking lot and glared at him. "There's no need to snap at me."

Scowl still firmly in place, he turned and leveled his own glare at her. "What are you doing, Katherine?"

Despite the obvious warning in his tone and the responding nervous flutter in her stomach, she simply raised an eyebrow. Two could play that game as far as she was concerned. "I'm not going anywhere with you until you apologize. All I did was ask if you were all right, because you are obviously in pain. Biting my head off was uncalled for."

The hard lines of his stupidly handsome face smoothed out and he sighed. "You're right. I'm sorry I snapped at you."

"Apology accepted." Allowing him to take her hand again, she fell in step with him. "Are you going to tell me what that was about?" she prodded when he didn't offer up an explanation for his overreaction.

"Just a rough practice. Knee's been giving me a little trouble. Nothing major."

There was an undercurrent there, one that warned her to tread carefully. As his financial advisor, she needed to know if he was looking at retirement sooner than the five years he'd so forcefully quoted in her office. But they weren't in her office, and she wasn't sure how to broach the topic without upsetting him.

Deciding to let it drop for the time being, she followed him into the crowded restaurant. He gave their name to the harried-looking hostess before pulling Kit into a corner and shifting so he was shielding her from the crowd with his lean, hard body.

"I really am sorry I snapped at you back there," he murmured, taking one of her hands in his and running his thumb across her knuckles.

A not-at-all-unpleasant shiver ran down her spine. Jesus, the man was potent. "It's fine."

"It's not. I had a shitty day, but that's no excuse to be an asshole."

"No, it's not." Feeling bold, she smirked up at him and lowered her voice. "Does that mean I get to spank you?"

"Hell, no." Laughing, he lifted her hand to his lips, his ice blue eyes blazing as he grazed the back of her hand with his lips. "You're a fascinating woman, Katherine."

"I bet you say that to all the ladies."

"Nope. Just you."

Before her brain could formulate a response, his name was called and they were led to a corner booth covered in red vinyl. Old records decorated the walls and there was what looked to be a vintage, working jukebox in the corner. All in all, the place was charming in an unexpected way, not unlike the man who'd brought her here.

Sliding in first, she looked up in surprise when he nudged her further into the circular booth rather than taking the spot across from her. And when he settled in beside her, with his arm draped around her shoulder as if it simply belonged there, her skin felt like she'd been lit on fire.

"Delicious," he murmured, and she was certain she would spontaneously combust right there at the table.

"What?"

"The menu." Amusement dancing in his eyes, he held up the single laminated sheet they'd been given. "Everything looks delicious."

Right. And she was the queen of fucking England.

Narrowing her eyes, she studied his seemingly open, honest face. This obviously wasn't a prank, or if it was, it was an incredibly elaborate one. For the life of her, though, she just couldn't figure out his angle.

Well, no better way to find out than to ask, right?

"What exactly are you angling for here, Mr. Barrick?"

That dark promise she'd heard in his voice earlier flashed in his eyes. "What do you mean?"

"I've looked at this from every possible angle and I can't figure out what a baseball star could possibly want with a—with me," she corrected herself hastily when he tensed, "when he could have his pick of women."

"Why wouldn't I be interested in you?"

"You're being deliberately obtuse, Mr. Barrick."

His lips tilted up in what she could only describe as a predatory smile. "All right. You want to know what I'm angling for, kitten?"

"Yes?" She'd meant to sound confident, assured, but the word sounded like a question even to her own ears.

Leaning in, he dropped his voice to a low, sexy purr. "Then let me show you."

CHAPTER 4

KATHERINE

Holy shit. Holy shit. Holy shit. Those two words raced through her mind over and over. "Show me what?"

Pulling back a bit, he studied her, his intense gaze making it hard to not squirm in her seat. "Exactly what I want from you."

"Couldn't you just tell me?"

"I could, but this is more fun. What do you say, kitten?"

It wasn't smart to agree to anything without knowing the terms first. But a part of her she barely recognized was urging her to throw caution to the wind and follow him wherever he wanted to lead. "Um, okay. I guess."

"If you want to stop, just say so. We're just having some fun."

Oh, God. What the hell was she getting herself into here? "Okay."

"Good girl." His voice lowered again, and she swore she could feel the rumble of those words on her clit. "Go to the bathroom and take off your pantyhose and panties, then come back to the table."

"What?" she squeaked in return, glancing around to ensure nobody had overheard his outrageous request.

"Do you not understand what I asked you to do?"

"No!" The man had basically just told her to strip half naked in the bathroom of some cheesy diner. So, no, she absolutely did not understand.

"What part didn't you get?"

"I don't understand why you'd ask me to... you know. Do what you said."

The corners of his lips kicked up in obvious amusement. "I didn't ask if you understood *why* I asked you to do it. I asked if you understood *what* I asked you to do."

"Well, yes, I understood the instructions. But, I—"

"Then that's all you need. Now, go. I don't like to repeat myself." When she didn't move, he raised an eyebrow in a way that made her want to simultaneously punch him in his gorgeous face and throw herself at his feet. "Waiting for an invitation, Katherine?"

"I just want to know why, then I'll go." Maybe.

"You'll find out when you come back to the table." His expression softened. "Unless you want to stop. Just say the word and I'll drop it."

Stopping would be the smart move. Common sense and decency practically demanded she get up and walk out without a second thought. She barely knew him, and he'd given her no reason to trust him enough to follow his outrageous orders. And yet... "What if I don't want to stop?"

"Then I expect you to do as you're told. Little girls who don't listen don't get their rewards."

"Reward?"

"Mmhmm. You'll see — if you're a good girl."

"Fine." Huffing out a breath, she grabbed her purse and scooted out of the booth. Although she knew it was unlikely, it felt as though every eye in the diner was following her to the bathroom. Would they know? Would anyone notice when she emerged without her pantyhose?

Again, unlikely. But the idea that someone might notice, that some stranger might realize she was completely naked under her conservative pencil skirt, sent butterflies dancing in her belly. Normally, she didn't care to be noticed. In her experience, it was rarely a good thing when people paid too much attention to the big girl.

Austin was paying attention, though. And so far, he'd shown no signs of being disgusted by her. Riding high on that knowledge, she slipped into a stall and hung her purse on the hook. With a deep, bracing breath, she hooked her thumbs in her pantyhose and wiggled them down her hips. Carefully balancing on one high heel, she slipped her foot from inside the stocking before slipping it back into her shoe, then repeating on the other side.

Already she felt deliciously naughty. Not once in her adult life had she gone to work without pantyhose, unless she was wearing pants. The satin lining of her skirt brushed against her skin, a sensation she'd felt hundreds of times before, but now it felt positively sinful.

With her pantyhose stashed in her purse, she reached for her panties and pulled them down over her thighs before she could change her mind. Letting the scrap of satin drop to the floor, she stepped out of them and snatched them up to shove them in her purse.

She hadn't even left the stall and already her cheeks were flaming. Closing her eyes, she took several deep breaths until she felt the heat fade. If she walked out of there looking like a tomato, people would definitely be staring, and not in the way that gave her those butterflies she'd gotten during her walk to the bathroom.

Once she felt passably under control, she opened the door and stepped out. Studying her reflection in the mirror as she washed her hands, she looked for any outward sign that she was engaged in some weird sex thing in the middle of a diner.

When her careful perusal of her reflection didn't turn up anything untoward, she dried her hands and headed for the bathroom door.

The noise hit her first. Had it been this loud just a few minutes ago? Or was she more aware of her surroundings now that she was so scandalously clad?

Then she saw him, watching her from their table, his hungry gaze glued to her, and everything else faded away. When had a man ever looked at her like that, like she was his last meal and he'd worn out his welcome on death row?

Never that she could remember. She wasn't the type of woman men looked at with need burning in their eyes, a fact she was reminded of every time she stood in line at the grocery store and came face to face with rows of women with lush breasts and flat tummies on the cover of every magazine. Or when she tried to find something—anything—in her size in an actual store without being relegated to the "fat girl" section or forced to shop online. And that was just the passive, day to day crap she'd learned to live with. It didn't even begin to take into account the active bullying she'd endured. She'd heard mooing from more people than cows in her lifetime.

No, most men didn't want women like her. They lowered themselves to fuck the fat girls on occasion, but they didn't crave them. Nobody wanted squishy thighs and round tummies in their beds if they had another option.

But Austin had other options. Hundreds of them. And unless she was way off base, he wanted her. She just had no fucking clue what to do about it. Sliding back onto the bench beside him, she tried not to freak out about being so completely and utterly out of her depth.

"Good girl," he murmured when she was settled in beside him once again.

"You don't even know if I did it."

"Yes, I do. You weren't walking that stiffly on your way to the bathroom." Brushing her hair back from her face, he leaned in, his breath tickling her ear as he whispered. "Tell me, kitten, does it turn you on? The idea that everyone in this diner might discover that you're naked under that sensible skirt?"

"No." But even she wasn't convinced.

"Little liar," he said with a low, rumbling laugh. "You know what happens to liars in my world?"

Before she could decide if she really wanted him to tell her, the waitress popped back up in front of the table. "Y'all decide what you want yet?" she asked, boredom and irritation coloring her words.

"We'll both have the bacon cheeseburger," Austin said, ignoring Kit's glare. "And a chocolate milkshake with two straws. We're celebrating."

"Congratulations," she drawled without a hint of excitement as she scribbled down their order and turned on her heel.

Turning her head, Kit narrowed her eyes at him. "What if I don't want a bacon cheeseburger?"

"You said you wanted a cheeseburger. If you don't want the bacon, then more for me."

"I don't need a milkshake."

"Sure, you do." His grin flashed, simultaneously filled with boyish charm and smug satisfaction. "You landed Austin Barrick as a client today. That calls for a celebratory treat. Besides, I promised you a reward and I don't think you're ready for the rewards I normally give."

Deliberately ignoring both his ego-stroking and the not-so-subtle comment about her *reward*, she scowled at him. "Still, you shouldn't have ordered for me without asking."

"I could apologize, but I won't." A wicked gleam lit his eyes. "I wanted her out of our hair."

"Why?"

"So I could see if you were lying to me."

"I wasn't lying."

"Hmmm. And if I told you to spread your legs so I could test my theory? What would I find?"

His voice was low enough nobody could have heard him, but to her ears he might as well have been screaming. "You wouldn't."

A warm, calloused hand rested on her thigh, pushing her skirt higher up her leg. "I could. And you'd let me, wouldn't you? Because underneath the prim, proper businesswoman, you're just a good girl desperate to please."

The hand on her thigh slid higher, leaving a trail of fire in its wake. "Austin, this is inappropriate."

"Yeah. But it's fun."

There was no point in denying it since her heart was pounding against her ribcage and her thighs were now slick with her arousal. Anybody could look over and see them. She'd die of embarrassment if she didn't implode first.

"Are you going to tell me the truth, kitten? Or do I have to find out for myself?"

His hand inched higher and the blood rushing in her ears drowned out the noise of the diner. When the tips of his fingers brushed against her outer lips, she grabbed his wrist. "Yes," she hissed at him, pushing at his arm. "Yes, I'm... you know."

"Say it, kitten." His voice was a low rumble that seemed to go straight to her clit. "Tell me how wet you are."

"Oh my god. I'm... I'm wet, okay?" Wetter than she'd ever been in her fucking life, but she wasn't about to tell him that. "Happy?"

Pulling his hand away, he gave her thigh a squeeze and

brushed a kiss across her cheek. "Good girl. I'm going to go wash my hands. Keep those legs spread for me until I get back."

A low whine escaped her before she pressed her lips together and glared up at him. With another kiss to her cheek, he slid from the booth and headed for the men's room.

∽

Austin

HE HADN'T MEANT to move so fast. But when she'd looked up at him with suspicion burning in those gorgeous brown eyes and demanded to know what he was "angling for", common sense had taken a back seat to the need to claim, to conquer.

And he couldn't seem to muster up any guilt over it, even though he was pushing the boundaries of acceptable behavior. He knew from his quick perusal of the restaurant that they were hidden enough nobody could see what was actually going on under the table, but it had still been a risk. One he normally wouldn't have taken until she'd agreed in no uncertain terms to be his, to follow his rules, to obey without argument. *Soon*, he promised himself, shifting in his seat in a vain attempt to ease the pressure of his zipper pressing against his erection.

For now, he'd have to settle for knowing she was bare and wet under that business suit, even as his mind conjured images of what she'd look like as he peeled it from her lush curves. It didn't ease the ache in his cock any, but it soothed the beast inside of him, the one demanding he stake his claim as soon as possible.

It killed him to slide off the worn vinyl and force his feet to carry him across the restaurant to the bathroom, but he didn't have much choice.

And it was worth the brief separation just for the sweet, hesitant smile she greeted him with when he returned. There were layers to his little kitten, and he couldn't wait to peel them all away until he found her core, the self she kept hidden from the world under that no-nonsense attitude and those stuffy suits.

There was a fiery, passionate woman buried deep inside Katherine Callahan, and he wasn't going to rest until he'd exposed her.

CHAPTER 5

KATHERINE

The burger was everything she'd been anticipating. Thick, juicy patties, perfectly melted cheese, slabs of crispy bacon. And the fries, good lord, a girl might be tempted to do some dirty, awful things for those beer battered potatoes.

Heat crept up her cheeks as she bit into another crispy, salty fry. She almost *had* done some dirty, awful things for this dinner.

And she didn't even feel bad about it.

Embarrassed, maybe. But the shame she'd expected to feel never really came. Instead, she felt strangely empowered. The knowledge of what she and Austin had shared, out in the open, and yet without anybody's knowledge, was a strangely heady feeling.

"Penny for your thoughts, kitten."

Oh, hell no. There was no way she was telling him she'd been daydreaming about him touching her. But judging by the glint in his eye when she looked up at him, he didn't need her confession.

Since she didn't want to tempt him into doing something

else outrageous by lying to him again, she dodged the question. "You'll need to get some additional documents together for me before our meeting next week. Should I send the list to you or your agent?"

"Ask Mary. She knows where to find all that stuff. And I know you weren't thinking about work, not with that pretty blush on your face."

"I'm thinking about work now, Mr. Barrick." His brows drew together at the use of his last name and she had to fight back a grin. It was fun to tease him. At least, it was fun here, where he couldn't really do anything about it. His previous threats still lingered in the back of her mind, and she briefly wondered what he would do if she provoked him in private.

"And I'm thinking about you spread out on your desk, naked, begging me to let you come."

The heat in her cheeks suddenly seemed to engulf her entire body. "You're assuming a lot about our relationship, Mr. Barrick."

Something flickered across his face, but before she could place it, the charming smile flashed again. "I know. It's not my usual style. But you make me forget my manners, kitten."

"Focus, Mr. Barrick."

"I am, Ms. Callahan."

But not on his finances. No, he was completely, one hundred percent focused on *her*. Couldn't he text someone, check his social media, take a call—something to pull even an ounce of his scrutiny away from her?

"Austin, I…"

"Here's your check. Y'all let me know if you need anything else."

Kit nearly sighed with relief when the surly waitress gave her the distraction she'd been hoping for, before she spilled all her deepest, darkest secrets right there in the middle of a damn diner.

"I can cover my half," she said when Austin reached for the slip of paper on the table.

"Nope. Dinner was my suggestion, so I'll pay."

Warmth filled her at the easy refusal. "Thank you. I'll get the next one."

A slow smile spread across his face, knocking the breath from her lungs. God, the man was gorgeous. "Are you asking me out, kitten?"

Gathering her courage, she lifted her gaze to his impossibly blue eyes. "I suppose I am."

"Just name the time and place."

"Saturday," she said, not giving herself a chance to overthink it. "You could come over after the game. I'll make you dinner."

His smile transformed to a knowing grin. "You know my schedule, Ms. Callahan?"

"I just assumed you had a game since it's in the middle of the season."

"Liar, liar, pants on fire. Sure, I can do Saturday. Send me your address."

Pulling his wallet from his pocket, Austin tossed a crisp hundred-dollar bill on the table before sliding out of the booth and holding out his hand. After a brief hesitation, Kit let him take her hand and guide her out of the booth to stand beside him.

"As your financial advisor, I should tell you that literally throwing cash around isn't going to help you keep your finances on track, Mr. Barrick."

"Guess you'll have your hands full with me, huh?"

His tone was playful. Teasing. But there was an undercurrent that sent a shock of need straight to her pussy, reminding her that she was completely bare beneath her skirt. Bare because he'd asked it of her. Because he'd wanted to touch her, to tease her, in public.

Having her hands full was the least of her worries if he kept this up. She was in way over her head, and that knowledge kept her quiet during the ride back to her office.

To Austin's credit, he was the perfect gentleman and didn't even hint at her hidden nakedness as he walked her to her car.

Steeling herself, determined not to let him knock her off balance again, she stopped by her driver's side door and turned to him with a polite smile. "Thank you for dinner, Mr. Barrick. I'll see you Saturday?"

She'd been shooting for strong and confident; the kind of statement a woman who never doubted her sexual appeal might make. But even to her own ears it sounded unsure, even a little needy, and she inwardly winced.

If Austin noticed, he didn't mention it. He didn't say anything, in fact. He simply lifted his hands to cup her face, sending her heart into overdrive with the simple touch.

His lips brushed against hers, the barest hint of a kiss, and she sighed.

The hands on her face tightened, and for a moment they were frozen in time, neither of them daring to move or so much as breathe. In an instant the kiss changed, and he was taking, claiming, demanding her surrender.

A surrender she was all too willing to give. With a whimper, she opened for him, wrapping her fingers around his wrists, clinging to him to keep herself from drowning under the flood of sensation and need crashing over her.

When it ended, they were both panting, and she wondered if her eyes had the same wild look in them that his did. She certainly felt wild, and a little desperate as she took a step back and willed her frantically beating heart back under control.

Reaching around her, he opened her car door and helped her inside. "Drive safe, kitten. Text me when you get home."

"Okay."

"Good girl."

He closed the door and she forced herself to focus on buckling her seatbelt, checking her mirrors, then carefully backing out of her spot which she somehow managed to do without running him over.

She was halfway home before her breathing evened out again.

In over her head? Snorting out a laugh, she fought back a rising wave of panic. She was fucking lost at sea, with no rescue in sight.

~

Austin

STRETCHED out on the plush leather couch in his study, Austin tried to focus on the replay of one of last year's games against Houston, the one where they'd blown a three-point lead in the third inning and ended up losing by eleven runs. At the time, he'd felt like he'd played a damn good game, but he'd been in the game long enough to know there was always room for improvement, especially with Houston coming into town for a three-game series tomorrow.

Problem was, he couldn't focus. His attention kept drifting back to the phone in his hand, waiting for it to light up with some indication that Kit wasn't ignoring him. It had been a long time, if ever, since a woman had gotten so deep under his skin. And they'd only been on one date. During the day, they'd texted back and forth a bit, but she hadn't answered him since she'd let him know she'd made it home from work.

What the hell was it about her? She was sexy and smart and sweet, but he'd been with plenty of women who were all of those things. There was a sort of innocence about her that just begged to be corrupted, and there was no denying it was part of her appeal.

But there was something…more. Something he couldn't quite put his finger on, and apparently he wasn't going to be able to focus until he did.

"Fuck it," he muttered, jabbing his thumb at the phone to dial her number.

She answered on the third ring, her sultry, smoky voice automatically making his cock ache. "Mr. Barrick."

"Hey, kitten. How's it goin'?"

Seriously? That was the best opening line he could come up with? Closing his eyes, he lightly banged the back of his head against the arm of the couch.

"Ah, it's going. Is everything all right?"

"Yeah." Maybe he should just be honest. Chicks loved it when a guy was open and vulnerable, right? "I, ah, just wanted to hear your voice."

"Oh." The word was more of a sigh and he grinned up at the ceiling.

Bingo.

"How was your day? Anything interesting going on in the world of finance?"

"I wouldn't know, as apparently I'm an idiot and the degree on my wall is just a pretty paper I had printed up and not the product of six years worth of education."

He swallowed a laugh at her obvious irritation. "Bad day at the office?"

Another sigh, though this one was nearly a growl. "Not entirely. I just have a client who's being difficult and seems to think that because he downloaded some app on his phone, he knows more about the stock market than the woman he's paying to oversee his investments."

"Then why is he paying you?"

"I have no earthly idea. I'm considering cutting him loose."

"Really? You can afford to just get rid of clients?" As soon as the question left his mouth, he winced. "Don't answer that. You know what you're doing and I shouldn't have asked."

"I appreciate that. But yes, I'm at a point I can afford to be choosy. Just ask your agent," she added, and he could practically hear her grinning through the phone.

"Mary did threaten me with bodily harm if I missed our meeting yesterday. Sorry you had a rough day, kitten."

"It's all right. I came home and poured myself a very large glass of wine and did a little online retail therapy. I'm feeling decidedly better than I was two hours ago."

"Good. So… what are you wearing?"

"Do you want the truth or an image to jerk off to when we get off the phone?" She gasped, as though she was shocked by her own words. "Oh my god. Forget I just said that. I can't believe I said that. No more wine for me."

"No, no, pour yourself another glass. I like the honesty."

"I'm sure you do. Which is why I'm changing the topic now. How was your day? Off day, right?"

"Right." It pleased him, probably to a ridiculous degree, that she knew his schedule. "Had a quick practice this morning, ran some errands. I was trying to brush up for the Houston series starting tomorrow but I kept getting distracted."

"By what?"

"You."

"Me?" Surprise turned her voice to a squeak. "I wasn't even texting you."

"I know. Your silence was very distracting, kitten."

"Was it?" The squeak disappeared, and her tone turned thoughtful. "I guess it was naughty of me to keep you waiting like that." Her voice went a little breathless, and he couldn't help but grin.

"It was. You know what naughty girls get, kitten?"

"What?"

"They get their pretty little panties pulled down, and then they get spanked on their bare bottoms until they're kicking and begging and promising to be good forever."

His answer was met with a long pause, broken only by the sound of her slightly ragged breathing. "What if they don't want that?"

"Depends. Are they being honest about not wanting it?"

"Maybe."

"So, if I told you to touch yourself right now, you wouldn't be soaking wet?"

"Austin! That's inappropriate."

Chuckling, he reached down to cup his own painful erection through his baggy sweatpants, giving it a gentle squeeze to help alleviate some of the pressure. "So is lying, isn't it, kitten?"

"I'm not lying, really. I'm just... unsure."

The sudden seriousness in her tone had him sitting up, the teasing tone leaving his voice. "Unsure about what?"

"I've never done those things. I don't know what I like or what I don't like and what if I'm just really bad at all of it? What if you do something I don't like and I want you to stop? I have so many questions."

Poor little kitten. He hadn't expected so much honesty, and it made him wonder how big that glass of wine was. "Well, first things first, we don't have to do anything you really don't want to do. And you will always have a safe word. Even when you're being punished, all you have to do is say 'Red' and everything stops. 'Yellow' lets me know you're unsure or you need to slow down."

"But how do I know what I even want to do? I mean, I've read some books but I don't really *know*."

She sounded so frustrated, he wished they were having this conversation in person so he could pull her into his arms and assure her everything was going to be all right. "Tell you what. I've got a worksheet I can email you. Take the next couple days, look it over, and fill it out. If there's anything you're confused about, you can always call me. I can't promise to be available all the time, but I'll call you back as soon as I can. How's that sound?"

"What kind of worksheet?"

"The kinky kind," he said, relaxing when she snorted out a laugh. "Seriously. It's basically a list of every possible kink out there and you just mark off if it's definite yes, a maybe, or a hell no."

"What if there's something that's a hell no for me and a yes for you?"

"Then it's off the table."

"Really?" Skepticism colored her tone. "That easy? Even if, say, I put spanking down as a no?"

"I know you're joking, but it's important to be honest here, kitten. If I can't trust you to be honest with me on this, then I can't trust you enough to play with you. And I really, really want to play with you."

"Is that what this is? Play?"

"We'll start there. I do have some basic rules I've always expected my submissives to follow in the past, in and out of the bedroom."

"Oh. What kind of rules?"

"For starters, no talking shit about my woman. And if we take this next step, you will absolutely be my woman. I don't share well, kitten." Just the thought of another man having his hands on her made him see red.

"It's not exactly like I'm in high demand here, Austin. I don't think sharing is going to be a big issue for you."

"Angling for a spanking already, kitten?" He didn't bother to hide the hardness in his voice. Better for her to get a taste of what she was getting into with him now.

"Oh. Um, no? What did I do?"

"Did I not just tell you that the first rule is not talking bad about yourself?"

"Oh. Well, yes, but that's not really talking bad about myself. I was just stating a fact."

"If you can honestly tell me you meant it as a completely neutral statement of fact, with not even a bit of a negative connotation, I'll let it slide."

Silence met his pronouncement, and he let it grow, listening to the sounds of her moving around. His imagination conjured an image of her, all flushed and guilty looking, shifting in her seat as she considered his words.

Finally, a quiet sigh broke the silence. "Okay, so maybe I was being a tiny bit negative."

"Then consider this your one and only warning. Say 'Yes, sir' if you understand me."

"Yes, sir."

"Good girl." A quick glance at the clock made him wince. "You should be in bed. I'll text you a link to the worksheet. Take your time with it, and we'll go over it together on Saturday."

"This feels a lot like homework."

"Yeah, I guess it is. Know what happens to naughty girls who don't do their homework?"

"They get spanked?"

"Nah. They have to write lines. 'I will do what my Sir tells me to do' a hundred times."

"Ew. I'd rather have the spanking."

He couldn't help but laugh. She was so damn cute. "That's kind of the point, kitten. Get yourself to bed and call me if you have any questions."

"Yes, sir."

"Fuck, baby. You're killing me here. Sleep tight."

"You too, sir."

Tossing the phone on the coffee table beside him, he hit play to resume the game. But he knew before the next pitch was thrown it was a lost cause. All he could think about was getting his hands on a Kit's ample curves and working his way down her list of "yes" kinks.

CHAPTER 6

KATHERINE

"Dad! You here?" Arms laden with grocery bags, Kit pushed through the front door of her childhood home and headed for the kitchen.

"In the living room!"

Grinning at the predictability that was her father on game day, she dropped the groceries on the kitchen table, grabbed a bag of sour cream and onion chips, and headed for the sound of his voice.

And there he was, perched in his favorite chair, wearing his favorite black and orange jersey. It was how she always pictured him in her mind. With everything they'd been through, the ups and downs, the loss and pain, it was soothing to know some things never changed.

Like his favorite baseball-watching snack. "Here," she said, tossing him the bag before dropping into the chair beside him.

"Thanks, pumpkin." He shot her a grin and ripped open the bag. "How's work?"

"Work is good." It was the perfect opening, but she still

hesitated before stepping through. "Landed a pretty big client the other day."

Dad snorted, but she caught the way his mouth tilted up at the corner despite his derision. "Another one of those D.C. assholes?"

"Well, he lives in D.C., but he's not a politician." Although he might consider Austin an asshole if he'd heard the conversation they'd had two nights ago. Or if he'd had a chance to read over the 'homework' Austin had assigned her. She'd had to Google half of the list, and half of *those* she'd quickly written off as no way, no how.

But that other half... sweet Jesus. Her trusty vibrator had gotten a hell of a workout by the time she'd finished her 'assignment'.

"Yeah? Who is it? Anybody I'd know?"

The questions jerked her back to the present and she said a little prayer of thanks that dear, sweet ole dad couldn't read her mind. He'd probably have a heart attack right there on the living room floor. "Probably. Austin Barrick."

"The shortstop for the Hawks? That Austin Barrick?"

"The one and only." Reaching into her purse, she pulled out the ball Austin had signed for him after their impromptu date. And even though she knew they weren't destined for some grand love story, her heart did a quick jerk in her chest at the awe that filled her father's face when she tossed him the souvenir. It was a simple act of kindness, one that had taken Austin all of thirty seconds, but obviously meant the world to her dad.

In turn, it meant the world to her.

Why did he have to be so damn sweet? She might have been able to resist the good looks and the boyish charm—even those hints of dominance he'd let trickle through. But she was helpless against the kindness which seemed to underscore his entire personality.

"This is incredible. You're incredible, pumpkin."

"Thanks." This next part was a little trickier, in part because she still wasn't sure she hadn't dreamt the whole thing. "We, ah, had dinner."

"Makes sense. A man like that probably doesn't have much free time. Hope he at least picked up the bill if he made you work through your dinner," he said absently, rolling the ball over in his hands.

She'd had plenty of 'working dinners' with clients over the years, and none of them had featured her stripping off her panties in the women's room and letting her client finger-fuck her under the table. "Ah, it wasn't really a work thing. We had an appointment at my office. He asked me to dinner afterwards."

That finally pulled his attention away from the ball in his hands. Lifting his head, he frowned at her. "Like a date? You had a date with Austin Barrick?"

If the disbelief in his voice stung, she did her best to ignore it. "Yeah. And we're having dinner again tonight, so I can't stay too late. I promised I'd cook for him."

"You invited him to your place?"

Something about his tone worked its way under her skin. "Yes. Is that a problem?"

"No. You're an adult. I know you..." Trailing off, he waved his hand around, red staining his neck as he implied things he'd obviously rather not imply. "Just be careful."

"I'm always careful, dad." Because she knew it would fluster him, she smirked. "I've known how to use a condom since I was seventeen."

"Jesus. That's not what I meant." Just as she'd expected, the embarrassed color crept up to his face and his eyes went a little wild, reminding her of a trapped animal looking for an out.

"What did you mean, then?"

"Guys like that, you know, they have lots of… fans."

Fans. Right. 'Fans' thinner than her, prettier that her, the type of women Austin and his ilk usually went for.

"I'm aware."

"I just don't want you to get hurt."

It was harder to ignore the sting this time. Or the anger that followed quickly on its heels. "Because a guy like Austin Barrick wouldn't be interested in me, right? Why would he want the fat girl when he could have his pick of supermodels or cute little baseball groupies?"

His frown deepened and he shook his head, but his eyes seemed to look everywhere but at her. "I didn't say that."

He didn't have to. But there was no point in making a big deal out of it. "You want a beer?" she offered instead, dropping the conversation for now.

Relief flooded his face and she felt a twinge of guilt for upsetting him. "Yeah."

The trip to the kitchen gave her an excuse to dawdle, which helped her nerves settle. Fighting with her dad always left her feeling shaken, like her whole world could flip itself over at any moment.

And the worst part was, she couldn't even be mad at him because he was right. Austin could have his pick of any woman he wanted, and she still couldn't wrap her mind around the idea of him wanting her. Especially considering the list he'd given her. Those books she kept hidden away on her Kindle, the ones where they did all those deliciously naughty things Austin apparently liked to do, they almost all had one thing in common. In damn near every one, the heroine was *tiny*. Short, slender, small enough to be picked up and carried places.

What would he think when he couldn't just pull her over his knee? Or toss her over his shoulder? Sitting on his lap was definitely out. Is that what it would take for him to realize what a horrible mistake he'd made?

Maybe it was better to break things off now, before she got too emotionally invested. Like that time Gregory Hartman, her high school crush, had asked her to prom right there in the middle of the cafeteria. She'd turned him down before he'd had a chance to humiliate her with whatever prank he and his buddies had cooked up. He'd taken Tiffany Willis instead, the tall, svelte captain of the cheerleading squad. They'd been prom king and queen, and last she'd heard, they had two wild preteens and a yappy little dog.

She'd done them all a favor, it seemed. And spared herself a humiliating heartbreak in the process. It was probably for the best to do the same with Austin before she did something completely stupid like fall in love with him.

Pulling her phone from her jeans pocket, she typed out a quick message and hit send.

Hey, sorry for the last-minute notice, but something came up and I have to cancel. Probably better if we don't reschedule. I'll see you at our next meeting.

The meeting would be hard, but she was nothing if not professional. She tucked the phone back in her pocket, grabbed two beers from the fridge, and returned to the living room.

Settling into her seat, she handed her dad his beer and did her best to ignore the buzzing in her pocket.

∼

Austin

AUSTIN WASN'T sure what had happened between the conversation he'd had with Kit two nights earlier and the text he'd gotten right before the game, but he was sure as hell going to find out. The guys had given him a wide berth in the locker room, and even the coaches hadn't given him any shit over what had been, arguably, the worst game of his career.

A fact which just pissed him off even more than the text itself. He prided himself on being a professional, and that meant not letting a woman get under his skin. Before the game, he'd been riding high, certain they were going to kick some Houston ass. Worst case scenario, he'd figured he'd be able to work off his frustration by testing his new little subbie's limits.

Instead, he'd gotten a text from her calling off their date five minutes before he had to lock his phone up and hit the field. He'd sent her a dozen texts in those five minutes, all of which had still gone unanswered by the time he pulled into a visitor's spot in front of her cute little townhouse.

Slamming the car door behind him, he stalked up to the front door and jabbed a finger at the doorbell.

No answer. Maybe she wasn't home. An emotion he vaguely recognized as jealousy twisted in his gut as he imagined her out with someone else, laughing and flirting. Probably some white-collar guy like her, with a row of degrees and awards lining the walls of his high-rise office.

He wasn't stupid. An almost washed-up baseball player wasn't exactly the catch of the day. Especially for a woman as classy and smart as Katherine Callahan.

Well, fuck that. He wasn't going to just be cast aside like yesterday's newspaper. If she wanted to end this thing between them before it was barely even started, she was going to have to look him in the eye and explain why.

A few more jabs at the doorbell netted him nothing. He'd pulled out his phone to call her and demand to know where the hell she was when the door flew open.

And he realized in about two seconds he'd seriously misjudged the situation. Her hair was piled up on top of her head in a messy but still weirdly sexy way, and she wasn't exactly dressed for seduction in her pale blue tank top and her matching pajama pants decorated with... were those pineapples? With sunglasses?

What really tipped him off was the red around her eyes. It might have been a while since he'd comforted a woman, but he recognized the remnants of a crying spell when he saw them.

The anger that had fueled him up until then fled. "Aw, kitten. What's wrong?"

"What are you doing here?" Her bottom lip wobbled, breaking his heart. "I canceled."

"I know. Can I come in?"

She studied him for a moment with the same wariness a hen might give a fox requesting access to the chicken coop before giving him a reluctant nod. "Sure."

Stepping through the door she held open for him, he took in the spacious living room and kitchen, his eyes widening in surprise. He'd expected something more like her office—simple, almost sterile. Instead, he was greeted with bursts of color everywhere, from the fun, cheerful pillows on the couch to the art decorating the walls. Not prints, he realized as he moved to study a rendering of downtown Annapolis. Actual paintings. He could see her in his mind, clear as day, carefully selecting them from some little local shop tucked away in the heart of downtown.

All in all, her home was charming. And he recognized it for what it was: her sanctuary. The one place she apparently felt safe enough to let her personality shine instead of hiding behind the cold, professional woman he'd met at her office.

Turning, he found her standing by the couch, her arms wrapped protectively around her waist, watching him. "Why are you here, Austin?"

At least it wasn't *Mr. Barrick.* "I'm here because you tried to dump me with a text and I want to know why."

"Because this isn't going to work."

"Did I do something?" He took a step forward, and it pleased those dark, carefully hidden parts of him when she stepped back in retreat. Tears or not, she was still going to give him the answers he'd come here for. "Did I piss you off? I'm good at pissing people off. Just ask my agent or my coaches."

Another step forward for him, another back for her. "I'm sure you are. But no, you didn't do anything to upset me."

"Then why are you running, kitten?"

Her eyes widened with surprise, then narrowed. Straightening her spine, she glared at him. "I'm not running, Mr. Barrick. I think it's time for you to leave."

"No."

"No?" she squeaked, and he barely suppressed a grin.

"Not until you tell me why, Katherine. And it's only fair to warn you, I'm not above spanking that sexy ass of yours until I get some answers."

Color filled her cheeks and her breasts swelled as she sucked in a breath. "You wouldn't."

"Wanna bet?"

"No. You need to leave, Mr. Barrick."

"Not until I have some answers. Why did you call things off?" This time when he stepped forward, she caught herself before moving backward. Equal parts pleased and disappointed that he wouldn't have to chase her, he closed the distance between them and lifted his hands to cup her tear-stained cheeks.

"What happened, baby?" he murmured, brushing his thumbs across her cheekbones. "Why are you so sad?"

"I… I don't know."

"Naughty little kitten. What have I told you about lying to me?"

"Please go."

The words were a plea, and for the life of him, he couldn't understand why. "Talk to me, baby. What happened?"

Tears shimmered in her eyes, but then she blinked and they were gone, replaced by a fury he hadn't been expecting. "You want to know what happened?"

"Yes," he replied automatically, with more certainty than he felt. For someone who'd just told him he hadn't done anything to upset her, she looked plenty pissed off to him.

"I realized what a fucking idiot I was being, so I called things off before I—before someone got hurt."

Irritation rose to shove aside the concern he'd been feeling since she opened the door. "What the hell are you on about, girl?"

Her eyes narrowed. "Excuse me? Girl?"

Oh, she didn't like that at all. Good. Maybe it was petty of him, but he had a sudden need to put her in her place. "Yeah. You're about two seconds from getting your ass blistered, so it seemed appropriate."

"You can't just keep threatening to beat me when I do something you don't like, Austin!"

"You're right," he conceded, dropping his hands to his sides.

"I am? Of course, I am," she corrected herself hastily, leveling another one of those icy glares at him.

"If I keep threatening, but not following through, it sends the wrong message."

He saw the moment his words registered in the widening of her eyes and the shake of her head. "That's not what I meant!"

"I know." And dammit, she had a point. He was moving too fast, and he knew it. Instinct was pushing him to claim, to conquer, and he was dangerously close to letting those instincts take over.

But he damn well knew better, so he took a step back. "If you want me to leave, I'll go. But I would like to know why, first."

"I already told you." Some of her bravado faded, leaving her looking sad and exhausted. "This thing between us isn't going anywhere, and we both know it. So it's better to just call it off before someone gets hurt."

"What makes you think it isn't going anywhere? Is it because you're too smart for me? Because I know that but I figure my dashing good looks make up for it." He flashed her a smile, which seemed to surprise a laugh out of her.

"You know it's not that."

"Then tell me what it is, kitten, because I'm at a loss here." Not entirely true — he had a pretty good feeling what was going on, but he wanted to hear her say it.

"Because we both know you're not going to stick with the fat girl, okay? Happy?"

"Not exactly. What did I tell you about speaking badly about my woman?"

A pink flush crept up her neck and she sucked her bottom lip between her teeth. "I'm not your woman."

"Why? Because you don't want to be or because some voice in your head says you don't deserve to be?"

Her eyes narrowed, but he could still practically see the wheels turning in her head. "The second one, I guess."

"Well, tell that voice to shut up. I want you, Katherine, and as far as I'm concerned anyone who has a problem with it can fuck off. Including that damn voice in your head."

"I want you, too, it's just not that simple for me."

"Yeah, I guess I get that. But isn't it worth a shot, at least? Do you really want to walk away from this and spend the rest of your life wondering 'what if'?"

Silence fell between them and he resisted the urge to keep pushing as she considered his words. It seemed like an eternity before she nodded. "Okay."

"Okay, what, kitten? Tell me what you want."

"I want to be with you. To be your woman."

Stepping forward again, he cupped her face in his hands and did what every instinct he possessed had been urging him to do since he'd walked in the door — he claimed her. And to his delight, she surrendered, melting against him with a quiet little moan that had him deepening the kiss until they broke apart, panting like a pair of horny teenagers.

"Now that we've gotten that out of the way." Turning with her, he guided her over to the couch, pushing her down so her ass was lifted high. "What did I tell you about talking bad about my woman, Katherine?"

"Oh, god. Can't we talk about this?"

There was a bit of a whine in her voice and he grinned down at her. "What's there to talk about? You agreed to be mine, and I already warned you what would happen if you kept talking shit about yourself. Now, did you do your homework?"

"Yeah."

His hand positively itched to spank the sulk right out of her voice, but he forced himself to hold back. "And what did you mark down for spanking?"

"Pretty sure you already know it was a 'Yes', Austin," she said, her voice surprisingly prim given her current position.

"Yeah, I figured, just wanted to be sure." The cute pjs she was wearing stretched taut across her backside, and he didn't bother to hide his groan as he ran his hand over the rounded curves of her ass. "Goddamn, baby. This is better than all those dreams I've been having about you."

She lifted her head to look over her shoulder at him,

surprise written all over her face. "You've been dreaming about me?"

"If I haven't been playing ball, I've been imagining you just like this. And on your back under me, screaming my name. And quite a few other little fantasies I can't wait to try out."

"I swear you had to have been dropped on your head as a child," she mumbled, turning her face back towards the couch.

Some of the anger he'd worked up on his drive to her place pushed through and he drew his hand back and landed two heavy smacks on her ass, one for each jiggling cheek. "What the hell does that mean?"

"Um. I don't think I want to say."

"But you will, unless you want to make your first spanking a hell of a lot longer and harder than I was planning." He waited, letting the silence drag out before he heaved a deliberately heavy sigh.

"All right, kitten. Have it your way. What do you say if you need me to stop?"

"R-red?"

"Good girl. I'm going to pull your pajama bottoms down, now. Do you know why?"

"Because you're a man and you like getting women naked?"

Fuck if he didn't love that cheeky sense of humor. But he forced himself to at least sound stern when he answered her. "No, it's because spankings are always given on the bare."

Her squeak could have been a protest, or maybe it was just surprise. Either way, it wasn't her safe word, so he did as he'd promised and tugged her pjs down to her knees, followed slowly by her lacy panties. As much of a hurry as he'd been in to finally claim her as his, now he wanted to draw things out a bit, let the tension build.

When she was bared to him, he rubbed a hand over her

skin, warming it up a bit. "What color are you, kitten? Red, yellow, or green?"

"What's green?"

"Green for go. Like a traffic light."

"Oh. Um, green. But maybe a bit yellow. I just...this is really hard," she blurted out, her voice already thick with unshed tears.

"What's really hard, baby?"

"Letting you, um, see me. Like this. Naked," she finished on a whisper, as though it were some kind of shameful secret.

His heart fucking broke for her. This should have been the easy part, but whatever she'd been through had her already near her breaking point. "Do you want to stop?"

"No, Sir. I want this. Please."

Well, then, who was he to deny her? Lifting his hand, he swung it down, the *crack* of skin meeting skin echoing around her living room, followed swiftly by her cry of surprise. It seemed like a bad idea to give her too much time to think, so he spanked her again, setting a fairly brisk pace as he peppered her ass with swats. At one particularly hard swat to her sit-spot, she jolted upward, but he braced a hand at the small of her back to hold her in place.

"Oh, shit that hurts!"

There was more surprise than distress in her tone, so he didn't bother to slow down until her entire backside was covered in a beautiful shade of pink and she was squirming and whimpering under his hand. He paused then, running his hand over her heated skin. "Now, kitten. Are you going to explain that remark about being dropped on my head?"

CHAPTER 7

KATHERINE

Too much.

It was all too much. The pain that had flared to life across her ass cheeks, the humiliation of being bent over and spanked like a naughty little girl, the unexpectedly fierce arousal throbbing between her thighs.

Too much. And still, somehow, not enough.

"Katherine? Are you going to answer me, little girl?"

Shit. She hadn't even realized he was asking her a question. "Um, I don't… could you repeat that?"

"Are you going to tell me why you asked about being dropped on my head when I said I'd been dreaming of fucking you?"

Good lord, that shouldn't be so damn hot. But she had to bite back a moan at his words and the responding pulse of her pussy. "I don't really want to, Sir."

"I know. But I need you to talk to me, baby."

The pet name and the sweet, almost pleading tone chipped away at her walls until she felt them begin to crumble. Maybe she should stand up and gather what was left of her tattered dignity, but it was actually easier to talk to him when she didn't have to look him in the eye.

"I don't understand why you want me. I'm not skinny or sexy or beautiful." Pretty, maybe. She had a good hand with makeup, and she took care of her appearance. Enough so that she would consider herself pretty most days. But not beautiful. Nowhere even approaching the level of gorgeous she usually associated with the women who married sports stars.

"Are you kidding me? You are so fucking sexy. This ass?" He cupped her heated flesh and squeezed, and this time she couldn't hold back the moan. "I love the way it jiggles when I slap it. The way my fingers sink into it when I grab it. You're sexy as fuck, kitten. And gorgeous. Smart as a fucking whip on top of it."

"But you could have any woman you want."

"I do have the woman I want. I have you."

It was impossible to ignore the way he'd looked at her, like he could eat her alive and still be hungry for more. But what about when the novelty of fucking the fat girl wore off? What happened when he realized he wanted someone he could show off for the cameras and not be embarrassed by her or the inevitable comments people would make?

There was no way she could explain any of that to him, not without dying of humiliation. "I still just don't understand *why*."

Calloused fingers dug into her bottom and she hissed at the renewed flash of pain. "What did I tell you the other day, kitten? You don't need to understand why. You just need to do as you're told. And right now, that means getting that beautiful ass of yours in the bedroom so I can prove to you exactly how sexy I think you are."

Longing and need filled her at his growled command. In a perfect world, she'd have the confidence to strut her half-naked self into her bedroom and let him have his way with her. But as soon as her mind conjured an image of her doing just that, all she could see were the dips and dimples of her thighs, the rolls of her belly, the flab in her arms.

"I can't," she whispered, her vision blurring as tears filled her eyes.

"Okay."

Disappointment flooded her, and a tear slipped down her nose, leaving a small wet mark on the upholstery.

"Right here works just as well. Spread your legs, kitten, so I can taste you."

"Austin! That's not what I meant!" She tried to push up off the couch when she felt him tugging her panties over her ass and down her legs, but he easily pinned her in place.

"Do not move, little girl." His voice was a low, sexy growl that sent a shiver of anticipation down her spine. "You stay right where you are until I give you permission to move."

"I don't need your permission to do anything, Austin Barrick."

Leaning in, his breath tickled the back of her neck as he spoke. "Pretty sure you stood right here a few minutes ago and agreed to be my woman, didn't you?"

"Well, yes—"

"Then right now, you do need my permission to move. And it's not Austin, or Mr. Barrick. It's Sir. Understood?"

"No, I do not understand."

"Hmm, what don't you understand, kitten?" The teasing note in his voice set her antenna quivering a split second before his hand slipped between her thighs. "How much I want you? Or maybe you don't understand how much you want me? You're so fucking wet for me, baby."

That wasn't at all what she'd meant, but the pleasure flooding her at his simple touch stole the breath from her lungs and she couldn't form the words to tell him so.

Behind her, he shifted, and the pressure on her back eased.

But she didn't move. Couldn't move, because she was frozen in place as soon as she felt the hot, wet brush of his lips across the backs of her thighs.

"Fuck, you're beautiful. I want to taste every inch of you."

"That's a lot of acreage to cover. Sure you have the time?"

Dread settled in her stomach as soon as the words left her lips. She braced for her punishment, but it didn't keep her from crying out when his hand connected with her ass, harder and faster than before.

The spanking ended as abruptly as it had begun, leaving her breathless in its wake. A hand fisted in her hair, yanking her head back, and his low growl of a voice filled her ears. "That was a very naughty thing to say, Katherine. What happens to naughty little girls?"

"They get sp-spanked?"

"They do." The hand in her hair tightened, pulling a whimper from her throat as her back arched and pain flashed at the base of her skull. "But when they're especially naughty, that's only the tip of the iceberg, kitten. *Very* naughty girls get spanked until their bottoms are nice and red and welted, until they're promising to be on their best behavior forever and ever. Then, they get their sore bottoms fucked good and hard. But you know what the real punishment is, baby?"

"What?"

"They don't get to come."

Fuck. His words had already sent her senses into overdrive and the throbbing between her legs was nearing unbearable levels. If he didn't give her some relief soon, she was going to die right there over the back of her couch, she was sure of it.

"I'll be good, I promise. Forever and ever."

Her desperate attempt at humor was met with a short, harsh bark of laughter. "The next time you say something nasty about yourself, you'll get the exact punishment I just laid out for you. Understand?"

"Yes, sir."

"Goddamn, I love the way that sounds. Now, I'm going to eat that pretty pussy of yours and you can moan or cry or scream all you want, but you will not say a word unless it's to use your safe word."

He didn't ask if she understood before he moved behind her and pressed his lips to her thigh once more. She wanted to object, to warn him she hadn't shaved in days, that she wasn't *prepared*, but his warning echoed in her mind. And the overwhelming need his touch inspired overrode any desire to try and argue with him.

But then those strong, callused hands, the same hands that had spanked and caressed her earlier, gripped her bottom cheeks and spread her wide, exposing every inch of her most secret places to his view.

"Austin!"

"Are you allowed to speak, little girl?"

"No, but—"

"Then I'll have to punish you, won't I?"

Oh, god. Was he really going to fuck her *there?*

She jumped when his hand appeared in front of her face. "Open your mouth, kitten. You're going to prep my fingers for your punishment."

For a moment, she simply stared at his fingers, not comprehending his words. When his meaning finally clicked, she felt her eyes grow wide and she shook her head wildly.

"What did you put down for anal play on your homework, baby?"

"Umm." She'd checked it off as something she wanted to try, but it didn't seem wise to tell him that just then. But once he checked the worksheet for himself, he'd know she'd lied, and that would just make her punishment worse.

Damn him.

"I said I'd like to try it," she confessed quietly.

"Then be a good girl and open your mouth."

Her lips parted almost of their own accord at the command in his voice. Two thick fingers filled her mouth, and she instinctively ran her tongue over them.

"Good girl," he crooned as he pulled his fingers away. "Has anybody ever fucked you here, kitten?" A slick digit pressed against her back entrance and she immediately tensed, clenching her muscles against the intrusion.

"No, sir," she whispered, shame heating her face at the thought of anybody having their fingers there, never mind their… anything else. "Please, sir, I'll be good." It was humiliating to realize he'd so easily reduced her to a whiny, begging mess, but dignity didn't stand a chance against the onslaught of fear and, god help her, lust coursing through her.

"I wouldn't be a very good Dom if I let you get away with disobeying me. Relax, kitten. I don't want to hurt you."

"Tell that to my ass!"

"Your bottom can take a lot more punishment than what I doled out. I guess I should have been more specific," he continued conversationally as he pushed the tip of his finger past the tight ring of muscle that was working so hard to keep him out. "I don't want to harm you. This will hurt, but it will hurt less if you relax."

"Easy for you to say," she mumbled. He wasn't the one with a finger up his ass.

"Yeah, it is easier to relax when you're not on the receiving end," he admitted with a low chuckle. "Come on, baby. Let me in."

It was hard to take a deep breath with the back of the couch digging into her stomach, but she managed to drag in enough air to work through her breathing exercises. Bit by bit, she felt her muscles unclench.

"There's my good girl. I'm letting you off easy, since this is your first time. But from now on," he continued, ignoring her low whine of discomfort, "when you disobey me, your bottom will pay the price, one way or another. Do we understand each other, Katherine?"

"Yes, sir!" At that moment, she would have said anything to make him stop, to put an end to the burning sensation in her bottom as he stretched her with his finger.

"Good choice. Because my cock is a lot bigger than my finger, and what do naughty girls get in their bottoms, Katherine?"

"A... your... that," she finished lamely, pressing her face into the couch cushions.

"They get their Sir's cock in their bottoms, that's right." His finger slid from her, and she collapsed against the couch with relief. "I'm going to wash my hands. Stay here."

Suddenly wishing she'd listened earlier and just gone to the bedroom like he'd asked, she shifted her hips and tried not to think about what she must look like, bent over the back of her couch, all of her naughty bits on display in the middle of her living room.

"Cute place you have here," he called from the bathroom over the sound of running water. "It suits you." The water stopped, and a moment later she heard his footsteps across the hardwood as he made his way back into the living room. "Having you on display for me really brings the room together, don't you think?"

Since all of the responses dancing on her tongue were liable to get her in more trouble, she pressed her lips together and pretended not to hear him.

"Of course, I think you, naked, would look good in pretty much any room. We'll have to test that theory at my place some time. I'm particularly curious about how you'll look tied to my bed."

Even though she'd never set foot inside his home, her

mind conjured the image all too easily, and she let out a soft whimper at the flash of heat between her thighs.

"Oh, my little kitten likes that idea, doesn't she? Use your words."

"Yes, sir." The words slipped out of her on a moan when he ran his finger through her soaking wet curls again.

"Then you won't mind staying in place for me like a good girl while I eat your pussy, will you?"

Even though she knew it wasn't really a question, she nodded and whispered, "Yes, sir" anyway.

"Good girl."

She sensed him moving behind her, and then his mouth was on her, and every ounce of her being focused on the sensation of his tongue on her clit. Gripping the edge of the cushion, she forced herself to stay in position while he licked, sucked, and teased her just to the edge of orgasm.

And then he stopped.

"Austin! Why did you stop?"

His laughter vibrated against her leg and she fought back the urge to kick him. "What did I say you should call me, kitten?"

"Sir," she said with a huff. "Why did you stop, *sir*?"

"I'm not ready to be done with you just yet. The view from back here is stunning."

The words were shocking enough, but they were nothing compared to the unmistakable feel of his teeth sinking into the flesh of her bottom.

"Sir!"

"Sorry. I should have made sure biting wasn't on your hard limits list. I just couldn't resist this ass. You okay, baby?"

"I'd be better if you'd let me come, sir." When the hell had she become so brazen? She had never, in all her life, so much as said the word *come* to a man and here she was, practically begging him for an orgasm on what amounted to their second date.

"Poor little kitten." Warm air blew across her pussy and she squirmed. "I do have to point out, I only promised to eat you out. I never promised you an orgasm. And you were a naughty little girl."

"Oh no," she moaned, then flushed with embarrassment at the needy sound.

"Beg me, kitten. If you beg prettily enough, I might let you come."

"Please, sir." The words tumbled out of her despite, or maybe because of, how utterly humiliating this entire scenario had become. "I need to come, sir, please."

"And if I let you come, you'll be a good girl?" His thumb brushed against her clit, sending a shiver of pleasure up her spine. "No more nonsense about not being sexy enough? No more mean comments about my girl?"

Ignoring the little twinge of guilt, she nodded, knowing it was a lie. She couldn't just turn those thoughts off, but she could be better about hiding them from him. "Yes, sir. I'll be good as gold, I swear."

"Naughty little subs always make promises they can't keep when they want something bad enough. But I think you'll try, and that's really all I can ask for."

Thank god. If he'd insisted on denying her, she might have gone through with the urge to kick in his handsome face.

Staying still became an internal battle she was determined to win as he caught her throbbing clit between his teeth and sucked—hard.

"Oh, fuck! Sir, please!"

His little hum of pleasure vibrated against her in the most delicious way, and she couldn't resist lifting her hips and pushing back, desperate for enough pressure to relieve the ache building in her core. A sharp slap to the back of her thigh reminded her to be still and she settled again with a whine of protest.

Who was this needy, wanton woman in her living room, wiggling and writhing while a man lavished pleasure on her? If the rush of sensation hadn't been so overwhelming, she probably would have convinced herself she was dreaming.

But it was all so real, right down to the scream that tore from her throat as the orgasm crashed over her. And he didn't even stop there. He kept going until every last ounce of pleasure felt like it had been drained from her very bones, and she collapsed against the couch.

"Good girl. Stay right there and I'll get you cleaned up."

Since she couldn't have moved even if she'd wanted to, she obeyed, letting her eyelids drift closed as she listened to the sound of running water.

CHAPTER 8

KATHERINE

"Kit? Are you okay? You seem a bit distracted today. Again."

Jerking her attention from the darkened computer screen she'd been staring mindlessly at for god only knew how long, Kit looked over at her trusty admin standing in the doorway to her office. The look on Donna's face was a mix of concern and admonition.

"Sorry. Head's a little in the clouds today," she admitted sheepishly.

With a shake of her head, Donna turned and left, muttering something about men ruining everything. Embarrassed at being caught daydreaming again, Kit dropped her head into her hands.

Distracted didn't even begin to cover the obsession consuming her. Even though Austin had insisted on staying the night with her on Saturday, they hadn't done more than cuddle, and he'd been gone when she'd woken up. She'd spent all of Sunday and most of Monday in a funk, and her Tuesday wasn't turning out to be much better if her admin had noticed.

Logically, she knew his job was demanding, to say the least. She knew he'd had to get up before dawn on Sunday to catch a plane to their game in Miami that afternoon. He'd be back on Wednesday, and then he'd be in town for a couple of weeks, but only because they had a string of home games before he had a day off. Even being an avid baseball fan her entire life, it had never occurred to her how much time the players dedicated to the sport, or how exhausting it must be.

And still, he'd made time to call her. Sometimes just for a quick check-in to see how she was doing. Other times for longer talks where he asked about her day and regaled her with tales of life on the road that left her laughing so hard it brought tears to her eyes.

So why was she having so much trouble shaking this feeling that something was wrong? That everything was going to come crashing down around them soon, and she was powerless to stop it?

Because she was being ridiculous, she decided, scowling at her blank monitor. Nothing was wrong, and she wouldn't become some broody, mopey girl pining after her crush. She was a woman with a career, a damn good one at that, and it was time she started acting like it again.

Giving the mouse a shake, she logged back in and pulled up Austin's files. Maybe diving into his finances would be enough to distract her from missing him.

It worked, at least until she started sifting through his monthly finances to see where he could trim things up a bit. It wasn't a service she provided for every client, as most who came to see her had a pretty decent idea of how to budget. The majority of people who made gobs of money were very careful with it, which was how they kept those gobs.

Austin wasn't one of those. He wasn't hemorrhaging funds, the way she'd seen with some of the other sports stars she'd worked with, but if he wanted to continue living comfortably after his retirement, he'd need to cut back on his expenses.

"Do you guys eat at five-star restaurants every night? Good lord," she muttered to herself as she sorted through what could easily be identified as dining expenses. And wasn't the team responsible for providing meals on the road? Shaking her head, she jotted it down as something to discuss before moving on.

Everything else seemed to track. Union dues, his agent's fee, various purchases from sports stores. But there was one payment, made on a monthly basis to "Cartwright-Davidson Enterprises" for twenty-five hundred dollars that she couldn't pin down.

Exactly the same amount, around the same date every month. Some kind of monthly membership or fee? But what the hell could he have a membership for that was costing him nearly as much as her mortgage?

Maybe it was a mortgage. Or rent. But as far as she knew, the Cartwright-Davidsons weren't in the mortgage game. She'd been watching them closely for years, desperately wishing she could get her hands on their portfolio. Or even a five-minute sit-down with Jaxson to pick his brain. The man was a genius when it came to making his money work for him.

Rent was a possibility, though. If she was remembering correctly, they'd purchased a few apartment buildings a couple years back and renovated them. But had that been here on the east coast or in California?

Abandoning Austin's finances for the time being, she dove head-first into digging up everything she could find about Cartwright-Davidson Enterprises. Talk about diversifying your investments. She nearly came on the spot when she realized how expansive their empire really was.

A few startups, almost all of which had done incredibly

well over the years. Some real estate, as she'd remembered, on both coasts. Runway East and West, of course, the twin nightclubs again on both coasts.

There was a "doing business as" filed for something call Black Light, but she couldn't find anything beyond that. Nothing else in their holdings, nothing online. So, what the hell was it? A front for something? She couldn't see Jaxson Davidson risking his business or his family with anything criminal, so there was probably some boring explanation for the odd DBA.

Right then, she was more interested in this monthly fee her, ah, client was paying out. Her mind skittered away from the word ' boyfriend'. It was somehow too permanent, and at the same time, not encompassing enough for what she had with Austin.

Her hand froze over the mouse and the number on the screen became a blur. He'd told her he didn't like to share, but that didn't necessarily mean that exclusivity went both ways. What if he had a more permanent girlfriend set up in a nice apartment somewhere outside of D.C., where he had easy access to her?

What if he had a whole family, for that matter?

Giving herself a mental shake, she refocused on the screen in front of her. If Austin Barrick had a family, she would know. Everyone would know. The man might be able to keep a secret girlfriend or two, but he couldn't hide a whole damn family from the world.

Nausea bubbled in her stomach as she started working her way through the Cartwright-Davidson holdings on the east coast. They didn't own a ton of apartment buildings, and based on the amount Austin was shelling out, she was able to narrow it down to a handful of options.

Sitting back in her chair, she studied the website for the one she'd deemed most likely, based on its ease of access from the Hawks stadium. The apartment building was run by a property management company, as most were. So why wasn't the rent showing up under their name? She'd never seen a payment billed to an umbrella company like that, especially not one the size of Cartwright-Davidson Enterprises.

Maybe it wasn't a rent payment. But if it wasn't, what the hell was it? The professional thing to do would be to wait until their next meeting to discuss any odd expenses, but she knew the wait would just give her more time to come up with increasingly outrageous scenarios. And if there *was* some secret girlfriend or something, didn't she deserve to know sooner rather than later?

Picking up her phone, she tapped out a message.

Call me. We need to talk about something.

There. That was all she could do for now. Doing her best to ignore her burgeoning unease, she shifted her attention to the real estate mogul she was meeting with that afternoon. Austin Barrick and his secrets would have to wait.

Austin

SCOWLING down at the phone in his hand, Austin silently willed the plane to move faster. As spacious as first-class might be, it didn't offer near the privacy for the conversation he apparently needed to have with his girl.

Call me. We need to talk about something.
About to get on the plane. What's up?
Call me when you get home.
What's going on, Katherine?

After that, crickets. His palm itched with the need to show her how little he appreciated being ghosted in the middle of what was, obviously, an important conversation.

But mostly, he had a headache from trying to figure out what the fuck would prompt a text like that. Obviously, she'd gotten something into that pretty head of hers again, and god help her if it was anything like last time. He really would wear his belt out on her ass if she so much as hinted at not being pretty enough or sexy enough or whatever enough for him.

"You keep glaring at it like that, the phone might burst into flames."

Relaxing his death grip on the phone, Austin looked up at Torres, who was watching him with a teasing smile on his baby face. The kid looked fucking twelve, and Austin felt irritation claw at his chest, eager for an easy target.

"Something on your mind, Torres?"

"You obviously got something on yours. Lady trouble?" The waggling eyebrows would have been amusing from someone his own age—from Torres, it just made his jaw clench and his fingers close into a fist.

"None of your fucking business, kid."

And just like that, he felt like the asshole he was obviously being. Torres's expression took on the look of a wounded puppy for a second before he closed himself off. "Man, fuck you. We're stuck on this plane for the next two hours. Figured you might wanna talk or something."

"Sorry." Unclenching his fist, he scrubbed his hand over his face. Torres wasn't the problem, and he knew damn well the kid had some idol-worship still left in him. Just because he was feeling twice his fucking age and he was pissed off at Kit's cryptic texts didn't mean he had to be a dick. "Yeah, my girl said we need to talk but won't tell me why."

Tony let out a low whistle and shook his head slowly. "Never good, man. Here's what you do. Go straight to her place when we land. Stop for some flowers, if you can find any place open. Your girl, does she like roses or mixed bouquets?"

"How the fuck should I know? We just started seeing each other." And yet, it still irritated him that he didn't know. He wanted to know everything about her. Wanted her stripped bare to him, body and soul, without any hidden places or secrets.

"And she's already got you all tied up in knots, huh? You got it bad, Barrick."

"Tell me about it," he muttered, shooting his phone another glare.

"Okay, so is she classic? Like old school romance, fancy restaurants, stuff like that?"

Images of her colorful apartment, with its eclectic mix of colors and styles popped into his head and he grinned. "No. She pretends like she is at work, but inside she's… colorful. A little wild."

It was part of what he adored about her. The way she presented one image to the outside world, when the reality of her was so completely different. Not like some of the women he'd dated in the past, who had been masters at being whoever they thought their audience wanted at any given time. With them it had seemed more…dishonest. With Kit, it was a defense mechanism. Why she felt she needed it was still something of a mystery to him, but that just made him all the more determined to strip her of those defenses until he finally found the real Kit she'd so expertly hidden away. The glimpses he'd gotten so far weren't nearly enough.

Torres nodded decisively. "Then those are the flowers you want. Colorful, and a little wild."

"I don't even know what I did, though. And that's what's pissing me off."

"Doesn't matter." Torres shrugged and gave him a rueful grin. "Sometimes you gotta get the apology out of the way and then figure out where you went wrong."

"Sounds like you've had some practice."

"Been with the same girl since I was fourteen. Married her as soon as we graduated high school. Four years ago in June. Love of my fucking life. Her and our two little boys."

Had he known Torres had a family? It seemed vaguely familiar, but he'd never really bothered to get to know him, and guilt niggled at him. There was a time when he'd known every man on his team, and their families. But he'd been so wrapped up in the idea of his inevitable retirement that he'd shut himself off from the rest of the team. Even the guys he'd known for awhile; he couldn't remember the last time he'd heard about Jameson's new baby or O'Connell's latest fling.

Somehow, without meaning to, he'd become the grumpy old man in the locker room. He'd work on that, starting with this conversation with his eventual replacement.

"Tell me about your girl."

From the grin on Torres's face, his wife was one of his favorite topics. "We grew up together. Our mamas were best friends. They even bought houses next door to each other when they got married, and our birthdays are only a week apart. Really, we've been together our whole lives, but I didn't really see her *that way* until our freshman year when Kyle Pickett started telling everyone how he'd kissed her and a whole lot more under the bleachers after the homecoming game. I gave Kyle a black eye, stormed over to Claudia's house, and asked her what the fuck she was thinking, screwing around with that asshole."

"And you lived happily ever after?"

"Shit, no." Torres threw his head back and let out a whoop of laughter. "She told me what she did under the bleachers was none of my business and that she'd waited fourteen years for me to kiss her, and since I obviously didn't want to, she was damn well going to find someone who did. Then she kicked me out of her house and didn't speak to me for a month, and even then, it was only after I got my head out of my ass and apologized about a hundred times."

"How many times have you had to apologize since then?"

"Too many to count, man. I can be kind of an asshole, but she puts up with me for some reason. You know she wanted us to sign a prenup when we got married? Said she knew I'd be famous someday, and she didn't want people saying she married me for my money."

"Did you sign it?"

"Hell no." The corner of his mouth lifted in a smirk, and a satisfied gleam lit his eyes. "I told her if she ever said that word to me again, I'd wash her mouth out with soap. *Then* we lived happily ever after."

Austin blinked in surprise, a dozen questions suddenly racing through his mind. But he restrained himself from asking any of them. He and Torres might have started working their way toward being friends, but some things he didn't need to know about his teammate. Or need his teammates knowing about him. Inside Black Light, he loved putting on a show with his submissive for the night. Outside of the club, he preferred to keep those tendencies to himself. Public opinion was a mercurial beast, with the power to boost or kill a career, and he wasn't going to let his kinky bedroom activities be the thing that forced him from the field.

Still… maybe he should have Torres and his childhood sweetheart over for a cookout or something. Might be good for Kit to see they didn't all date supermodels or whatever other stereotype she had in her head.

Something to think about. For now, he had a naughty little kitten to get home to. Flowers and preemptive apologies might work for Torres, but Austin had his own plans for getting to the bottom of whatever was bothering his girl.

CHAPTER 9

KATHERINE

Although she'd been expecting it, the buzzing of her phone nearly made Kit drop the pan she was holding. Setting it back on the stove, she hit the button for speaker. "Hello?"

"Hey, kitten. I'm on my way to your place. Don't suppose you'd be willing to feed a starving young ball player some dinner?"

How was it that just the sound of his voice seemed to soothe away the stress of the day? She caught herself smiling dreamily at the phone before she straightened her spine, bracing for what seemed like an inevitable fight. "We need to talk, Austin."

"So your text said. I'm going to assume it's not a good talk?"

"Well, I don't know. I guess that depends on your answers."

"Then it sounds like something we should discuss in person. I'll be there in five."

The phone went silent before she had a chance to argue. Five minutes? He was giving her five minutes to get ready?

Asshole.

Plating the asparagus so it wouldn't burn in the pan, she checked on the chicken in the oven and decided it was fine for another few minutes while she rushed to the bathroom to check her appearance. Some part of her must have been wishing he'd come straight to her when he got in, because she hadn't taken off her makeup when she'd gotten home, and she'd chosen a cute t-shirt and leggings that gave her ass a nice little boost over her usual pajamas. Once she pulled her hair down from its messy bun and ran her fingers through it to smooth it out a little, she looked almost presentable.

Her doorbell rang just as she finished slicking on a new coat of lipstick, and she forced herself to walk instead of racing for the door like an eager virgin on prom night.

The strange monthly payments, her suspicions, her anxiety, all of it seemed to disappear when he grinned down at her. She'd somehow forgotten how gorgeous he actually was up close. Too gorgeous. The kind of gorgeous that made smart women stupid. It certainly made her feel like she'd lost a few dozen IQ points whenever she opened her mouth around him.

"Hey, kitten. You look as delicious as dinner smells. Gonna let me in?"

"What? Oh." Realizing she was standing in the doorway staring up at him like some wide-eyed groupie, she took a step to the side to let him in and closed the door behind him.

"Austin, we need…"

"To talk. Yeah, I know. But I need something first."

"What?"

He moved in before her brain registered what was happening, one arm sliding around her waist, the other moving up to wrap her hair around his hand and pull her head back. "You."

Then his mouth was on hers and her mind went blank. Everything disappeared, leaving only him, her, and this wild, nearly desperate kiss.

"Need you. God, I fucking missed you."

Hot, wet kisses trailed down the side of her neck to her collarbone and she let her head fall back further, a needy moan escaping her at the flash of need.

"Bedroom. Now." Releasing her abruptly, he turned her and laid a heavy smack to her ass, propelling her forward.

"But—"

"We can talk after. Go, or I'm going to think you need a reminder of who's in charge here."

She still wasn't sure how she felt about him being "in charge" but her pussy loved it. Arousal flooded her panties and her clit throbbed at the growl in his voice.

For just a moment, she hesitated. If they slept together, what would happen when she confronted him about the monthly payments? If he had some deep, dark secret, would this be their last night together?

Maybe. But if it was, didn't she deserve to know what being with him could be like? Would she regret it more if she didn't let herself have this one night with him?

Her mind made up, she hurried up the stairs and into the bedroom. Austin was right behind her and she was barely through the door before he was reaching for the hem of her shirt.

"Wait!"

"Baby, if I have to wait much longer, you're going to end up on your knees with my cock down your throat. What's wrong?"

God help her if part of her wasn't tempted to keep stalling just for the thrill his threats gave her. But if this was their last night together, she wanted him inside of her. Just maybe not with every light in the house glaring, highlighting every dimple and roll. "Turn the lights off. Please?"

A wicked gleam lit his eyes, and she instantly knew she'd lost this argument. "Absolutely not. I want to see you, Kit. Every inch of your beautiful body. Arms up."

She opened her mouth to argue that it wasn't beautiful, that it was fat and gross, but his warning about what happened to naughty girls who spoke badly of themselves was still fresh in her mind, so she clamped her lips together and slowly lifted her arms in the air.

The brush of fabric against her stomach and back sent a shiver up her spine.

"Cold, kitten?"

"A little," she lied, jerking her arms down to cover her bare stomach as soon as he'd freed them from the shirt.

"Arms down," he snapped, and she jumped a bit at the command in his voice.

"Austin, please." She could barely whisper the words and tears burned at the corners of her eyes. Great, the only thing worse than letting him see her naked would be crying about it in front of him.

She'd half-expected another barked order, but instead, his hands came up to cup her face, forcing her to look up at him. "Arms at your side, baby. Let me see you. Let me show you how beautiful you really are."

It felt like ages as she stood there, staring into those clear, ice-blue eyes. However long it was, she finally found the courage to lower her arms to her side.

"Good girl." The soft, sweet murmur was followed by a kiss so tender, her knees buckled. If he hadn't been holding her, she might have melted into a puddle right there at his feet.

A soft chuckle vibrated against her lips. "You like being a good girl, don't you, kitten?"

"Yes, sir."

"If you can keep being a good girl for me, you can have a reward soon, okay?"

"Okay." Hopefully, the reward would be some kind of release for the unbearable ache between her thighs. Even as humiliating as this whole experiment was, her need for him hadn't ebbed in the slightest. If anything, it was worse now than when he'd ordered her into the bedroom.

"Don't move your hands. If you try to cover yourself, you won't get your reward. Understood?"

"Yes, sir," she whispered.

When he reached for the waistband of her leggings, she screwed her eyes shut, unable to bear the disgust she just knew she was going to see on his face.

"Nope. None of that either, little girl. Look at me."

It took every ounce of willpower she had, but she managed to open her eyes again. Relief washed over her when she didn't see any of what she'd expected to. There was only him, smiling down at her, approval etched into every line of his gorgeous face.

"There we go. Eyes on me, kitten."

Dread settled in her stomach as he reached for her leggings again and began tugging them down over her hips. There was a small voice in the back of her head, reminding her he'd already seen her like this so there was nothing to worry about.

But she hadn't had to watch him, then. She'd been able to hide in the couch cushions, which was a completely different experience than watching him peel her leggings down, inch by agonizing inch.

"Hands on my shoulders and lift your foot up."

She obeyed almost mechanically, first her right foot and then her left, until she was left in just the lacy pink bra and panty set she'd put on this morning in anticipation of exactly this.

Thank god early morning Kit hadn't known what she'd find at the office, or she might be standing here in her favorite comfy cotton bra and a pair of superhero panties.

"Fucking beautiful." Stepping back, Austin let his gaze roam over her, and she had to fight back the rising wave of panic and the urge to cover herself. What was she going to do if he turned his back on her? If he decided she wasn't at all what he'd been expecting?

But when his eyes met hers again, all she saw was her own need reflected back at her, a raw kind of hunger that made her feel… everything.

Beautiful.

Desirable.

Wanted.

Emboldened, she reached behind her back, and with trembling fingers, flicked open the first hook of her bra. Approval flashed in his eyes and she moved on to the next hook. Then the third, before sliding the straps over her shoulders and down her arms. She hesitated, briefly, holding the lacy fabric to her chest, but braced herself with a deep breath and let it fall, baring herself to him.

"Put your hands on the back of your head and lace your fingers together." The order was given in a rough, gravelly voice, almost like he'd forgotten how to use it.

He wasn't faking it. He wasn't just humoring the fat girl, or using her to get his rocks off. There was no way to fake those raw reactions, and it gave her the courage to obey his orders without the slightest hesitation.

"That's my good girl." Stepping closer, he cupped her breasts in his palms, running his thumbs over the hardened nipples. "You put breast torture down as a maybe. Would you like a sample tonight?"

Yes. She wanted everything and anything he wanted to give her. Maybe it was the knowledge that this might be their only time together, or maybe it was just the way he looked at her, but she knew there was almost nothing she would deny him tonight.

"Please, sir."

"Such a polite little kitten, asking so nicely for her Sir to hurt her." He caught her right nipple between his thumb and forefinger, squeezing tightly enough that she let out a little whimper at the flash of pain. "Give me a color, baby. Green if you're good, yellow if you need me to slow down."

"Green, sir."

"Excellent." The pride in his voice carried her through as he repeated the torture, adding a little twist at the end that brought her to her toes.

"Still green, kitten?"

"Yes, sir."

"Hmmm." Ducking his head, he ran his tongue over her nipple, soothing the abused flesh. "Doesn't seem fair to only play with one of these beauties, does it? Wouldn't want the other to feel neglected."

It was all the warning she got before the familiar pain laced through her opposite breast, straight down to her throbbing clit. "Ow! Austin!"

Her outburst was met with a raised eyebrow. "It's sir when we're playing, kitten."

"Sorry, sir."

"Try to remember. You've been such a good girl for me, I'd hate to have to punish you before you get your reward."

There was something in his voice that told her he wouldn't hate it *that* much, but she nodded her understanding. "Yes, sir."

"Good girl. You can put your arms down now."

She obeyed, wincing at the unexpected stabbing in her

shoulders. To her surprise, he reached up and massaged each of them in turn until the pain faded.

"Better?"

"Yes, sir. Thank you."

"Welcome. Now, get those panties off so I can eat that pretty pussy."

CHAPTER 10

AUSTIN

Watching the blush creep up Kit's face, Austin couldn't help but grin. Poor little kitten, completely out of her depth. But she'd kept up with him so far, and he had no doubt he could push her further without even coming close to her limit.

He gave her to the count of ten, which he ticked off silently in his head, before he hardened his expression. "Are you going to do as you were told, Katherine?"

The use of her full name got her attention, and she moved her hands to the lacy waistband of her panties. She hesitated again, looking up at him with that uncertainty in her eyes that made him want to throttle every man who'd come before him. Fuck that; every single person who'd ever made her feel less.

Knowing she'd probably dealt with more than her fair share of people who had put those thoughts in her head, he took pity on her. "I'm going to get undressed. By the time I'm done, I expect you fully naked and kneeling on the bed."

Relief flashed in her eyes, and he knew he'd made the right choice. Turning away from her, he pulled his own shirt over his head, grinning at the wall when he heard her whispered, "Holy shit."

"Like what you see, kitten?"

"Yes, sir."

Still facing the wall, he unbuckled his belt, slowly sliding it through the loops. Though he wasn't watching her, he heard the hitch in her breathing that told him she was definitely watching him.

"Are you naked yet, kitten?"

"No, sir."

"You have about thirty seconds," he warned her, right before he popped open the button on his jeans and pushed them down to his ankles. The sound of her moving around behind him, the quiet squeak of the bed, filled him with pride.

His little kitten wanted to be a good girl. She just needed to get out of her head a bit.

And he knew just how to help her.

He finished stripping down and turned to her. The sight of her kneeling on the bed, watching him expectantly, had his cock twitching painfully. He was already harder than he could ever remember being, and her eager submission nearly made him embarrass himself before he even had a chance to taste her.

"Good girl," he praised as he climbed onto the bed, settling his head on one of her pillows. "Come here, baby. I'm starving."

Confusion twisted her features, followed by a horrified expression when understanding dawned. "You want me to let you… like that?"

"Yes, kitten. I want you to ride my face while I eat you out."

"I can't!"

He'd expected the argument, but he wasn't about to give in. "Why not?" he asked, deliberately giving his words a hard edge of warning.

"You won't be able to breathe! I'll smother you!"

"If that happens, I'll die a happy man." Ignoring her horrified gasp, he continued, "But it won't happen, because I can handle you, kitten. All of you. So get over here."

Again, he counted silently, but he only got to eight this time before she slowly lowered herself to all fours and crawled towards him. He thought he might burst with pride when she knelt by his head.

"You're really sure about this?"

"Yes, baby."

Grabbing hold of her padded headboard, she shifted so her knees were on either side of him. When she was mostly in position, he hooked his arms under her thighs, reveling in the soft curves pressing against him.

"There's my good girl," he crooned, grabbing a handful of luscious ass in each hand and massaging as she gradually relaxed. When he heard her sigh, he scooted down the bed so she was directly above him and lifted his mouth to her dripping pussy.

"Oh! Sir!" Her body jerked, then went still. "Are you okay? Austin?"

Instead of answering her, he set about allaying her concerns the only way he knew how— he ate her like she was his last meal. He licked from the bottom of her lips up to her clit and back down again, then caught that sensitive nub between his teeth and sucked.

That got her attention. With a shocked gasp, she rocked her hips forward. He didn't know if she even realized she was doing it, but soon she was writhing and wriggling atop him, her body instinctively searching for release.

The part of him that craved her submission crowed with delight. Normally, he would draw things out, torturing and teasing until she was begging to come. But he wanted to show his girl how fucking proud of her he was, so he went straight for the kill.

A moment later, she went rigid over him, her entire body shuddering as the orgasm hit her, his name a hoarse shout on her lips.

Hearing her call for him drove him over the edge and he rolled with her, shoving her knees wide. Bracing himself, he drove into her and nearly came when her pussy contracted around him.

"I can't go slow," he warned her, but judging by the way her eyes lit with excitement, he didn't need to worry about it.

"Fuck me, sir. Please."

There was no finesse, no perfectly timed movements, no practiced maneuvers. There was only him, her, and the primal need to claim his woman. To mark her as his own. He fucked her, hard, holding off as long as he could until her back arched, those gorgeous breasts thrust towards him like an offering, and her wet heat clenched around him. When she screamed his name again, he was lost, and he followed her over the edge into bliss.

∼

Katherine

SHE WASN'T sure if someone could actually pass out from an orgasm, but she'd come damn close. At the very least, she'd fallen asleep for a bit, her head nestled against Austin's hard, warm chest.

When she came to, he was stroking her hair, and the sweet, simple gesture nearly made her sigh. It was perfect.

Except it wasn't.

And once her mind latched on to that tiny little detail, she couldn't turn it off. Shifting beside him, she snuggled in closer, chasing the peace and contentment she'd felt a moment ago.

"Hey there, sleepyhead. How are you feeling?"

"Mmm. Wonderful." Physically, anyway. If she could get her mind to shut up, she could follow her liquid muscles back to dreamland.

But even if she'd been able to turn her brain off, apparently Austin had other ideas. Rolling on top of her, he gathered her wrists in his hands and pinned her to the bed beneath him. When he claimed her lips in a kiss that was brutal in its tenderness, she tasted herself on him, and her cheeks heated at the memory of him beneath her, driving her wild with his tongue.

"Ready for round two?" He moved his lips to her jaw, then down her neck, and even though she was more sexually satisfied than she'd ever been in her life, her pussy clenched at his touch.

But unlike before, when she'd managed to convince herself she deserved to experience being fucked by Austin Barrick at least once, this time his clever mouth couldn't quiet her overactive mind.

"Actually... we still need to talk, Austin."

He went still, and she felt him sigh a moment before he shifted back to the side, still keeping her pinned beneath him but giving them both some space. Not enough space, in her mind, for the conversation they needed to have, but when she tried to move, he simply swatted her hip and told her to stop squirming.

"You want to talk, so talk. What's going on in that beautiful brain, Katherine?"

The use of her full name made her stomach jump, but she refused to be cowed into backing down from this. "I started going through your financials today. If you're going to be retiring soon," she sent him a cool look when he growled at her, "*when* you retire, however soon that may be, you'll need to tighten up your monthly budget. I was looking at ways you could start doing that now."

Pausing, she waited for some sign of alarm or shock, but he simply shrugged. "Sounds smart. So, what? I need to stop partying with the guys? I haven't really done much of that lately, anyway, but I've never been good at budgets so I'm sure there's plenty of places I can save some cash."

"Well, yes. Your dining and entertainment budget is a bit outrageous," she admitted, feeling suddenly unsure of herself. Did he think she hadn't found the mysterious monthly payment? Or did he truly have nothing to hide? "But there's one expense in particular, it looks like a recurring fee or membership of some kind, and I don't know how to categorize it." There. She'd made her point without coming off like a crazy, jealous girlfriend. All business.

"A fee? What kind of fee? For how much?"

"Twenty-five hundred dollars a month. To Cartwright-Davidson Enterprises."

The lines on his forehead drew together in obvious confusion, then smoothed out again when he grinned. "Oh. That. Yeah, I'm not canceling that."

"What is *that*, exactly, Mr. Barrick?"

She knew he hated it when she was so formal, especially when she used her customer service voice on him. Which was exactly why she'd done it. Why should she be the only one feeling put out at the moment?

Sure enough, his eyes narrowed and his mouth thinned into a dangerous line. "What's this about, Kit? Why are you getting all snooty on me? Is this what got your panties all knotted up: that I didn't tell you about the club?"

"My panties were not 'all knotted up'! As your financial advisor, I need to know…"

"Bullshit. Don't fucking lie to me, little girl. A woman

doesn't send a 'we need to talk' text to her boyfriend unless she's pissed about something. What are you so upset about? I would have told you about it eventually."

Ignoring the flutter in her belly at the word 'boyfriend', she lifted her chin. "I wasn't upset. I simply need to know how to categorize your expenses."

With a low growl, he rolled off the bed and stalked to the other side of the room. She braced herself for him leaving, for never seeing him again.

So when he turned back to her, his wide leather belt dangling from his hand, it took a moment for her to process his intent. When it finally clicked, her stomach twisted itself into a knot. "Austin, you can't spank me for asking you a perfectly reasonable question."

"I'm not. I'm going to spank you for lying to my face and trying to dance around the question you *actually* want to ask me. Get on your knees with your chest on the mattress and your ass in the air."

"Can't we talk about this?"

"Sure. After your punishment. I warned you about lying to me, kitten. I'm not a big stickler for rules, but that's the one thing I won't allow. On your knees, unless you want to do this the hard way."

She wasn't entirely sure what the hard way entailed, but if the easy way was him whipping her ass with his belt, she was absolutely certain she didn't want to risk it. Kicking the covers off of her, she moved into position, doing her best to not think about how on display she was in this position.

"Arms out in front of you. Good girl," he praised when she shifted. "Ass a little higher. That's it, just like that. I'm going to give you three with the belt, and then I'm going to ask you again why you're so upset. Lie to me again, and it'll be six. Rinse and repeat. Got it?"

"Yeah."

There was a *whoosh* and then a line of fire exploded across the back of her thighs. Lurching forward, she let out a shriek at the unexpected agony.

"Try that again, with a little more respect this time."

"Yes, sir. I'm sorry."

"Back in position."

Whimpering, she moved back to her original position with her cheek pressed against the mattress and her ass in the air.

"Just so you know, that one didn't count. It's only three, kitten. You can take it, because you're my good girl. Isn't that right, baby?"

His steady assurance eased some of the fear slithering around in her belly and she nodded. "Yes, sir. I'm ready."

From the corner of her eye, she saw his arm swing back, then there was another *whoosh*, another line of fire, this one directly across the middle of her bottom. Gritting her teeth, she squeezed her eyes shut and braced for the next two.

They were delivered right on the heels of the first, covering her backside in searing pain. But the initial agony only lasted for a few moments, and the fire had already started to fade to an almost pleasant burn by the time he spoke again.

"What was it that upset you so much, kitten?"

Even though it wasn't as bad as she'd thought it would be, she *really* didn't want another six. "I thought it was for rent, or something. For another house or apartment."

"Why would I need another house? The one I have is already too damn big for one person."

The frustration in his voice might have been amusing if her ass wasn't already wearing welts from his belt. "For someone else. Like another girlfriend, maybe."

Silence filled the room for several long, tense seconds before he sighed. "Oh, kitten. Come here."

She heard the clunk of the belt hitting the floor, felt the

bed dip beside her, and practically threw herself into his arms. "I'm sorry. It was stupid. I know it was stupid, and it didn't make any sense, I just... I couldn't figure out what else it could be, and I was hurt and confused."

"Would you like to know what it's for?"

"You said it was a club of some kind. I don't really need the details. Just tell me how to categorize it and I can work it from there."

"All right. But I still want to tell you."

"Okay. But only if you're sure."

"I am. It's a membership for a BDSM club called Black Light."

Of all the horrific confessions she'd prepared herself for, that one hadn't even been on her radar. "Oh."

"See? Nothing nefarious. Look at me." Placing a finger under her chin, he tilted her head back so she was forced to look up at him. "I don't want there to be any secrets between us. All you have to do is ask, and I'll tell you whatever you want to know. All right?"

"Yes, sir."

"Good girl. Now," his lips curved up in a wicked smile, "would you like to hear about Black Light?"

CHAPTER 11

KATHERINE

*D*id she want to hear more about the secret kinky sex club her self-professed boyfriend belonged to? Duh.

"Sure," she replied as nonchalantly as she could with her stomach doing somersaults.

"Let's get you cleaned up and warm up our dinner, and I'll tell you all about it."

"Cleaned up?" The sticky sensation between her thighs registered and she sat straight up. "Oh no! I'm so sorry, I can't believe I forgot to get a condom!"

"Calm down, kitten. It's my fault. I got carried away." He smirked, then sobered quickly. "I've been tested, so I'm clean. I wouldn't risk you like that."

"Okay. Me too." She'd gotten tested several times after her one and only one night stand a while back. "And I get a birth control shot, so no surprises."

"So, we're covered. I am sorry, though. I usually don't get so carried away I forget basic safety precautions."

Had she done that to him? Stripped him of his self-control? Turning away to hide her grin, she held that knowledge close to her, a prize she'd never in a million years imagined winning. "It's all right."

"Lie back down and I'll go get a washcloth."

She swallowed the argument that instinctively sprung to her lips. If it pleased him to take care of her, then who was she to deny him? Settling back against her pillows, she pulled the covers back up over her naked body while he disappeared into the en-suite bathroom.

When he returned and stopped beside the bed, frowning down at her, she squirmed under the blankets. "Why are you glaring at me?"

"I'm not glaring. I'm wondering who gave you permission to cover yourself up."

Oh.

"I, um, thought we were done playing."

"Fair enough," he admitted, though he didn't look at all mollified by her explanation. "We need to talk about that, though." Kneeling on the bed beside her, he tugged the blankets off and nudged her knees open so he could swipe the washcloth over her thighs and the too-sensitive skin of her pussy.

"Talk about what?"

"I already told you that I would have rules for you to follow if we were together. I don't expect you to walk around calling me Sir all the time, but I do prefer to have a certain amount of control in a relationship." Settling back on his heels, he cocked his head to the side and studied her with serious eyes. "Think you could be okay with that?"

"How much control? Are you going to pick out my clothes and make me crawl around naked all the time?" Need flared to life again between her thighs, but she had a feeling the reality wouldn't be quite as sexy as the fantasy her imagination conjured.

"Just sometimes," he assured with the flash of a grin. "You

already know about not putting yourself down. No lying. No more calling me 'Mr. Barrick'. And definitely no clothes when we're alone together."

"Uh huh, sure." With an exaggerated eye roll for what she was sure must have been a joke, she sat up and reached for the bra she'd abandoned during their play. But before she got very far, a hand fisted in her hair, jerking her back against a firm, hard body.

"Did you roll your eyes at me, little girl?"

"I—I thought it was a joke, sir."

The use of his honorific seemed to settle him and the grip on her hair gentled. "Not a joke, baby. I want you naked and accessible at all times. Besides, it's good practice for the club."

Her heart slammed against her ribcage at the insinuation. "You can't be serious, Austin."

"I'm very serious. I like the idea of being able to spread your thighs and eat that sweet pussy whenever I get the urge."

She liked that idea, too. She liked it very much. "But the part about not wearing clothes in the club. That was a joke."

"Not a joke. If we're going to scene in public, you'll most likely be naked. You and most of the other subs there."

"No. Absolutely not." Panic wrapped its tendrils around her chest, squeezing until she couldn't seem to drag in enough air.

"Hey. Breathe, kitten. You'll have your safe word if you need it. Even for something as simple as taking your clothes off."

"You won't be mad?"

"Look at me." Turning her head at the stern command, she let out a whoosh of breath at the understanding she found in his eyes. "I will never be mad at you for setting limits. If you *don't* tell me that something is upsetting you, or if you refuse to use your safe word when something gets to be too much, then I'll be pissed as hell. And I can promise you, *that* punishment would be a hell of a lot more than three measly strokes from my belt. Understood?"

Oddly enough, it was the threat of a punishment, delivered in that hard, strict tone, that finally settled her system. "Yes, sir."

"Good girl." He pressed a kiss to her forehead before nudging her out of the bed. "Let's go get dinner. I'm starving."

"Can I at least put my panties on? I'm not going to sit on my fabric dining room chairs naked."

"We'll put a towel down."

Sensing this was an argument she wouldn't win, she huffed out a breath. "Fine."

Austin

"A CATTLE PROD? NO WAY!"

Grinning at the shock on his girl's face, Austin nodded and stabbed at another spear of asparagus. "So I heard. I couldn't make it this year, but everyone's been talking about it. Hopefully we can get tickets to next year's Roulette."

It wasn't like him to start making plans seven months out with a girl, especially so early in, but every time he thought about not having Kit around, there was a weird sort of pressure in his chest. So he didn't think about; he just made plans.

Problem solved.

"That, ah, sounds nice." There was a pink tint to her cheeks that hadn't left the entire time they'd been having dinner. Part of him hoped she never completely lost that sweet shyness, but he did have some concerns about visiting Black Light. If she couldn't handle it, he'd deal with it, but he couldn't deny that part of him that wanted to show her off, parade her around for everyone to see what was his, the spectacular treasure they'd never get to touch or taste.

Hopefully she'd feel more comfortable after she spent some time naked with him. "Shoulders back, kitten. Don't hide yourself from me," he chided gently when he noticed her hunching over to take a bite of chicken.

Her face screwed up in a petulant way he found inexplicably adorable, but she straightened up as he'd instructed. At least for a second, until she leaned in for another bite of her dinner.

Hmmm. "Put your fork down."

She frowned slightly before asking what he was beginning to think of as her favorite question. "Why?"

Cocking an eyebrow, he gave her a cool stare. "Do you need to know why? Or are you supposed to do as you're told?"

"Is that a rule?"

One look at her serious, dark eyes told him the question wasn't borne out of snarkiness or a desire to be a brat, so he didn't slap at her for it. "Yeah, it's a rule."

With a quiet sigh, she placed her fork on her plate. "Happy?" she asked, the sulk clear in her whiskey-smooth voice.

"I'm always happy when you're a good girl."

Some of her annoyance faded at the praise and the pink in her cheeks darkened. Picking up his own plate, he switched chairs so he was sitting in the one just to her right. "Put your hands under your bottom and press your shoulders back against the chair."

She opened her mouth, probably to ask her favorite question, but she shut it again without voicing it. Her bottom lip pushed out in a bit of a pout, but he overlooked it since she'd done as he'd asked without argument.

"Thank you. Chicken or asparagus?" he asked, picking up her fork.

"Ah. Chicken?"

He cut off a small piece and held it up to her mouth. The blush he loved so much spread from her cheeks down her neck as she accepted the bite and chewed.

"Anything else you'd like to know about Black Light?"

"Um." She took the bite of asparagus he offered, chewing carefully before answering. "I don't even know what to ask, really. I'm worried I'll do something wrong and embarrass you, so just tell me what to do."

"You won't embarrass me, kitten. We'll go over some protocol before we go, but even if you get something wrong, I won't be upset. Nobody will judge you." He felt his lips twitch as he fought back a laugh. "Well, if you're intentionally being a brat, they might. But mostly they'll just enjoy watching you get your bottom paddled if that happens."

"You'd spank me there? In front of other people?"

"If I think you need it. But you're such a good girl, I can't see you earning a public punishment like that."

Something strangely close to disappointment flitted in her eyes before she smiled. "Thank goodness."

Hmmm. Maybe his kitten had more of an exhibitionist streak than she was letting on. It would fit nicely with his own needs if she did, but he didn't want to read too much into it at this stage.

"Well, if you think of any more questions, you can ask me any time. But now it's my turn to ask you something."

"What?"

"Would you and your dad like to come to the game on Saturday? I have some tickets, right behind home plate."

"Seriously?" Her entire face lit up, and in that instant, he knew he was sunk. There wasn't anything he wouldn't do to see that expression of pure joy as often as he possibly could.

"Yeah. I already have the tickets, so somebody needs to use them."

"Thank you! Dad is going to lose his mind!" She threw her

arms around his neck, technically without permission, but he didn't have the heart to correct her. Besides, she'd finished her dinner and apparently forgotten all about being naked in front of him, which had been his end goal anyway.

"Any time, kitten. I, ah, also invited Tony and his wife over for dinner after the game, if you guys wanna come hang out."

"Tony Torres?" Pulling away, she frowned. "Your replacement? Won't that be a little awkward?"

"I prefer to think of him as my understudy." He'd tried for a light, joking tone, but going by the way her face crumpled, he'd missed the mark. "Shit," he mumbled, blowing out a breath. How much of an asshole could he be? "I'm not mad at you, baby. I'm just... this is all I've ever done, you know? Other than washing cars when I was a teenager and I'd really prefer not to go back to that. The idea of retiring is just, I dunno. It's weird."

"I understand. Well, as much as I can, not being in your shoes. But I know how much my business means to me and I'd be devastated to lose it. Starting over is hard, but you have options."

"So they say. Pretty sure I'd make a shit coach, though."

"I don't know." She tilted her head to the side, and he was suddenly keenly aware of how much intelligence those shrewd brown eyes held. "You've been coaching me through all of this," she waved her hands at her naked form. "And there's not just coaching. There's sports TV, radio, podcasts. Or you could do something completely different. Surely baseball isn't the only thing you enjoy."

"Hmm." Leaning in, he captured a bare nipple between his teeth and tugged, drinking in her gasp of surprise. "There's plenty I enjoy that's not baseball. But I'm not sure I can make a living eating you out every night."

"Don't be so sure about that. I'd be willing to pay good money for those orgasms you've been giving away for free."

"Is that so?" Delighted by her, and relieved to be talking about anything other than his pending retirement, he pulled her to her feet and into his arms. "Guess I should get as much practice in as I can before I go pro, then, right?"

"It's the smart thing to do."

CHAPTER 12

KATHERINE

Staring at her cell phone, which she'd deliberately left sitting out as a silent reminder to call her dad, Kit nibbled on her bottom lip. She'd never been this nervous about talking to her dad before. But then, she'd never really done anything he remotely disapproved of before, and he'd made his feelings about her dating Austin crystal clear the last time she'd seen him. What if he still thought she wasn't good enough for him?

"Oh, stop being ridiculous," she snapped at the empty room, snatching her phone off the desk and hitting the button to call her dad.

"Hey, pumpkin! How's my favorite girl? I thought you'd forgotten all about your dear old dad."

Guilt nagged at the back of her mind. She hadn't intentionally been avoiding him, she'd just been busy. At least, that was what she'd been telling herself. "Just swamped at work, dad. But I have something that might make it up to you."

"Yeah? What's that?"

"Home plate tickets to the Hawks home game this weekend."

She winced and pulled the phone away from her ear at his loud whoop of excitement. "Fucking A! You serious, pumpkin?"

"Yup." Dragging in a breath, she fought through the tightness in her chest to drop the next bomb. "Austin got them for us."

"Barrick? You still seeing him?"

"Yes, I'm still seeing him." She winced at the defensiveness in her tone and forced herself to relax. "He's a really good guy, dad. I think you'll like him."

A long silence met her declaration, and she was about to ask if he was still there when he spoke again. "He treat you good?"

"Yeah, dad. He's amazing. And he makes me feel... beautiful." Heat filled her cheeks at the admission, and in that moment, she missed her mom like her own arm. The way she felt about her body, and the way Austin made her feel, were all things she could have spent hours dissecting with her mom. But it wasn't anything she'd ever really talked to her dad about.

"Well, you're the prettiest girl in the whole damn world, so why wouldn't he make you feel beautiful?"

She snorted out a laugh. "Not hardly, but thanks anyway. I know he could do a lot better than me, but he seems happy." *For now.* But she wasn't going to think about that. She was just going to enjoy the time she had with him.

"You listen to me, Katherine Marie. If that boy thinks he can do better than my little girl, then he's a complete moron and he doesn't deserve to breathe the same air as you."

Shock robbed her of the ability to speak for a long moment. "Dad, we both know all he'd have to do is whistle and a dozen pretty little groupies would come running." *You said so yourself.*

"Maybe so, but he'd be an idiot to so much as look at any

of them when he's got someone like you, who's not just a pretty face, but smarter than that whole damn team put together. Is he an idiot?"

Her world, which she hadn't even realized was a little off balance until that moment, righted itself again. "No, he's not an idiot."

"There you go, then. If he gets stupid, you let me know and I'll take care of it. Just because he's Austin Barrick doesn't mean he gets to be an asshole."

"Duly noted. So, I'll pick you up about ten on Saturday?"

"It's a date."

∼

THE CONFIDENCE BOOST her dad's little pep talk gave her lasted right up until they were escorted to their seats a few days later. She hadn't seen Austin since he'd barged into her apartment and given her the best sex of her life, and she'd spoken to him less than she had when he'd been on the road.

And when an adorable, tiny little blonde introduced herself as "Tony's wife but you can call me Claudia", all of her insecurities came rushing back to the surface. Maybe Claudia wasn't a supermodel, but she definitely fit the idea of "baseball player's wife" better than Kit.

"Your seats are next to me. Tony said it was your first time. You're here with Austin?"

A distinctly feminine snicker had Kit glancing over her shoulder at a pair of brunette beauties with their heads together. Her gaze collided with one of them, who quickly looked away, but the smirk on her face told Kit she didn't feel an ounce of guilt about being caught.

Turning back to Claudia, she forced a smile. "Yes. I'm Kit, and this is my dad, Charlie."

"Nice to meet you, Mrs. Torres." Reaching around her, dad

shook the little blonde's hand, giving it a little squeeze that made Claudia giggle.

"It's just Claudia. Are you two big baseball fans?"

"The biggest," Dad confirmed with a grin, slinging his arm around her shoulder. The casually affectionate move calmed some of the anxiety churning in her stomach. "Kit's first word was 'OUT!'. I don't think her mother ever really forgave me for it."

"That's adorable!" Claudia gushed, pressing a hand over her heart. "Tony Jr., he's just learning to talk, and I keep telling Tony he's gotta be careful about what he says 'cause once they start, babies pick up every word you say. And the only ones they want to repeat are the naughty ones."

"That's the god's honest truth there, Claudia. This one time, Kit was with me at the store and..."

"I don't think Claudia really wants to hear all about me, dad," Kit rushed to cut him off. She'd heard that opening enough to know it wasn't a story she wanted repeated in public, especially with the stares she swore she could feel boring a hole in her back.

"Oh, I want to hear *all* about you," Claudia insisted, mischief sparkling in her eyes. "But there's time for that at the cookout later."

Kit could have sworn she deliberately raised her voice, a suspicion that was confirmed when Claudia jerked her head towards the bimbo twins and rolled her eyes.

"How old is Tony Jr.?" Kit asked, more out of a desperation to turn the conversation away from her than any real desire to know. But thirty seconds into Claudia gushing over her sons —Tony Jr. had a younger brother named Gabriel—Kit found herself forgetting all about the snickers and stares for awhile.

Her phone buzzed in her pocket, and she grinned when she saw Austin's name on the screen. "Shouldn't you be getting ready, Mr. Barrick?"

"I was born ready, baby. And don't think I didn't catch that. You think I won't punish you just because we have some people coming over?"

Suddenly keenly aware of the fact that she was seated between her dad and an almost complete stranger, she quickly made her way over to the stairs for a little privacy. "You wouldn't," she shot back, with more certainty than she felt.

"I could teach you a very painful lesson without making a sound, kitten. You really want to risk that?"

"Ah," a quick glance around confirmed nobody was close enough to hear her. "No, sir. I'm sorry."

"There's my good girl. God, I miss you. I changed my mind, cookout is canceled."

"It's at your house, Austin," she reminded him, doing her best to ignore the sudden aching need in her pussy. "You can't skip your own dinner party."

"Sure I can. I'll give Torres a key and we can go to your place, instead."

While that sounded infinitely better than making small talk over burgers, she shook her head. "No can do. You promised my dad dinner with not one, but two professional shortstops. He'll be devastated."

"Fine. But I'm having you for dessert."

"Austin!"

"What? You're my favorite sweet treat."

"You're ridiculous."

"I dare you to say that to me when I've got you tied to my bed and you're not allowed to come until I let you."

"I'm hanging up now, Austin."

"I gotta get going, anyway. Enjoy the show, kitten."

"Yes, sir."

Was her face as bright red as it felt? She hoped not, or her dad was going to have questions.

When she returned to her seat, Claudia handed her a

bottle of water. "Looks like you could use this," she whispered, her lips twitching with obvious amusement.

Oh, god. "That obvious?" Kit whispered back.

"Only because I was paying attention. Looked like that was some phone call."

It might have been fun to share if her dad hadn't been sitting right beside her, his eyes locked on the empty field in front of them. Twisting the cap off the bottle, she took a long pull just as the players started to file onto the field. Austin took his place beside his teammates for the anthem, but he turned to scan the crown behind him.

Her heart stuttered in her chest when his gaze slammed into hers. There was heat there, even from a distance, but even more than the heat was the joy. His entire face lit with pleasure when he found her, and he gave her a little wave.

Lifting her hand, she waved back, even stepping out of her comfort zone enough to blow him a kiss. The goofball pretended to catch it and stuff it in his pocket before turning back around.

And it was then she recognized another bonus to watching him play in person: getting to see his incredible ass in those tight uniform pants.

Everything would have been perfect if it hadn't been for the whispers gradually building in volume behind them.

"Seriously, her? I don't get it. Think he's got some kind of weird, fat girl fetish?"

"Oh! I've heard of that. Eww, what if he's one of those guys who gets off on feeding women and watching them get bigger and bigger?"

"If she's even with him at all. I bet that wasn't even him on the phone."

"God, how desperate is *that*?"

Fixing her gaze on the scoreboard, she tried to drown out

the mocking voices, but each new barb dug its way under her skin until she could barely stand it.

It was high school all over again. And as much as she silently lectured herself that she was a grown ass woman, that words from two bitches she didn't even know shouldn't have the power to hurt her, she felt that familiar burning in her gut. That bone-deep shame she'd learned to live with from the first time she'd stepped out of the "Juniors" section and into the "Womens" at a department store, because her hips no longer fit in the pin-straight jeans.

Even twenty years later, the shame had never really faded. She buried it, as deep as she could, but it never went away. She covered it with stylish clothes and perfectly applied makeup, hid it behind a successful business she'd worked her ass off to build.

But it was never enough. And no matter what Austin said, no matter how beautiful he tried to make her feel, she was beginning to think nothing would ever really be enough to rid her of that shame.

"Want me to have them removed?"

Claudia's quiet question jerked her back to the present and Kit shook her head. "No. Just ignore them. I am."

"Sweetie, you may be pretending you don't hear them, but you aren't ignoring them. Don't let those groupies ruin this for you. They're just bitter that you have something they'll never have."

"What's that?"

"They may be able to get into these guy's beds, they'll never get into their hearts. Not like you have with Austin."

"That's sweet." Austin might care for her, but she wasn't stupid enough to think he'd fallen in love with her or anything.

Claudia snorted. "I am not sweet. Look over at the dugout. What do you see?"

Tearing her gaze from the scoreboard, she looked over to the home team's box. Austin was there, his steady stare locked on her.

"He's been watching you the whole game. That man adores you, Kit. Don't forget it."

"Maybe," she conceded, unwilling to put too much meaning on the fact she'd caught him looking at her.

"Are you always this stubborn?"

The exasperated tone pulled a giggle from her and Kit felt her muscles loosen. "Maybe."

"Brat."

CHAPTER 13

AUSTIN

Why the hell had he invited them to dinner? Not that he wasn't having a good time. Tony's wife was a little spitfire, and she brought out a sassier side of Kit he normally didn't see. Not so much that she got herself into trouble, but enough that he'd pulled her aside and whispered a reminder of what happened to naughty girls in her ear.

Unfortunately, the threat seemed to have more of an effect on him than it had on her. Standing in front of the shiny, barely used grill on his back deck, he silently willed his cock to stand down, at least until their guests left.

Would it be rude to pack everyone to-go bags and send them on their way when the food was ready?

At the sound of the glass door sliding open and shut again, he turned, hoping to find Kit had escaped for a few minutes alone. Instead, he found her dad, two beers in hand and a carefully guarded expression on his face.

"Thanks," he said when Charlie handed him the extra bottle.

"Welcome. Good game today." Joining him in front of the

grill, Charlie stared down at the burgers sizzling over the charcoal.

"We won." Barely. As much as he'd enjoyed having Kit in the stands, he'd definitely been distracted. "Coulda been better."

An awkward silence settled between them, and Austin frantically searched his brain for something to say.

"So. You and my Kit."

A panic he hadn't felt since his rookie days gripped him by the throat, forcing him to swallow hard before he could speak.

"Yes, sir. She's great." *Great* didn't begin to encompass his sweet, sassy, brilliant little kitten, or the all-consuming need he felt for her, but he knew damn well there were some things you couldn't say to a woman's father.

"She's the best person I know. She just doesn't see it."

Austin shifted to study the older man. Red was creeping up his neck, just like it did with Kit when she was forced to talk about something she'd rather not.

"I don't get it, either," he said, shrugging when Charlie glanced over at him. "She's the whole package, but she's got this idea in her head that since she's not a size two, the rest of it doesn't count."

"And you? You care she's not a supermodel?"

"Fuck, no." Shit. He was just going to have to come out and say it. "Mr. Callahan, I'm crazy about your daughter. I think she's about the sexiest damn woman I've ever known, body, soul, and mind."

"Good. That's good." Charlie took another pull of his beer. "There were these women at the game. Making nasty comments. Just thought you should know."

So that was why she'd been so stiff for awhile. He'd caught her staring at the scoreboard like it held the meaning of life, but then she'd looked his way and he hadn't noticed the stiffness again the rest of the game.

"What women? What did they say?"

"I don't know who they were. Pair of brunettes sitting behind us. They never said anything to her, but they made sure she could hear it, and any idiot could tell they were talking about my Kit. Pissed me the fuck off."

"So why didn't you handle it?"

The look Charlie sent him was filled with wry amusement. "You ever try handling things for Kit? Fastest way to piss that girl off. Look, son, I'm not in the business of giving grand speeches or putting my nose where it doesn't belong. But I'll give you this bit of advice, if you want it."

"Sure."

"She doesn't need a knight in shining armor to sweep in and rescue her from the big, scary world. Ever since her mom died, she's learned to be her own knight. I know there's lots of things she's never told me, 'cause she wanted to handle it on her own. But she knows I'm in her corner, no matter what, and I figure that's what she'll want from you."

"All right. I can do that." It grated a bit, to not be able to protect her, to keep her tucked up and safe from people who wanted to hurt her. But he figured Charlie knew what he was talking about. "So, no tracking these women down and getting them banned from the stadium for life?"

"Well, now, I reckon what she doesn't know won't hurt us."

Grinning, Austin turned back to his burgers.

∼

Austin

"Thank god they're gone." Kit collapsed on the couch beside him, and Austin reached for her, pulling her into his arms.

"You took the words right out of my mouth, kitten." Pressing his lips against the side of her neck, he tugged at the hem of her jersey. "What's the rule about clothes when we're alone?"

"They just left!"

"Five whole minutes ago. That's five minutes you've been wearing too many clothes. Strip, little girl, before I decide to get mean."

"You're already mean," she muttered, pulling the jersey up over her head.

"Oh, I can definitely be meaner. Stand here." With a snap of his fingers, he pointed to the floor in front of him. "I want to watch you."

"You can see me fine, Mr. Barrick," she snapped irritably.

All it took was a quick tug and she was sprawled across the couch, her ass propped up high on his knee. Cupping one cheek, he gave it a hard squeeze that had her squealing and drumming her feet against the leather.

"Is that how you talk to me, Katherine?"

"I'm sorry," she whined, drawing the words out and wiggling against his grip. But he figured she wasn't too sorry since this was what she'd obviously been angling for whether she was really aware of it or not.

With that in mind, he put plenty of steel into his next order. "After you strip for me, you're coming right back here. Up."

She scrambled to her feet, pink staining her cheeks as she reached for the button on her jeans. Her movements were slow, hesitant, as she pushed the curve-hugging denim over her hips with a little wiggle of her ass.

"Fuck, baby. You're so beautiful." Reaching inside the baggy sweatpants he'd changed into after the game, he stroked his already impossibly hard cock.

As always, her eyes lit up at the compliment. But tonight, there was something... more. Something almost desperate in her gaze. Thanks to the heads up from her dad, at least he had an idea of what had put that look in her eyes. He'd also tracked Claudia down before dinner and she'd spilled the whole sordid story, peppered with a few choice words about the bimbos who'd insulted her friend.

When she was completely bared to him, he let go of his cock and patted his knee. "Over you go, kitten."

Her bottom lip moved into a pout. "Am I in trouble?"

"Now, Katherine."

She sighed, her gorgeous breasts swaying with the effort, but she moved to his side. "What about your knee? You've been favoring it."

Her concern warmed him, but he didn't soften. "This position won't bother my knee. Quit stalling, little girl."

Pouting again, she stretched out across the couch cushions, her ass perfectly positioned for her punishment.

"That's my good girl," he murmured, rubbing each of her cheeks in turn, warming up the skin. "Do you like getting in trouble, kitten?"

"No, sir. It just slipped out."

"Did it?" Leaving it at that, he lifted his hand and brought it down hard on her right cheek. "Count them. One, sir. Two, sir. Maybe that will help you remember how to properly address me."

"One, sir," she repeated obediently, if a little sulkily.

Chuckling, he repeated the action on her left cheek, this time earning him a small gasp before her count. "Two, sir."

"See how easy it is, kitten? I don't believe for a minute it 'just slipped out'. You're too smart for that." Another swat, hard enough to make her jolt forward.

"Three, sir! I didn't mean anything by it!"

"Didn't you? I know that tone, kitten. It's the one you use when you're irritated or when you're struggling with submitting to me."

Number four earned him a low whine, and he was

rewarded with the delicious sight of her ass jiggling when she wiggled her hips to escape the burn. "Four, sir."

"Not gonna try and argue that, are you, kitten?" He aimed the next swat at the sensitive spot where her thighs met her ass.

"No. Five, sir."

"Because you know better than to try and lie to me. I'm not mad. But you were trying to get a reaction out of me, so I'm not going to go easy on you, either."

The next swat was met with a whispered, "Six, sir."

"This is exactly what you'll get every time you try to provoke me. Understood?"

"Yes, sir, I understand."

"Good. You can stop counting now."

It was all the warning he gave her before he shifted his grip on her waist and lit into her bottom. Kit let out a shriek at the sudden assault and before long, she was a wild, thrashing thing over his lap, wiggling and fighting to be released. His knee throbbed in protest, but he gritted his teeth through the pain and focused on delivering a thorough lesson.

Bringing the punishment to an end with a few extra hard swats to the sensitive spots where ass met thigh, Austin let his hand rest on her heated skin. "Who is in charge here, kitten?"

"You are, sir," she said on a groan, her breath coming in short, sharp pants.

"Good girl. We're done for now. But just know that there will be a time when that attitude of yours will earn you more than just my hand on your ass."

"Yes, sir."

Satisfied he'd made his point, he patted her bottom and leaned back. "Stand up, hands on your head."

Scrambling to obey, she stood, linking her fingers behind her head like he'd taught her. "Place your feet shoulder width apart."

When she was positioned how he wanted her, he stood, circling her, taking his time and letting her feel his gaze on every inch of her exposed body.

Standing behind her, he reached around, cupping her breasts in his hands. "I love your breasts. But you already know that, don't you, kitten?"

"Yes, sir," she replied, a small smile curving her lips.

Releasing her soft mounds, let his hands drift down to her round tummy. "And I know you don't believe me, but I love your stomach, too." He gently pressed his fingers into the soft flesh. "Your hips. Your ass. Your sweet pussy."

As he spoke, he trailed his fingers down her stomach to the thick thatch of curls between her thighs. "I can't get enough of this. Of you."

Using one hand to grip her hip, he slipped a finger between her lips, grinning when he found her wet and ready for him. "Seems like the feeling's mutual."

"Yes, sir."

"Ready to up the ante, kitten?"

"Sir?" she asked, her voice just a little breathless, a little uncertain.

"I want to hurt you." Pulling her back against him, he pinched her clit, drinking in her shocked gasp as she went up on her toes. "Do you remember your safe words?"

"Y-yes, sir. Yellow to slow down, red to stop. Like a traffic light."

"Good girl. And you know I won't be mad if you need to use them?"

There was the slightest hesitation before she nodded. Frowning, he pulled away and turned her to face him, catching her chin between his thumb and forefinger to force her to look up at him.

"We don't go any further until I'm absolutely convinced you'll use your safe words if you need them, little girl."

"I will, sir. It's just…" Trailing off, she sucked on her bottom lip and tried to look away.

"No. Eyes on me." He waited for her to obey and granted her a tight, approving smile. "Good girl. Now, what did you want to say?"

"I just want you to be happy with me," she whispered, tears shimmering in her eyes.

"Oh, baby. I am beyond happy. Even if you shout red before I put the first clamp on, I could never be anything less than thrilled with you."

Her eyes widened, and she sucked in air. "Clamp, sir?"

"Yes. I think you'll enjoy them. But you'll never know if I can't trust you to tell me when it's too much. Can I trust you, kitten?"

"Yes, sir."

Much more believable this time, but he'd still be keeping an eye on her. "All right. Come with me, then."

CHAPTER 14

KATHERINE

Kit obediently took the hand Austin offered and followed him down the short hallway to his bedroom. Every nerve ending in her body felt like a live wire about to snap. If the anticipation was this nerve-wracking, what was the actual experience going to be like?

His bedroom was much like the rest of the house. Modern and stylish, in a very laid-back kind of way that reminded her of him. The focal point was obviously the king-sized bed in the middle of the room, with the twisted metal headboard and footboard.

"Do you remember how I taught you to present yourself for my belt the other day?"

"Yes, sir."

"Good. Up on the bed. I need to get some things ready."

With a nod, she moved away from him, toward the bed. She turned to ask if she should take her clothes off, then remembered with a start that she was already naked. She'd been so caught up in their play, she'd somehow forgotten that she was parading around his house in her birthday suit.

It should have been embarrassing. But all she felt was…

free. Like she'd shed some kind of weight she hadn't even realized she'd been carrying with her.

Austin gave that to her. He gave her the power to simply be, without worrying about the way her tummy jiggled or her thighs rubbed together.

And in return, she would give him this. Her submission. Her obedience.

Her pain.

Trembling a little at the thought, she climbed onto the bed and arranged herself as best she could remember. On her knees, ass in the air, arms stretched out on the bed in front of her.

"Perfect." His praise filled her with warmth and she turned her head to smile at him.

"Thank you, sir."

"You're welcome, baby. Do you know what this is?"

He held up a ball of some kind, with a flat bottom and a pointed head. Her mind reached for the term. "Is that a plug, sir?"

"Yes, it is. Where does it go?"

"My, um, oh geez." Cheeks flaming, she buried her face in her arm.

"No." The curt order was followed by his hand in her hair, pulling her head up. "You don't get to hide from me, kitten. Not here. Tell me where the plug goes."

"In my butt," she mumbled.

Grinning, he leaned in for a quick kiss. "You're so cute when you're embarrassed. A guy could get addicted to it. Yeah, baby, it goes in that gorgeous ass of yours. You're gonna want to relax for me, okay? I don't want to hurt you. Yet," he added with a wink.

If her face got any hotter, his whole damn bed was going to go up in flames. Closing her eyes, she focused on relaxing her muscles. Relaxing, so he could shove a giant chunk of plastic up her butt. Was this really her life?

Cold liquid dribbled between her cheeks and she let out a whimper.

"You okay, kitten?"

"Yes, sir."

"Katherine. What color are you?"

"Green, sir. As long as I don't die of embarrassment, I'm perfectly green."

"You won't die of embarrassment," he assured her with a laugh. "But I gotta tell ya, kitten. The more you blush, the harder I get. You've got me wondering how red you'll be when I'm prepping your bottom for my cock. Or when you're strapped to a bench at Black Light, waiting for my cane."

The mention of being naked in a club, of being punished so publicly, sent a familiar flash of panic through her system. But it wasn't the same overwhelming, nausea-inducing fear she'd felt the first time he'd brought it up. This was more akin to what she often felt before a first date, or before meeting a client for the first time. Nervous but… expectant. Excited, even.

Interesting.

"Hmm." A thick finger slipped between her thighs and she gasped at the unexpected intrusion. "Fuck, baby. You're dripping wet. I think you like the idea of being on display. Does that make you horny, the idea of all those people watching you, admiring how you take your punishment? Touching themselves while you take your Sir's cock in your ass?"

The orgasm rocked through her, not nearly as powerful as the ones he'd given her before, but the rush of pleasure was unmistakable.

"Naughty little kitten. From now on, you only come when I give you permission. Understood?"

"Yes, sir." She tried to sound repentant, but she couldn't

feel too guilty when the quick orgasm had taken the edge off enough for her to relax and enjoy the feel of his hands on her.

"I can't wait to show you off, kitten. But for now, I'm happy to have you all to myself. I'm going to stretch your bottom a bit so I can put the plug in."

"Um, okay."

It wasn't as painful as the first time, probably thanks to the liberal amounts of lube he'd coated her with. There was a bite of pain when the tip of his finger pushed past the initial resistance, but then her bottom seemed to accept its intruder and all she felt was a strange kind of pressure.

"Still green, baby?"

"Yes, sir."

"Excellent. I'm adding a second finger now."

The pressure inside her eased, but a moment later there was another shock of pain and she nearly lurched forward to get away from it.

"Easy, baby," he murmured, his voice low and soothing. "Give it a minute and it won't hurt anymore."

"Easy for you to say," she snapped, hissing at the burn as his fingers stretched her past the point of simple discomfort.

"Watch the attitude or I'll find something to occupy that naughty mouth."

"It hurts." She hated the whine in her voice, but she couldn't seem to help herself. It did hurt, though the burn was already fading to that odd fullness.

"I told you I wanted to hurt you, baby. But you can take it, can't you? Because you're my good girl and you can take whatever I give you."

The easy praise uncoiled some of the tension that had settled low in her belly. "Yes, sir."

"That's what I thought." He pumped his fingers inside of her, and she had to fight the urge to bury her face in the covers at the feel of them inside of her, stretching her.

Then they were gone, and she was left feeling empty again. But only for a moment, before something hard and round pushed against her hole.

"Deep breath in and let it out slowly. Push back against the plug and that will help it slide in."

Slide turned out to be a bit of an overstatement. Even with the lube, she could feel him forcing the rubber inside of her, no matter how hard she tried to relax and accept the foreign object.

Just when she thought it was too big and would never fit, the widest part of it pushed past that tight ring of muscle and she felt her bottom close around the base.

"You can lie down now, kitten. I know that's a hard position to hold and you've been there for awhile already. I'm going to go wash my hands and I'll be right back."

Since her muscles were starting to scream at her, she gratefully accepted the opportunity to stretch out on the bed, pillowing her head on her arms with a soft sigh of contentment. Did it make her weird to feel so perfectly happy with a plug in her ass and the promise of more pain to come?

Maybe, but Austin was obviously the same kind of weird, and if their shared weirdness had brought them together, then who was she to question it?

"All this time I thought your ass couldn't be more perfect, but I was wrong. My handprints on your skin and my plug inside you takes it to a whole new level."

Unease and pleasure warred inside of her, as they often did when he was complimenting her body. "I don't know that I would call it perfect."

Leaning over, he tapped her on the nose. Despite the playful gesture, his eyes were serious. "New rule. Whenever I give you a compliment, you aren't allowed to argue with me. If you absolutely have to say something, you can say 'Thank you, sir' but that's it."

"I wasn't arguing, I was just saying I don't think my ass is perfect."

"Well, I think it is. And since I'm the one who gets to spank, fondle, and fuck it, I get the final say."

"Since I'm the one who has to force it into ten different pairs of jeans in the dressing room to find anything that fits, I think I should get the final say." She didn't know why she was pushing back so hard; there just seemed to be something inside of her that refused to back down. Compliments had always made her uncomfortable, and the idea of simply accepting them with nothing more than a "Thank you" twisted her stomach into knots.

"You're forgetting one vital piece of information here, kitten."

"What's that?"

Using her hair to pull her head back, he growled into her ear. "You're not in charge, are you, little girl?"

And just like that, everything faded but him. She could worry about her too-big ass later. For now, all she had to do was focus on pleasing him. "No, sir."

"So, when I say your ass is perfect, what do you say?"

When she hesitated, he tightened his hold on her hair, the flash of pain prompting her obedience. "Thank you, sir."

"Much better." Releasing her, he straightened, his fingers trailing down her spine, leaving a line of gooseflesh in their wake.

"Roll onto your back with your arms stretched over your head."

She rushed to obey, eager to see what he had planned for her next. Her answer came in the form of a long length of rope he pulled from a walk-in closet the size of her bedroom.

"Have you changed your mind about being tied up?"

"No, sir." If anything, she was more eager now than when she'd filled out the kinky survey.

Moving to the bed, he climbed up with her, straddling her chest as he went to work. There was something almost hedonistic about being completely nude while he was still fully dressed. It was as if she were on display for him; nothing more than a plaything to be used for his pleasure as he saw fit.

Fuck, she needed to come again.

By the time he'd finished, her hands were clasped together, the soft rope twining around her wrists and forearms. Tilting her head back, she watched in fascination as he secured the remaining rope to the headboard.

"Give it a tug," he instructed as he climbed off of her.

She pulled lightly, then harder, her heart pounding against her chest when she realized how securely he'd tied her. Not only was she his plaything, she was completely at his mercy. No matter how hard she fought, there would be no breaking free. No escaping whatever torment he had planned for her.

Now she *really* needed to come again.

Pressing her thighs together, she squeezed, hoping to alleviate some of the ache building in her pussy. But her attempts didn't go unnoticed.

"None of that, kitten. Knees apart. Wider." The order was punctuated with a sharp slap to the inside of each thigh when she inched them further apart. "As far as they can go, little girl."

Huffing softly, she spread her legs wide, fully exposing herself to him. "Happy?"

"I'm always happy when you follow instructions. I am not happy with the attitude you have right now."

"Sorry, sir."

"Pull your heels up to your ass but keep your knees open."

When she was in position, he smiled. Not the playful grin she was used to, but the kind of smile that promised pain and pleasure, as much of each as she could handle.

"Sir…"

"What color are you, baby?"

"Green, but…" she let the question trail off, not wanting to upset him. "I'm green, sir."

"But, what?"

"Nothing."

"Tell me or we stop now, I untie you, and you won't be allowed to come again the rest of the night."

"What are you going to do to me?" she blurted out.

"Sorry, kitten. I'm not going to tell you because you'll be fretting over the next step instead of enjoying what's happening."

Because she couldn't deny it, she settled for scowling up at him. "That hardly seems fair."

"You can use your haughty, professional voice on me all you want, little girl. It'll just make your screams sound that much sweeter."

"What is that supposed to mean?"

Instead of answering her, he disappeared into the closet again, this time reemerging with a short strip of leather in one hand, his opposite fist tightly closed around something else.

"What's in your hand?"

"You'll see in a minute."

If she could have stomped her foot just then, she would have. "Why can't you just tell me?"

"Because I don't want to."

"Why?"

"Do you need to understand why? Or do you just need to listen and do as you're told?"

"I'm supposed to listen, but…"

"Then stop asking questions and turn off that beautiful brain of yours for a while. Just focus on what you feel. The pain." Dropping the strap on the bed, he reached out and pinched her nipple. "The pleasure." He ran his tongue over the abused peak. "Can you do that for me, baby? Just let go and feel?"

If anyone could make her brain stop working, it was him. He'd taken her there before, and if she'd let him, he would do it again. "I'll try, sir."

"Good girl. Let's get these clamps on you and see how much those pretty nipples can take."

CHAPTER 15

AUSTIN

Watching Kit's eyes go wide with surprise and need was always a delight. A man could get off on that look alone.

But since he had plans for his kitten, he ignored his rock-hard cock and focused on her.

"Will it hurt?"

Her tone was laced with fear, but enough curiosity to soothe his conscience. "Yeah, baby. It's going to hurt."

"Okay." Nibbling at her bottom lip, she moved her shoulders, her arms pulling at the rope he'd wound around her wrists.

"How are your arms? Any tingling or numbness?" Moving to the head of the bed, he checked her fingers for any signs of circulation issues. There was a bit of redness where the rope was rubbing her skin, but nothing dangerous.

"No, sir. I'm good."

"Tell me if that changes."

His instruction was met with a subtle eye roll. "Yes, sir."

Biting the inside of his cheek to keep himself from grinning at her brattiness, he raised an eyebrow at her. That was all it took for her to flush a delectable shade of pink and give him a sheepish smile.

"Sorry, sir."

"Much better." Palming a heavy breast in his hand, he rolled the nipple between his thumb and forefinger, drinking in her quiet sigh of pleasure.

Once the bud was nice and tight, he opened one of the clamps as far as it would go and placed it around her nipple. Watching her expression so he could gauge her reactions, he slowly twisted the screw to tighten the clamp.

"Oh!" After a few twists, she gasped and arched up. "That hurts!"

"Does it hurt more than when we played the other day?"

"No. It's," she paused, and he could practically hear her mind searching for the right explanation, "it's more like when you squeeze a little too hard."

"Good. Then you can take more."

The next twist of the screw was met with a low whine. He paused again, letting her adjust to the new sensation. A sheen of arousal clouded her eyes and he grinned down at her.

"Do you like it when I hurt you, kitten?"

"Yes, sir. Ow!" She let out a cry when he tightened the screw another turn. "Too much, that's too much!"

"Is it?" He ran a hand down her tummy to where her legs were still spread obscenely wide for him. "I don't think it is. You're soaking wet, baby."

Panting, she shook her head from side to side. "Sir, please!"

"What color are you, kitten? Take a second and really think about it."

Another soft whine, this one distinctly more petulant than the last. "Green, sir. But close to yellow."

"Good girl. Thank you for being honest with me."

If she'd been more experienced, he would have given the clamp at least one more twist, but he didn't want to tip her over the edge of what she could handle. There would be plenty of time for skirting those lines later, if he had his way about it.

For the first time that he could remember, he couldn't imagine growing bored with the woman in his bed any time soon.

"Next clamp, baby. You're doing so good. I'm so proud of you."

"Th-thank you, sir."

He took his time with the second clamp as well, letting her reactions tell him when she'd just about reached her limit. When both nipples were properly clamped, he stepped back to admire his handiwork, those rosy buds turning red between the silver of the clamps.

"So beautiful. Keep those knees open wide for me, baby."

Kit nodded, and it didn't go unnoticed by him that she didn't question him or argue. Whether she was actively learning to trust him or she was just too focused on the pain, he considered it progress.

Picking up the short, lightweight strap he'd pulled from his toy chest, he tapped it lightly against the curls between her thighs. Without a word of warning, he lifted the strap and snapped it down against her pussy.

"Fuck, fuck, fuck!" Back arching, Kit pulled at her restraints, but kept her knees spread. "That hurts!"

Good girl. "Aww, poor kitten. Do you want me to stop?"

"Yes!"

In response, he snapped the leather down again, this time drawing a howl of pained outrage from her. "Aus— Sir!"

"Good catch," he crooned, switching the strap to his opposite hand so he could gently stroke her swollen lips. "What color are you, kitten?"

"I-I don't know."

"Look at me, Katherine."

She forced her eyes open and he felt a rush of raw, primal need at the tears glittering like dew on her lashes. "Sir?"

"Can you take one more for me, baby?"

A single tear slipped from each eye and her lower lip trembled, but after a moment of hesitation, she nodded. "Yes, sir."

"That's my good girl. One more and then you can have your reward."

∽

Katherine

ONE MORE. *You can take one more, Kit.*

She could take anything if it meant seeing that gleam of pride in her Sir's cool blue eyes. That, and the reward he was dangling in front of her like the proverbial carrot.

The leather tapped against her sore, tingling pussy and she braced for the last blow. Pain, white-hot and shocking, zipped through her, straight up her spine, and a scream ripped from her throat as she arched up, desperate to relieve the fierce sting.

"Such a good girl."

She barely heard the praise over the sound of her own panting, but her heart did a slow roll in her chest as his words registered.

"Th-thank you, sir."

As the pain faded from nearly unbearable to that delicious burn she loved so much, she managed to pry her eyes open and focus on him, just in time to watch him yank his shirt up over his head.

Goddamn, he was perfect. Chiseled abs, arms, and shoulders that looked as though they'd been carved from rock. Everything about him was absolute perfection.

He'd stripped down to his boxers when he caught her

watching him. A slow, easy grin spread across his face as he pushed them down, letting them pool on the ground around his ankles. Her mouth literally watered at the sight of his cock, jutting forward like it couldn't wait to be inside of her. "You look so gorgeous, all flushed and glassy-eyed."

Was she? She hadn't given much consideration to how she looked. But judging by his words and the hunger burning in his gaze as he knelt between her thighs, he was more than happy with what he saw.

It was her own personal miracle.

Lifting her hips, she welcomed him inside of her, letting out a soft sigh as he pushed into her. Between the plug and his cock, she was full, impossibly full. And she was loving every second of it.

"Ready for your reward, kitten?"

"Yes, sir—oh!"

Clever, skilled fingers toyed with her clit, rolling and pinching the over-stimulated bundle of nerves until she yanked at her restraints, her head thrashing wildly against the pillow. "Sir, please!"

"Just a moment longer. Can you wait for me, baby?"

Words deserted her as pleasure took over, crowding out everything that wasn't pleasing him. The room filled with her whimpers and sobs, the soft slapping of their flesh coming together over and over, and his quiet murmurs of encouragement and praise.

"Good girl. Almost there. Wait for me, baby, wait for me."

Too much. It was too much, but she fought back the waves threatening to crash over her. Her Sir wanted her to wait, and she was going to wait if it killed her. And she wasn't entirely sure it wouldn't. The human body wasn't meant to withstand this level of torturous pleasure, was it?

"Fuck, baby." The fingers of his free hand dug into her thigh and his hips slammed against her raw, punished pussy.

Pain and pleasure melded together, until she couldn't remember which was which.

"Come for me, kitten."

The growled command was punctuated by an extra hard pinch of her clit and the flash of pain sent her careening over the edge of reason, screaming out his name as she bucked against him.

And just when she was certain she'd rode her pleasure to its end, he reached for the clamps on her nipples, ripping them off without warning. Pain lanced through her, pushing her back up to her peak and over again, this time dragging him over with her.

"Such a good girl," he murmured when he collapsed beside her, brushing soft kisses along her collarbone and up her neck, over the curve of her jaw to her lips. "My good little kitten."

"Sir." The word was a sigh against his lips. It was all she could manage with her heart threatening to beat out of her, and her chest shuddering with each deep, heaving breath.

"Stay here," he ordered with a twitch of his lips. "Let me get you cleaned up."

Even if she hadn't been tied to the bed, she wouldn't have been able to move more than an inch, not after he'd so thoroughly wrecked her.

"I could definitely get used to this." Returning to the bedroom with a damp washcloth in one hand and a bottle of water in the other, Austin paused to grin down at her. "Maybe I should just keep you here, tied to the bed all weekend."

"Mmm. Okay."

A low, deep chuckle reached her as he ran the cloth up the inside of her thighs and ever so gently across her sore pussy lips. "If orgasms make you this agreeable, I'll definitely have to consider keeping you tied here for awhile."

"I'm agreeable," she argued, but there wasn't much heat to

the response. Every part of her felt loose and floaty and she wasn't quite ready to return to Earth.

His only response was another quiet laugh before she felt the tug of the ropes and the pressure releasing from her arms. Pain stabbed at her shoulders when she tried to move, and she let out a soft groan.

To her surprise, Austin climbed on the bed behind her, pulling her up so she was sitting in front of him while he massaged the kinks from her shoulders.

"Thanks," she murmured, letting her head fall to the side.

"Gotta take care of my kitten." A comfortable silence stretched between them before he spoke again. "Want to tell me about the game?"

"Tell you what, exactly?"

"You had a good time?"

"We had a blast." And she had, mostly, so it wasn't really a lie, right?

Another stretch of silence, but this one seemed heavier than the last—expectant in a way. She had the fleeting thought that he was waiting for her to confess something, but there was no way he could know what had happened.

"Kitten… you know keeping things from me counts as lying, right?"

Shit. He did know. "What did dad tell you?"

"Just that some idiots were making comments and it upset you. Wanna talk about it?"

"Not really. I'm used to it. Different girls, same high school bitchiness." Old wounds, long since healed. And maybe today had ripped them open again a little, but it wasn't anything she couldn't handle.

"I'm sorry, kitten."

"It's fine." Or it would be, once the wounds closed back up. "We had fun, anyway. Thanks for inviting us."

"Any time, baby." Soft kisses feathered down the side of

her neck. "I liked having you there. My own personal cheerleader. Maybe I should get you a uniform."

"Don't you dare."

"Oh, I will definitely dare. But I think I'll save that particular outfit for home. Or Black Light."

At the mention of the club, everything else faded to the background. "I have to wear a costume?"

"Not every time. They do have theme nights, which can be fun."

"What am I supposed to wear?" Up until that moment, it hadn't even occurred to her that she might not have a single thing in her closet to wear to a BDSM club.

"I'll take care of it. You'll be getting a delivery tomorrow."

"What did you get me?"

"If I tell you it's a surprise, are you going to be worrying about it all night?"

"Probably," she confessed with a shrug.

"It's a corset and a skirt. I want you to promise me you'll give it a try."

"That doesn't sound too bad. How long is the skirt?"

"Shorter than what you're used to. Which is why you'll also be getting a long jacket to wear over it for the walk from the car to the club."

A corset. She could do that. Corsets gave you a waist, right? Maybe she'd actually look thinner than she really was. It was better than being paraded around naked, anyway. "Okay."

"That's my good girl." With a low hum of approval, he slid a hand around her waist and down between her thighs. "I think you deserve another reward."

An hour later, she'd decided any outfit was worth *that* reward.

CHAPTER 16

KATHERINE

True to his word, the next afternoon, a package was courier-delivered to her house. She'd hoped they'd be getting ready together, to help soothe the nerves she couldn't seem to keep under control on her own, but since he couldn't be sure when his game would be over, he was planning to get dressed at his house and pick her up later that evening. Since she didn't have him ready and available to answer the dozens of questions racing through her mind—on top of the dozens he'd already answered the night before—she'd settled for a cleaning spree. By the time the courier arrived, her kitchen sparkled like new and there wasn't a speck of dust to be found anywhere in the house.

Carefully cradling the white box in her arms, she carried it to her bedroom and placed it on the bed. The only thing keeping her from the outfit her Sir had chosen for her was a red silk ribbon wrapped expertly around the box. She wiped her sweaty palms on her leggings before tugging at the ribbon and slowly lifting the lid from the box.

A moan of purely feminine pleasure escaped her as she lifted the corset from its resting place atop the tissue paper. It was gorgeous. Nearly solid black, with accents of red ribbon laced down each side from nipple to waist, the top and bottom edges trimmed with black satin ruffles, it was possibly one of the most beautiful pieces of clothing she'd ever laid eyes on.

Shedding her t-shirt, she pulled it on. The fit was perfect, and each hook pushed her breasts higher until she worried they might smother her. But she didn't care. Looking down at the smooth skin threatening to spill over the top of the boning and her newly-cinched-in waist, she felt... *sexy*. Sexier than she could ever remember feeling.

Right up until she looked in the mirror.

Sexy went out the window. All she could see was how her fat bulged out under her arms and over the top of the corset digging into her skin. And speaking of arms, there was no way to hide her globs of flab in this thing. Sleeves were her friend for a reason. Her reflection blurred as tears filled her eyes. There was no way she could embarrass herself or Austin by going out in public like this, no matter how much he wanted her to wear it.

Maybe if she explained her issue with the corset, she could make him see reason. Surely if she told him how uncomfortable she was, he wouldn't be upset with her. And even if he was upset, she could handle whatever punishment he decided to give her.

Welts on her ass were well worth not humiliating herself in front of a bunch of strangers.

With her mind made up, she headed for the shower. And since she was actually feeling a little guilty about not wearing the outfit he'd chosen for her, she took extra care with curling her hair and painting on her makeup. Hopefully, she wouldn't sweat it all off by the end of the night.

Or cry it off. Would Austin really be upset enough with her to punish her to the point of tears? She'd read about it in books, but so far, his punishments had been fairly light by those standards. What if he followed through on his promise to punish her in front of the entire club and she couldn't take it? Would everyone think she was a horrible sub? Would they think Austin was a bad Dom?

Shit, shit, *shit*. Maybe she should just wear the corset.

No. She was going to wear the dress she'd picked out herself. With the off-the-shoulder sleeves and shorter hemline, it was the most revealing thing she had in her closet and the closest thing to "club wear" she could find, but it was still nowhere near as embarrassing as the corset and skimpy skirt Austin had sent over.

She'd just zipped the dress up over the black, lacy bra and panty set she'd chosen when her doorbell rang. Steeling herself against the argument to come, she took a deep, bracing breath and opened the door.

His eyes, lit with excitement, quickly clouded over with displeasure as he scanned her outfit and she nearly dropped to her knees to beg his forgiveness. How had she forgotten, so quickly, how much she hated disappointing him?

"Hi." Her voice shook with nerves, which seemed to snap him out of his thoughts.

The disappointment cleared and his eyes were once again that pale, stunning blue, sparkling with a dash of humor. "You're not dressed, kitten."

"I, um, decided to wear something else." There. She'd said it. No turning back now.

"Oh?" One single syllable, delivered in a casual, conversational tone. And somehow it still sent a chill down her spine.

"Yes. The corset is lovely, I just wasn't very comfortable."

Stepping across the threshold, he closed the door behind him before grasping her chin in his hand. When he tilted her head back, forcing her to look up at him, her breath caught in her throat at the predatory gleam in his eyes.

"Do you need to use your safe word?"

She'd expected a lecture, or at the very least, the promise of a spanking. "What? Of course not!"

"Then the corset isn't beyond your limits, is it?"

Shit. He was expertly backing her into a corner and she hadn't seen it coming. "I don't want to wear it, Austin."

"And are you going to tell me why?"

"I already told you. I wasn't comfortable."

"What are you supposed to say if something I'm asking you to do is beyond your limits? If you really, honestly, can't do what I've asked?"

Red. One little syllable was all she had to say and he'd back down. Let her off the hook. Probably not without a long talk about it at some point, but at least she wouldn't be in trouble.

And yet, she had no desire to say it.

"I don't need my safe word. I just don't want to wear the outfit." Or maybe, on some level, she did and that was why she was being so stubborn.

"Sweet, disobedient kitten of mine. I can guarantee by the end of the night you'll be begging to wear it. Go get the outfit I sent you. We'll take it with us."

"You're not going to... you know?"

"Is that how you thought this would work?" His hand slid from her chin to wrap around her throat, the pads of his fingers pressing into her skin. "You thought you'd openly defy me and I'd let you off with nothing more than a little spanking? No, kitten, you're going to get a long, painful lesson in obedience tonight."

Even through the anxious pounding of her heart, she felt the thrill of excitement, the pulse of need between her thighs. "I'm not wearing it. You can't make me."

"I could make you." The hand at her throat squeezed, and she could feel her pulse racing against his palm. "Trust me, after six of the best with the Delrin cane I have in my bag, you'd lick the bathroom floor clean if I told you to. But I have something very different in mind for you tonight. Go get the outfit and pack an overnight bag. You're staying with me again tonight. I'll take you to work in the morning, so bring whatever you need for tomorrow."

When he released her, she stumbled to the steps to do as he'd asked.

No, not asked. Demanded. Ordered.

The small, rebellious part of her wanted to march back into the living room and tell him where he could shove the scraps of clothing he'd so laughingly called an "outfit". But the logical, rational part knew she'd eventually pay for her disobedience one way or another, and there was no sense in making things any worse.

Her heart felt like it was going to beat out of her chest by the time she made her way back down the stairs. Ever the gentleman, he took the overnight bag and gift box from her before sliding an arm around her waist and jerking her up against his rock-hard body.

"Do you trust me, Katherine?"

"Yes. Yes, sir."

"I want you to remember that tonight. And that you have your safe word if you need it at any time. Understood?"

"Yes, sir."

"Good girl."

His praise did nothing to ease the nerves dancing in her stomach as she followed him to his car. The first ten minutes of their drive was filled with silence so tense it felt like it would strangle her. "I'm not being a brat," she finally blurted out when it became more than she could take.

"I didn't think you were," he assured her, his voice cool and calm like they weren't barreling towards the most terrifying event of her life.

"Oh." Her right leg began to jump up and down with nervous energy. "Okay. Good."

"If I had to guess, you have a perfectly logical reason why you don't want to wear what I picked out for you."

"I do!" She flashed him a relieved smile. "Thank you for understanding."

"You're welcome. But it's not going to save you, kitten."

"But… but… why not?" she sputtered.

"Because instead of calling me and asking to discuss it, you made a conscious decision to disobey me. You didn't give me a chance to hear your concerns. And honestly, I'm disappointed in you for it. You think so poorly of me that you didn't think I'd listen to you?"

Tears burned in her eyes but she ruthlessly blinked them back. She was not going to walk into Black Light with her makeup already ruined. "I'm sorry."

"Apology accepted. Now, why don't you want to wear the corset, baby?"

"I just didn't feel comfortable."

"You've said that already. Why didn't you feel comfortable?"

"I don't want to talk about it."

Glancing over at her, he shrugged. "You can talk now or after I tear your ass up at the club. Which is it going to be?"

"You said you weren't going to spank me!"

"No, I said I wouldn't be letting you off with *just* a spanking. I will definitely be whipping your ass raw at some point tonight, but that is only a small part of your punishment."

"That's not fair!" Her voice had pitched up to a whine, and she was sorely tempted to stomp her foot, which just served to embarrass her further. When had she turned into a spoiled child?

"I'm not the least bit interested in being fair. I gave you an order and you unilaterally decided to ignore it. I am interested in an explanation, but I'm perfectly fine proceeding with your punishment without one."

"Since when does the big bad jock use words like unilaterally?"

It was a low blow and they both knew it. As soon as the words escaped, she slapped a hand over her mouth, staring at him in horror. "I'm so sorry," she whispered, moving her hands to her lap. "That was uncalled for."

His knuckles went white on the steering wheel and a muscle in his jaw jumped. "It was. I expect better from you, Katherine."

"Take me home. I'll change and you can punish me and then we can go to the club. Okay?"

"Your punishment starts now. Not another word until I say so."

"You can't do that!"

"I can and I am, little girl. And you'll do as you're told unless you want all of Black Light to see how I handle mouthy, disrespectful subs."

Crossing her arms over her chest, Kit glared out the window. Guilt was churning in her stomach, right along anger and embarrassment. Being treated like a wayward child was absolutely humiliating and he had no right to treat her this way!

You gave him that right, a little voice reminded her. And yeah, that was technically true, but he didn't have to be such a hard ass about it.

And you didn't have to insult him.

Shit. The voice was right, as much as it grated her to admit it. She'd outright ignored his wishes, argued with him, and then insulted his intelligence. The only one in the wrong here was her, and she wasn't sure there was a spanking long enough or hard enough to ease her guilt.

Sniffling against the threat of tears, she dropped her hands back into her lap. An apology burned on her tongue, and her throat was tight with the urge to beg his forgiveness. But at this point, showing him she could behave properly and follow instructions seemed like the best apology she could offer, so she clamped her lips together.

Time seemed to stretch into eternity before he spoke again. "All right. I think I'm calm enough to continue this conversation. Tell me about the corset, kitten."

"It's beautiful," she whispered hoarsely, her throat working overtime as she fought to hold back the tears that wouldn't go away. "But not on me."

"Baby, that's not true. I guarantee you looked hot as hell in it."

"I did not! I looked fat and stupid and I didn't want anyone to see me that way. Especially you!"

"Katherine." The word was full of warning, and it cut through the panic building in her chest. "Take a deep breath. Good girl," he praised, his voice a low purr as he guided the vehicle off the interstate. "One more."

He pulled into the parking lot of a giant gas station and parked the SUV at the far end. Unbuckling both their seatbelts, he pulled her to him and pressed a kiss to her hair.

"Better?" he asked when her breaths were no longer short and shaky.

"Yes. I'm sorry."

"You never need to apologize for being scared, kitten. I understand this is hard and I know I'm pushing a lot of your limits. I want you to tell me when shit like this comes up, instead of waiting for it to turn into a panic attack on the beltway. Okay?"

"I'll try."

"Do you want to go home? We can turn around and try this another day."

Yes! Go home, where it's safe and there's nobody there to laugh at you!

But that was the cowardly part of her, and she knew, instinctively, she'd just keep finding ways to back out if she didn't push through now. "No. Let's go."

"All right. But I swear if you need your safe word and you don't use it, I'll paddle your ass every day for a week. You hear me?"

"Yes, sir."

CHAPTER 17

KATHERINE

Black Light, it turned out, was carefully hidden under *Runway*. Sneaky, but brilliant. Nothing less than she would have expected from the Cartwright-Davidsons.

But instead of taking her through the trendy, exclusive club, they somehow ended up in a small psychic shop. "Umm, sir?" she whispered as he reached for the door.

"Yes, kitten?"

"Where are we going?"

"Black Light. This is the secret entrance." His eyes danced with humor and she felt her own lips twitch in response.

"Secret entrance, huh? Is there a secret handshake or something, too?"

"No, just lots of paperwork."

He wasn't kidding. By the time she was actually allowed past the security table, her hand had started to cramp from all of the initialing and signing of the very extensive NDA that was required.

Austin stopped in front of a locker as it popped open and held out his hand. "Phone, baby," he reminded her gently.

Right. It was all in the stack of paperwork she'd just signed and the lecture she'd received before having her hand stamped with an invisible stamp. No electronics. Wouldn't want some senator's kinky evening activities ending up on TikTok for the world to see.

She handed over the small clutch she'd brought with her, and Austin stowed their belongings in the locker. After security checked it, he was allowed to keep the large duffel bag he'd pulled from the trunk of his SUV when they'd handed it off to valet. For the hundredth time that night, she found herself wondering what implements of torture it held. She already knew he'd moved her "outfit" to the bag before they'd left her house, and as far as she was concerned, that was more than enough torture for one evening.

It wasn't until they finally stepped into the cavernous room that she realized how incredibly overdressed she was compared to everyone else. All around her were acres of flesh. Bare chests and legs, completely nude submissives being lead around the room, some on leashes attached to thick leather collars around their throats.

And that didn't even take into consideration the men and women engaged in various scenes and sexual acts all around them. To her left, a naked woman dangled from an intricate web of ropes, and across the room she spotted a tall, thin man squirming against some kind of wooden X, his back crisscrossed with angry-looking welts.

It would have been revelation enough to see everyone so openly nude or in various stages of undress if they'd all been the perfect, thin, beautiful model-types she'd been expecting. But though there were certainly a few of those, there were plenty of people of all shapes and sizes wandering the room. A couple passed in front of them, older than herself and Austin, and she couldn't help but stare at the slight belly hanging over the man's leather pants. Then her attention shifted to the submissive behind him, and she drank in the calm, almost serene expression on her round face. If Kit had to guess, they were about the same size, but if the other woman felt any shame in parading herself around in front of everyone, it didn't show.

So much for not embarrassing herself, or Austin. Her 'daring' red dress suddenly seemed overly conservative, and she couldn't help but feel like she stood out more fully dressed than she would have if she'd walked through the doors naked. Both options were equally humiliating, in their own way, but if she'd worn the outfit Austin had given her, she would have at least been covered without being so painfully out of place. Obviously, he'd known what he was doing when he'd picked it out for her, and she felt another wave of shame for being so damn stubborn and refusing talking to him about it.

Just as she was turning to Austin to ask him to let her change, she heard a familiar voice call her name.

"Katherine?"

Oh, no. This wasn't happening.

Forcing a smile she didn't remotely feel, she turned to find one of her favorite clients, Kawan Park, smiling down at her. "Mr. Park. It's, ah, nice to see you."

"I thought that was you." His smiled deepened and his dark eyes warmed. "I didn't realize you were a member."

"I'm not. I'm, um, here as a guest. Sir? Am I supposed to call you that? I don't really know..."

"Calm down, kitten." Stepping forward, Austin slid a steadying arm around her waist and her nervousness eased at his touch. "I'm Austin. Kit's here as my guest for the evening."

"Nice to meet you. I'm Kawan, and this is my babygirl, Melody."

The petite brunette to Kawan's right grinned and gave a little wave. Melody was definitely not overdressed. Her cute, curvy figure was barely concealed behind a pink, see-through teddy. The pastel colors and the ruffles at the bottom gave the outfit an air of innocence most of the other 'outfits' in the room lacked.

"It's lovely to meet you, Melody. Kawan talks about you often."

Melody's brow wrinkled and Kit felt her cheeks heat at the sudden glint in the other woman's eyes. "During our meetings. In my office. I'm Mr. Park's financial planner."

"Oh!" Melody's expression smoothed out again and she grinned. "That's where I know your name from. Daddy's mentioned you a few times."

It took every ounce of willpower Kit had to not react to the cute, bubbly brunette referring to the prim and proper Mr. Park as *Daddy*. She'd read some books with Daddy kinks, so she wasn't a complete stranger to the concept. It just wasn't something she'd ever expected to hear someone say so... openly.

"It was nice to meet you both," Austin interjected smoothly. "But Kit and I have something to discuss, and I have a feeling she'd rather have this conversation in private."

At the look of surprise—and was that a hint of approval?—on Kawan's face, she wished the floor would open up and swallow her whole. "Yes, we should go. I'll, ah, see you soon, Mr. Park. Melody, it was nice to meet you."

"Enjoy your evening," Kawan called after them as Austin led her away.

"Did you have to embarrass me like that?" she demanded, dropping her voice to a low hiss.

"How did I embarrass you, kitten?"

"You practically announced to them that you're going to punish me!"

"And?"

"Mr. Park is a client! How am I supposed to ever look him

in the eye again? How is he ever supposed to respect me after this?"

They'd stopped in front of one of the semi-private alcoves along the wall. "Sit." With a hand at the small of her back, Austin urged her into the alcove.

Dropping onto the couch, Kit buried her face in her hands. "I'm sorry. I can't do this, Austin."

"Hey. Look at me, baby."

Reluctantly lifting her head, she met his ice-blue eyes and nearly wept with relief at the understanding she found in them. "Sir?"

"There's my pretty kitten. Breathe for me, baby. Deep breaths, until you stop feeling like you're going to puke all over this very nice carpet."

A laugh burst out of her, and she tried to pretend she didn't notice the people throwing curious glances their way. "It is nice," she conceded, pulling in a deep breath and holding it for a few seconds before slowly letting it out again.

"Good girl. Feel better?"

"Yes, sir. Sorry."

"No need to apologize. But we do need to talk about what happened."

"Could we not?" Moaning softly, she dropped her head back into her hands.

"Eyes up here, little girl."

Steel replaced the gentle understanding in his voice and, she discovered when she raised her head again, his eyes. It seemed like it should have pissed her off for him to be so stern when she was on the verge of a nervous breakdown, but her stomach instantly settled. It was as though he'd commanded all of her attention, not leaving her any room for the freakout she'd been trying to have.

"Sir?"

"Your eyes are on me until I give you permission to look away. Do you understand?"

"Yes, sir." Follow his directions. Baby steps, one at a time. She could do baby steps.

"If Kawan is a halfway decent dominant, he won't let tonight affect your professional relationship. He will understand and respect that you are *my* submissive, not his. And he will not look down on you for it in any way. In fact, he should respect the hell out of you."

"Huh?"

Austin's lips twitched, but the steel remained in his gaze. "I'm going to interpret that as 'What do you mean, sir?'"

"Oh. Yes, sir."

"Look, baby. I know this is hard. Submitting to someone else, letting someone else call the shots, letting them hurt you and humiliate you and punish you isn't an easy thing. No matter how much you crave it, it's fucking hard. Any good Dom understands that, and he respects any submissive who is able to give themselves over that way."

"I guess. It's still embarrassing."

"What are you embarrassed by?" His voice lowered, soft and silky in a way that she instinctively recognized was meant to embarrass her further. "That your friend knows you were a naughty little kitten and that your Sir is going to punish you?"

Heat threatened to engulf her, and she glanced around to see if anyone was listening, but everyone seemed to have found something more interesting than a Dom quietly lecturing his submissive. "Yes, sir."

Lifting a hand to her hair, he wrapped her curls around his fist, forcing her head back and her chin further up. "Good. Embarrassment helps a lesson stick, often times more than the actual pain. Stand up and strip."

The order sliced through her, freezing her to her core. "What?"

"Stand up and take off your clothes. All of them."

All of her clothes? Here, where they barely had the illusion of privacy? "I can't."

"You can, and you will."

"I can't. Sir. Please."

"Katherine. Take off your clothes. Now."

It was the whip-crack of his voice that spurred her into action. Forcing herself up onto trembling legs, she tugged the hem of her dress up over her hips, pausing to send him a pleading look.

"Good girl. Keep going."

He began circling her as she worked the dress up over her tummy. "If you'd worn the outfit I'd chosen for you, this all could have been avoided. But you chose to be a naughty, disobedient little girl, and now the whole club is going to watch as I teach you a very painful lesson. And stripping yourself bare for me is part of your punishment."

A whimper escaped and she faltered, teetering on the too-tall heels. He caught her, his hands on her waist as she pulled the dress off over her head, leaving her in the matching bra and panty set she'd so carefully chosen, and the ridiculous heels.

"God, you're beautiful," he murmured, running his hand down her spine. "It baffles me that you somehow manage to look in the mirror and not see how absolutely perfect you are."

"Would you like me to list all the reasons alphabetically or just start with the most obvious, sir?"

Two sharp spanks landed, one for each cheek, and she hissed at the sudden bursts of pain.

"Watch the attitude, kitten. You're already in enough trouble."

"Yes, sir."

"Let's finish getting you naked, and then I think I'd like a drink."

"May I have a glass of wine, sir?" she asked as he unsnapped her bra and pulled the fabric from her breasts.

"No. You're being punished. You don't get to hide behind a buzz."

"Sadist," she mumbled.

"Yeah, but you already knew that about me."

Since she couldn't argue, she settled for rolling her eyes and hooking her fingers in her panties. As slowly as she dared, she pushed them down over her hips until they pooled around her heels. Austin bent and picked them up, and she felt her face flame even hotter when he pressed the fabric to his nose and inhaled.

"I fucking love the way you smell." Tucking the discarded panties into the pocket of his pants, he sent her a cool, wicked smile. "Hands on your head, kitten. And leave them there until I get back."

"Back? Where are you going?"

"To the bar. I told you I was going to get a drink."

"You can't leave me here!"

"Why not?" There was steel in his voice again, demanding an answer.

Shame coated her stomach, and she felt her bottom lip tremble. "I'm scared."

"Oh, kitten." His voice dropped, losing some of its hard edge. "What do you say if you need me to slow down?"

"Um, yellow?"

"Good girl. Are you yellow?"

"A little, sir," she admitted reluctantly, dropping her head to avoid the disappointment she knew she'd find in his eyes.

Moving to stand in front of her, he cupped her face in both of his hands, tilting her face up. "Eyes on me, kitten."

She forced her eyes open, her knees going weak with relief when she found only understanding in his gaze. "I'm sorry."

"Don't apologize for using your safe word. Ever. Now, take a deep breath for me. Good girl," he crooned quietly as she dragged air in through her nose and pushed it out through her mouth. "Now, why are you scared?"

"I don't really know." Pleading filled her voice, though at this point she was beginning to suspect it wouldn't help. "I'll wear the corset. And the skirt. I'll wear whatever you want. Just please don't leave me here like this."

"I told you that you'd beg," he murmured, amusement coloring his tone. "Do you trust me, kitten?"

"I'm trying, sir," she whispered.

"I know. And I'm very proud of you for it. I promise I won't go far and you will never be out of my sight. Okay?"

Some of the panic ebbed. If he could see her, then he couldn't be too far away, right? Taking a deep breath, she nodded and lifted her hands to link her fingers behind her head.

"Good girl."

The praise slid through her, warming her, easing the tension in her arms and legs.

But then he stepped away, and she felt the loss of him down to her bones. Anxiety and fear crept back in, twisting her stomach into knots and shortening her breaths. Could everyone see her? The alcove offered some privacy, but not much. And if they could, were they laughing at her? Picking out all of her flaws and whispering about how much better Austin could do than a fat, disobedient sub?

Maybe. But Austin didn't want anyone else. He wanted her. Amongst a sea of rich, beautiful women, he'd chosen her. She focused on that single fact until her breathing returned to normal.

"Good girl." Austin's low growl behind her made her jump,

but she kept her position.

"This is her?"

At the sound of a stranger's voice, she whipped her head to the side to meet Austin's proud gaze. "Yeah. Isn't she lovely?"

"She is." A tall, almost obscenely muscular man stepped in front of her, kind eyes searching her face for… well, she wasn't sure what, but he apparently found it, as he gave her a small nod of what she took for approval.

"On your knees, kitten. Show Master Terrance what a good girl you can be."

"Yes, sir," she whispered before sliding to her knees in front of them, her gaze focused on a spot on the floor between their feet.

"Good girl. You might just earn yourself a reward after we're done with your punishment if you keep this up."

The promise of a reward immediately focused her attention on the wetness dripping down the inside of her thighs. Her mind might have been terrified, but her body was loving every fucking minute of this. From somewhere to her right, the sound of leather meeting flesh reached her, followed quickly by a cry of pain, and her pussy throbbed in response. The sights, the sounds, her own humiliation at Austin's hand — all of it seemed to come together in a perfect storm of sensation, leaving her hornier than she could ever remember being.

"Thank you, sir," she replied, letting her voice drop to a husky purr.

"You can kneel right here next to me while I catch up with Muscles here."

A hand settled on her hair, stroking her head, and she just barely resisted the urge to turn and press her cheek into his palm.

"She's fabulous, Austin. And gorgeous. I bet that peaches and cream skin marks up beautifully."

"It does," Austin agreed, and she heard the tinkling of ice in his glass indicating he'd taken a sip of his drink. "You'll get to see for yourself in a bit. My naughty kitten has quite the punishment coming."

Heat rose in her cheeks, but she fought the urge to defend herself or cover up. It was humiliating to be spoken of like she wasn't there, but Austin's hand in her hair centered her, and she tried to focus on his touch instead of their running commentary.

"Really? She seems so well-behaved. What did she do?"

Seriously, where was a submissive-eating hole in the ground when a girl needed it?

"I sent her very explicit instructions for her wardrobe tonight and she decided she knew better." The sweet, tender hand fisted in her hair, yanking her head back so her breasts thrust out towards their guest and she was looking up at her Sir's amused grin. "Isn't that right, naughty girl?"

"Yes, sir," she gasped out.

"So now she's not allowed any clothes until she's properly convinced me she deserves them. Once she's dressed in the outfit I chose for her, she can have her punishment."

A low groan escaped her and the fingers in her hair tightened, sending a flash of pain through her scalp and down her neck.

"Something you'd like to say, kitten?"

"No, sir."

"That's what I thought."

His hold on her hair loosened and he rubbed at her neck, relieving some of the tension he'd created. The conversation around her turned to sports and she gladly tuned them out, choosing instead to focus on the floor in front of her and pretend like she wasn't completely butt naked and on display for a complete stranger.

She'd expected more of a panic, but as she knelt there with

her Sir's hand stroking her hair, her mind was oddly calm. Practically empty. It was kind of peaceful, she decided, to have nothing more to focus on than silently keeping her position.

Then a pair of boots moved into her line of vision and Austin gave her hair a gentle tug, breaking the spell.

Taking the hint, she tilted her chin up. Master Terrance ran a finger down her cheek and gave her an approving smile. "Your Sir is very lucky to have you, Katherine. I look forward to watching your scene later."

"Thank you," she replied, equal parts embarrassed and thrilled by his praise.

"Come here, kitten. Time for you to convince me you deserve to wear the clothes I picked out for you."

Shifting on her knees, she turned so she was facing Austin. He'd settled on the couch, watching her. When she sent him a questioning glance, he grinned down at her.

"Go on, baby. You know what to do."

Well, in the most technical sense, she did. But what if he hated her technique? What if she used too much teeth or not enough? What if...

"Katherine." The cool, hard tone snapped her out of her indecision, and she focused on him. "If your mouth isn't on my cock by the count of three, there will be zero chance of you being allowed to come tonight. One."

It was exactly what she needed to spur her into action. Scooting forward on her knees, she hurriedly undid his pants and pulled his cock free. With one last glance up at him, she lowered her head and took the head in her mouth.

"That's my good girl. Slow and steady. I want to take my time with you, kitten."

It almost sounded like a threat, and she felt a delicious bolt of heat go straight to her clit. Digging her fingers into his thighs to keep her hands from sneaking between her legs, she focused on giving the best fucking blow job of her life.

CHAPTER 18

AUSTIN

If he lived a thousand years and fucked a million other women, Austin was certain none of them would ever rival his kitten. There was no artifice, just an obvious desire to please as her tongue danced along his cock, wrapping around the sensitive head, and her cheeks hollowed around him.

Sliding his hand into her shiny locks, he curled his fingers and pulled. Confusion and hurt filled her eyes when she looked up at him.

"What did I do wrong?"

His heart contracted painfully. His sweet, eager to please kitten always seemed to assume the worst.

"Not a damn thing, baby. I just wanted you to stop before I embarrassed myself."

Her lips pursed in a perfect "O" a moment before color flooded her cheeks and she grinned. "Sorry?"

"No need to apologize, kitten. Just take your time. I want to enjoy you for a good, long while yet."

"Yes, sir."

Jesus, that throaty little purr in her words was going to make him come before she even touched him again.

Leaving his hand in her hair, he guided her back down. She abandoned the suction in favor of exploring every inch of his rock-hard cock with her tongue. He had to give her a tug here and there to remind her to go slow, but once he was certain she knew what he wanted, he loosened his hold on her hair.

Closing his eyes, he let his head fall back, content to enjoy her attentions for as long as he could stand it. No doubt the floor was hard on her knees and her legs would feel like jelly by the time he decided they were done, but she was being punished, after all.

The thought caused another little twinge of guilt, just under his heart. It was tempting to let her off the hook, after she'd broken down on the way here. But he'd given her an out and she hadn't taken it. And she hadn't shown any signs of real distress when she'd knelt at his feet, completely nude in front of a complete stranger.

Progress. It was definite progress, and he'd never been so fucking proud of one of his subs.

"Such a good little kitten, sucking her Sir's cock for everyone to watch. I wish you could see how gorgeous you are with your mouth full of my dick, drool dripping down your chin."

The color on her cheeks deepened, but the look she gave him through her lashes was filled with need and, if he wasn't mistaken, pride.

"That's right, baby. You're a fucking mess, and it's just going to get worse." Tightening his grip, he forced her head down, groaning when her throat contracted as she gagged on his length. He held her there for a moment before jerking her head back up. His cock slid from her mouth with an audible *pop* and she let out a little mewl of surprise. "Maybe I should just go ahead and ruin you. What would you say if I wanted to come on that pretty face and make you walk around with your perfect makeup all smeared and my cum dripping from your eyelashes?"

The way her eyes widened and her breaths turned to short, sharp pants made the threat all too tempting. But he had other plans for his kitten, and he wasn't about to risk ruining them for some spur of the moment fun.

Maybe another time.

"Too bad we have other plans. The only place I plan on coming tonight is in that sexy ass of yours."

"Sir?" The word was a squeak of surprise, and he couldn't help but grin at her.

"How are naughty girls punished, kitten?"

"I, um." Her tongue darted out, wetting her lips, and the plea was obvious in her eyes.

"Tell me, kitten. How are naughty girls punished?"

"They, um, they get spanked." She glanced around like she was worried someone might hear her, which was about the cutest fucking thing he could imagine given their surroundings. Spanking was the most vanilla thing happening at Black Light.

But even as adorable as she was, he had a point to make. "And what else do they get when they've been extra naughty?"

"They, um, get fucked. In the, in their bottoms," she finished on a whisper.

"That's right. And I did tell you I was going to punish you here at the club, didn't I?"

Her eyes went wide as she pieced it all together. "I—I can't! You can't!"

"Sure I can, baby."

"Yellow! Yellow, please, Austin, I can't do this."

Shit. Releasing his hold on her hair, he cupped her face in his hands, forcing her to look up at him. "Breathe, baby. Just breathe." When she'd taken a few shaky breaths, he rewarded her with a small smile. "That's my good girl. Tell me what's wrong."

"It's just, I don't want everyone watching me and judging me. I've never let anyone, you know." An adorable flush crept up her cheeks and he couldn't resist needling her a bit.

"Fuck your ass, kitten? You can say it."

"Yes." She had enough courage left in her to glare at him, which soothed his conscience a bit. "That. And what if I screw it up or I can't take it and everyone sees what a horrible sub I am?"

"Oh, baby. That is not going to happen. If you can't take it, nobody will be judging you." As much as he wanted to stay and show her off, he wasn't going to risk hurting her to do so. "We can go home. Just say the word and we'll pack up and leave."

He watched the wheels turn in her mind before she finally shook her head. "No, sir. I want to do this, I'm just scared."

"I know. And I'm so fucking proud of you."

"For being scared?"

"First of all, for using your safe word and letting me know you were scared. I didn't have to ask this time, and I'm very proud of you for speaking up for yourself."

Pleasure filled her eyes at the praise. "Really?"

"Yeah, baby. Really. And I'm proud of you for doing this anyway, even though you're scared. For trusting me enough to follow my lead, even though you're scared of what's coming next. Think you can continue to trust me, kitten?"

"I think so, sir."

"Good. One last thing before we head out to the floor. Are you listening to me, little girl?"

"Yes, sir."

"You are not a bad sub. Even if you call red the second I strap you to that bench, you are not a bad submissive. Having limits, no matter how narrow or broad they may be, doesn't make you a bad submissive. It makes you an excellent one. You understand me?"

The brilliant smile that lit her face eased the last of the tension inside of him. It hit him then, that he'd do anything for that smile. Raze cities, destroy kingdoms, topple governments. Whatever it took to make sure she never stopped smiling like that, like he'd hung the fucking moon just for her.

"Yes, sir."

"Good girl. Do you want to wear the outfit I chose for you now?"

"Yes, please. I'm sorry I didn't do as I was told, sir."

"I appreciate that, kitten. Unfortunately, it's not going to save your ass from the punishment you have coming."

∽

Katherine

It should have terrified her. A smart woman would have taken off running at Austin's declaration. But instead of the urge to run, all she wanted to do was take his cock in her mouth again and prove what a good girl she could be.

If it made her weird, well, she figured she was in the right place for it.

Austin helped her to her feet, steadying her when she wobbled on her heels. Pins and needles danced up and down her calves and she winced as she tried to wiggle away the prickly sensation.

From the corner of her eyes, she saw Austin speaking with Muscles again. The large man sent her what she assumed was meant to be a reassuring smile as he took Austin's bag and headed out into the crowd.

"What's going on?"

"The bench I was hoping to use just opened up, and Master Terrance offered to take my bag over to claim it for us."

"Oh." What kind of bench? What was it made of? Oh, Jesus, what if it broke while she was on it? She'd die of embarrassment, right there in the middle of Black Light.

"Katherine, stop thinking whatever it is you're thinking. I can see the panic in your eyes."

"I just… how sturdy is this bench?"

"Do you trust me, kitten?"

"Yes, but…"

"Then trust me. It will be fine. Arms out."

With a little huff, she obeyed, holding her arms out to the side so he could wrap the corset around her middle. "It's not that I don't trust you."

"You don't seem to trust that I've done my research and that I wouldn't let anything happen to you."

"That's not what I meant." Well, maybe that was sort of what she'd meant.

"Mmhmm." With the last clasp hooked, Austin took a step back and grinned. "I changed my mind. There's no fucking way I'm letting anyone else see you in this corset."

"Sir?"

"Every Dom here is going to want a piece of you. I'm feeling unusually territorial about it."

"Really?" She couldn't help the smile she could feel pulling at her lips. "Is that so?"

"Yeah, that's so. I wouldn't feel too smug about it, kitten. That just means I'm more likely to leave my marks all over your ass so everyone here can see them."

"I'd like that, sir."

"Would you?" Tilting his head to the side, Austin studied her. "I think you might. But it won't be easy, kitten. This is a punishment, after all."

"I understand."

"Good girl. Kneel on the couch there and push your ass out so I can put this plug in, and we'll get started."

It took longer than it had the night before, and she realized with a flash of panic that he'd chosen a much larger plug. And if she had to guess, the plug wasn't even as large as his cock.

How the hell was she supposed to take him there?

Do you trust me, kitten?

She did trust him. Every step of their journey together he'd proven how seriously he took her safety. It might hurt like hell, but he'd never do anything to truly endanger her.

Clinging to that knowledge, she let him help her into the short, flirty skirt, and with one final deep breath, she followed him into the crowd.

In the alcove, it had been easier to pretend they were alone or at least not so completely on display. But out here, in the open, she was keenly aware of the gazes following her, the curious murmurs as they made their way to the spot Master Terrance had staked out for them. *Trust him, trust Austin, trust your Sir* ran through her mind like a mantra as she tried to block out everything that wasn't him.

The 'bench' he'd asked for wasn't so much a bench in the traditional sense as it was a series of padded, wooden slats obviously designed to position some poor submissive to receive the punishment of their dominant's choosing.

And tonight, she was that poor submissive.

Turning, Austin pulled her closer to him, his pale eyes unusually serious. "What color are you, baby?"

"Green, sir. I want to do this," she added quietly, for his ears only.

"All right. Up you go."

"You can do this, you can do this," she muttered under her breath as she knelt on the two pads closest to her. Austin guided her down so her arms rested on the far pads and a large section of the bench supported her torso. It also pushed her ass up and out, but she was doing her damnedest not to think of that just then.

"Still green, baby?"

"Yes, sir."

"Good."

A few minutes later, he'd pulled several leather straps tight across her wrists and ankles. Kit gave them an experimental tug, relieved to find she couldn't really move. If she couldn't move, there was less chance of her chickening out and making a run for it.

Since she was positioned with her head down, her hair fell in a curtain around her face, blessedly blocking out the crowd. But a moment later, a pair of familiar hands pulled her hair away and she was exposed to the crowd once more. Off to her right, she spotted Kawan and Melody. Her client had a hand under his girlfriend's cute little nightie, obviously playing with her nipples as Melody stared straight at Kit, her lips slightly parted and her eyes glassy.

All of the embarrassment Kit had been feeling up until that moment faded to the background. There was still an element of humiliation, knowing she was being disciplined in such a public way, but there was also a sense of…power. All these people standing around, watching her, they weren't there to gawk at the fat girl or to point out her flaws. The dimples in her thighs, the extra width of her hips—none of it mattered. Her body, her submission, the punishment she was about to receive, every part of it was enjoyable to the people watching.

Not just enjoyable. *Desirable.*

And that was something nobody could ever take from her. There was nothing a couple snotty sports groupies could say to cancel out the sheer exhilaration of knowing dozens of people were watching her, getting off to the show she and her Sir were about to put on.

In that moment, she knew she'd take whatever Austin dished out. Not because of some misplaced sense of pride or fear, but because she never wanted this feeling to end.

CHAPTER 19

KATHERINE

"Ready, kitten?"

"Yes, sir." Despite the pounding of her heart and the zing of excitement lighting up every nerve she had, her voice was steady.

A hand gripped her hair, pulling her head up at an awkward angle. The sweet, gentle Dom who'd coaxed her through her fears to get to where she was now had disappeared. A cold hardness had settled in his eyes and her core trembled at the sight.

"Tell me why you're being punished tonight."

Austin had raised his voice slightly, she assumed so the hovering crowd could hear. Taking his cue, she swallowed hard and spoke as clearly and loudly as she could without screaming. "Because I didn't wear the outfit you chose for me, sir."

"Do you get to decide which of my orders to obey, kitten?"

"N-no, sir."

"Tell our audience what happens to naughty little kittens who disobey their Sir's orders."

Oh, sweet Jesus. She prayed her face wasn't as red as it felt as she recited her line. "They get spanked and fucked in the ass, sir."

"That's right." Releasing his hold on her, he shifted, and for the first time, she caught sight of the long, thick piece of leather dangling from his other hand. It looked a hell of a lot scarier than his belt, and she had a feeling he wasn't going to be stopping at three quick stripes.

Before she could think clearly enough to dare to voice an objection or even a question, he disappeared, and a moment later the leather tapped against her upturned ass.

Squeezing her eyes shut, she braced for the blow. But nothing could have prepared her for the agony that pierced her with the first stroke of his strap.

Oh, *fuck*. If her lungs hadn't frozen, she might have screamed. It was so much worse than his belt, so much worse than anything he'd put her through before. And her mind had barely any time to register the pain before the second stroke landed, the edges of the strap digging into the tops of her thighs.

She lurched forward on pure instinct, but the straps around her wrists and ankles quickly reminded her she had nowhere to go. Her muscles clamped down in a fruitless attempt to protect her from the pain, which only served to remind her she had a giant plug in her bottom, which was its own kind of hell.

The third stroke landed right in the middle of her ass, and her chest finally loosened enough for her to drag in a deep, shuddering breath. Grinding her teeth together, she forced the air back out through her nose.

Do not scream, do not scream, do not scream. She would take her punishment like the good girl he claimed she was, and she would absolutely not embarrass him by carrying on like a hysterical little girl just because her ass was on fire.

Her resolve was sorely tested with the next two stripes,

but she made it through. When a familiar pair of boots appeared in her line of sight, she slumped against the leather, panting wildly.

"The next time I choose an outfit for you, what are you going to do, kitten?"

"W-wear it, s-sir. I'm sorry. I'm so sorry."

"Five more and then we can finish up your punishment."

Tears blurred her vision, but she ruthlessly blinked them back. She'd taken five without dying, she could take five more.

What she could not do, it turned out, was take five more in silence. Number seven was delivered straight across the tops of her thighs and she couldn't hold back the wail of remorse and pain it pulled from her chest.

"Am I making my point, kitten?"

"Yes, sir!" As far as she was concerned, the point had well been made and she had no intention of ever disobeying him again.

But she still had three to go and she was determined to make it through. The last three were delivered so fast, she barely had time to register anything beyond the searing burn in her ass before she went limp again on the bench.

A soft whimper escaped when he ran a hand over her swollen, heated skin. "Such pretty marks for a pretty little kitten," he praised, his voice almost too sweet. "Ready for the rest of your punishment?"

No! her inner voice wailed. "Yes, sir," she managed to whisper instead.

With a few gentle tugs, the plug slid free and the thick, hard head of his cock nudged against her bottom. After an initial pinch, there wasn't as much pain as she'd expected as he slowly pushed his way inside of her.

Full. She'd never felt so fucking full in her life.

"Color, baby. Give me a color."

His voice was strained, like he was in pain. "Green, sir."

"Thank god." The long, thick length of him pulled back, and a moment later, slammed back into her ass with enough force to make her gasp.

Her bottom burned, inside and out, and she'd never been so fucking turned on in her life.

"Sir, please," she whined, pushing back to meet his next thrust.

"Please, what, baby?"

"I want— I need— please, sir!"

"Such a needy little kitten, aren't you? Tell me what you want."

Face burning with humiliation, she tossed her head back and lifted her voice so he could hear her. "I need to come, sir, please!"

Something hard and round pressed against her clit, and she had about a second to wonder what it might be when the vibrations hit.

"You don't come until I say, kitten. If you do, the strapping I just gave you will feel like a warmup."

There was a harshness to his tone that drove his words home. Sensation after sensation washed over her and she knew there was no way she could obey.

But, somehow, she had to. Digging her fingers into the leather beneath her arms, she focused on holding back the waves of pleasure threatening to drag her under. Their audience faded until it was only her and her Sir and the brutal pleasure he was forcing on her with every thrust inside of her ass. The very air around them seemed to electrify as it filled with her whimpers and mewls of pleasure and pain, and the sound of flesh meeting flesh.

And just when she knew she was about to fail, he drove into her and pressed the device more firmly against her clit. "Come for me, baby. Come for me!"

The orgasm ripped through her, destroying her from the

inside out. Her blood went to lava in her veins and electric pleasure zinged up and down every nerve in her body. A scream tore from her throat seconds before she collapsed on the bench. She was dimly aware of people moving around her, of the straps being released from her wrists and ankles.

Then she was standing, and something soft and fuzzy was draped around her shoulders.

"Come on, baby. Let's get you back to the booth and get some water in you."

Letting her head fall to the side, she leaned into Austin as he led her away. "Did I do good, sir?"

"Yeah, baby. You were fucking fantastic." Soft lips brushed across the top of her forehead. "My good girl."

If anyone had told her a month ago she'd get such a thrill from those three words, she never would have believed them. But hearing them from Austin practically sent her soaring all over again. "Thank you, sir."

Back in their alcove, Austin carefully guided her to the bench and helped her ease down onto the seat. The low whine she let out when her body painfully reminded her of everything he'd just put her through earned her a quiet laugh.

"Not funny. Hurts."

"Awww, baby. I know it does. But did you learn your lesson?"

"Yes, sir."

"Then I did my job." Taking a seat next to her, he lifted a bottle of water to her lips. "Slow sips, kitten. Good girl."

When she'd polished off the water, he unwrapped a chocolate bar and broke off a piece to feed her. "I'm so fucking proud of you, Kit. You took your punishment like a champ and I swear I've never seen anyone look more beautiful than when you came with my cock in your ass. You were incredible."

"Thanks." The high from their scene was beginning to

fade, and she could feel the doubt creeping in. But she didn't want to ruin this for him, so she forced a smile and accepted another bite of chocolate.

"I'm going to get everything packed up," he said when she'd finished the candy bar. "Are you good for now or do you need me to stay a bit longer?"

"No, I'll be okay."

With a quick kiss to her forehead, he disappeared into the crowd.

Settling back against the bench, she closed her eyes and tried to cling to that feeling of complete peace she'd had during and after their scene. God, she wished she could feel like that forever. Was that why people did this? To chase that high?

Was she a BDSM junkie now?

The thought made her giggle just as Austin returned with his bag and another bottle of water. "What's so funny, kitten?"

"Just thinking." Opening her eyes, she looked up at him, studying the hard lines of his face. Even when he was amused, his face seemed to be carved from rock. "I think I could get addicted to this. And if I do, does that make me a junkie? Would you be my dealer?"

"I better be," he grumbled, but his eyes were light with humor. "You had a good time?"

"Yes. It was lovely. I just wish…" Unwilling to ruin his good mood, she shook her head. "Never mind."

"Oh, no you don't. 'Never mind' and 'It's nothing' are no longer in your vocabulary. What is it?"

"I swear it's—" Catching herself, she stopped and wrinkled her nose. "It's not important."

"Do you need another round with my strap, little girl?"

"No!" But even as she rushed to deny it, her body throbbed with need. She really was becoming a junkie.

"Then tell me what's going on in that pretty head of yours."

"It's silly."

"I don't care."

"It's just, I wish that feeling I had during the scene could last forever, you know? Like nothing in the world mattered but being your good girl. I felt so... I don't know. Free. And alive."

"You're dropping." Crouching in front of her, Austin captured her hands between his and squeezed. "It's totally normal. And for a lot of subs, the more intense the scene, the worse the drop. Let's get you home so you can take a nice bubble bath and we'll get ourselves some snacks. Whatever you want."

"Cheetos!" Blushing at her outburst, she tried to tug her hand from his grip. "Sorry."

"What are you apologizing for? Cheetos sound perfect. There's a convenience store on the way home, I'll pop in and grab whatever you want. Sound good?"

"That sounds perfect."

CHAPTER 20

AUSTIN

Bottom of the eighth, and the Hawks lead ten to two. Austin Barrick is showing us why he's the best in the league tonight. This may be the best game of his career.

Okay, so maybe the commentators weren't raving about his performance tonight, but in his head they sure as fuck were. It certainly felt like the best game of his life. Kit wasn't in the stands, but he'd coaxed her into heading over to his place after work, and he was enjoying the thought of her curled up on his couch in those adorable pineapple pajamas, watching him play.

"Down boy," he murmured when his cock pressed painfully against the cup he wore under his uniform. Giving himself a mental shake, he focused on the player approaching home plate.

Thoughts of Kit faded to the background as he watched number three roll his shoulders and lift the bat into position. Jameson stepped back on the mound, lifted his arms, and let the ball fly.

Strike one!

"That's it, Jameson. Strike this guy out so I can get home to my woman."

They still had one inning left, but if it went half as well as the rest of the game had so far, he had a good chance of getting some good, kinky fun in before she had to get to bed.

Another wind up and - *Strike two!*

Hell yeah. Grinning, Austin bounced on his toes as Jameson prepped for the next pitch. But this time, there was the unmistakable *crack* of ball meeting bat. A line drive, straight for him. All he had to do was scoop it up and wing it to first. It was a play he'd made a hundred times.

But as soon as he twisted to dive for the ball, he knew something had gone horribly wrong. There was the unmistakable feel of something stretching too far, maybe even ripping, and a white-hot, blinding pain.

And hot on the heels of the physical pain was the soul-crushing fear that he'd just played his last game.

∽

Katherine

LEANING BACK in her office chair, Kit pushed her hands to the ceiling, trying to stretch out the muscles in her back that had tensed up during her marathon of a day. She'd told herself she'd gotten behind, and that was why she'd packed her day with meetings both in-person and virtual. But the truth was, she wasn't looking forward to hanging out around Austin's huge, empty house all by herself all night.

After a final, quick perusal of the file she had open on her laptop, she forced herself to close everything down and pack up. If his game hadn't run over by too much, and if traffic was its usual shitty gridlock, she figured she'd get to his place about a half an hour or so before him.

It was just her luck that traffic was worse than usual. Glancing at the glowing numbers on her dash, she chewed her bottom lip as she weighed her options. She hadn't actually planned on telling him what time she'd left, as he'd made it perfectly clear he wanted her out of the office by six every night. It was fine if she wanted to come home and work a little extra, but he didn't like the idea of her staying at the office so late.

And considering it had been nearly eight before she'd powered down her laptop, she figured she'd be in for a hell of a lecture. Maybe even a spanking, but surely he'd let her off with a warning the first time, right?

Despite the fact that she was alone in the car, she could feel the blush warming her face when her panties instantly dampened. It was humiliating how her body seemed to crave his discipline. So far, she hadn't earned anything close to what he'd given her at Black Light, but a couple thoughtless comments about her weight had earned her more than one sore bottom over the past few weeks.

Secretly, she loved it, at least after the fact. And, well, it probably wasn't a secret from Austin since he always made it a point to comment on how wet she was after a spanking.

Tonight was his first home game after a string of away games, so maybe kicking things off with a good, hard paddling wouldn't be too bad. The sex was always incredible afterwards. But she should at least call him and let him know she was running late.

Before she could hit the button on her in-car touchscreen, a call rang through and Austin's name popped up on the screen.

Uh oh.

Tapping the button to answer, she forced herself to relax. Even if she was in trouble, it wasn't anything she couldn't handle. "Hey! Did your game end early?"

"Where are you?"

There was something in his voice, a dark edge that seemed disproportionate to her crimes. "Um. I'm on my way, I promise. Traffic was a nightmare."

"Go home."

"What? I'm less than fifteen minutes from your place. I'm not going home."

"You don't get a say in this, Katherine. Turn around and go home."

Silence filled the car and with a shock, she realized he'd hung up on her.

What the hell had just happened?

In a daze, she maneuvered the car off the beltway, taking the first exit she came to. Parking the car at a gas station, she dug her phone out of her purse. Tapping the screen to open it, she noticed a handful of missed texts from Claudia.

Are you watching the game???

Where are you? Austin's hurt. I'm at home and I can't get a hold of anybody.

Fuck. Tony just called. It's bad. Where are you??

The fear that had wrapped around her during the call from Austin tightened its grip. She hit the button to call Claudia.

"There you are! I've been texting you for an hour! How's Austin?"

"I don't know."

"What? Isn't he home yet?"

"I have no idea, I just left work."

"Girl, you have got to stop working these crazy hours. You're gonna put yourself in an early grave. Get your ass over there and let me know how he is."

"What happened? You said it was bad. How bad is bad?" Concern crowded out anything else as dozens of scenarios ran through her mind. It couldn't be life-threatening since she'd just talked to him, but that didn't exactly narrow things down.

"His knee. I don't even know what happened. He was going for the ball like he's done a million times before and then he was on the ground and they had to carry him off the field."

Bad, but not as bad as some of the scenarios her imagination had managed to conjure in the past thirty seconds. "Has Tony talked to him at all?"

"He tried, but Austin isn't answering his phone, which is why I called you. So get your ass over to his place and let us know how he is."

"I can't. He told me not to come." The pain she'd felt when he'd called came flooding back and she had to blink back the tears burning in her eyes.

"At the risk of repeating myself—*What?*"

"He called and asked where I was and then he told me to go home. I just thought he was mad I stayed at the office so late."

There was a beat of silence before Claudia snorted in disbelief. "You're not going to let him get away with that, are you?"

"Maybe he just wants to be alone right now."

"Well too fucking bad. If the tables were turned, do you think he'd let some temper tantrum keep him away from you when you were hurting?"

Despite the tightness in her chest, Kit giggled. "Never. Guess I'm not going home after all."

"Atta girl. Text me and let me know how he's doing."

After ending the call with Claudia, Kit gave herself a minute to take a few deep breaths. The fear and panic eased a bit, leaving behind only the dregs of nervousness as she pulled back onto the interstate and finished the trip to his house.

Other than the glow of the television coming from the

living room, the house was completely dark. Gathering the takeout she'd stopped to pick up from his favorite Chinese place, she grabbed her bags and made her way up the front porch. She didn't bother to knock, and thankfully, he'd left the door unlocked so she didn't have to juggle for the key he'd given her before he'd left for his last round of away games.

"Honey, I'm home!" she called out cheerfully as she bypassed the living room on the way to his sparkling kitchen.

The tightness in her chest returned as she heard the telltale thump of crutches on the hardwood behind her.

"I told you to go home."

Turning, she forced a bright smile and gripped the counter behind her for support. "And I decided you need me here. You can spank me for it later if you want to, but I'm not leaving."

A muscle in his jaw jumped and she wondered if he was considering doing exactly that. The blue of his eyes burned with a fury she'd never seen in him before and a coil of fear wrapped itself around her stomach, squeezing until she thought she might be sick.

"I don't need you here, hovering over me like I'm some fucking invalid. I can take care of myself."

"Fine, I won't hover. But unless you can convince me those crutches are just for fun and not because you're injured, I'm not leaving, either."

"Go home, Katherine. I don't want you here."

Tightening her grip on the counter, she fought back the hurt his words inflicted and lifted her chin. "I thought lies weren't allowed between us, sir."

"Go. Home."

"Fuck. You."

"Excuse me?"

Swallowing past the dryness in her throat, she pushed away from the counter and stalked over to him, jabbing a finger in his chest. Some dark part of her cheered when he wobbled on his crutches, even as she reached to steady him. "I said, fuck you if you think I'm just going to leave you here, alone, when you've been injured. Would you leave me?"

"Of course not, but that's—"

"I swear on all that is holy, if you say 'that's different' I will stab you." Anger had worked its way past the fear, righteous fury boiling in her veins. "You may be my Dom, and you may be the one who makes the rules, but I thought we were partners. I won't have you pushing me aside because your ego is a little bruised."

"It's not my goddamn ego!"

She was close enough now to see the fear he was trying so desperately to hide behind his anger. "What is it, then? Talk to me, Austin. I'm not going anywhere until you do."

"I'm done, Kit. I fucking ripped the tendons to shreds in my knee."

"That's what the doctor said?"

"I don't need a doctor to tell me what I already know, Kit."

Narrowing her eyes slightly, she weighed her words carefully. "What exactly *did* the doctor say?"

"Does it matter?" he snapped, bitterness coating his tone.

"Yes. If the doctor didn't flat out tell you that you're done, then how do you know you're done? Maybe you just need some time to heal and some physical therapy and you'll be good to go."

"I've been injured before, Kit. I know the drill."

Inhaling deeply, she reminded herself he was injured and hurting and scared, that the sharpness in his tone didn't really have anything to do with her. "Then help me understand why this time is different."

"Doc said I might have torn my ACL. That means surgery, especially if I want to play again. And there's no guarantee that will even work."

"Might have is a far cry from definitely. Don't go signing

your own death warrant before they figure out exactly what's going on."

The anger seemed to have faded, leaving behind just the fear she'd glimpsed in him earlier. "But what if 'might have' becomes 'definitely did'? What if they can't fix me this time?"

"Oh, honey." Cupping his face, she drew him down to press a gentle kiss to his lips. "I'm sorry. God, I'm so sorry. I can't imagine how hard this is for you."

"What am I gonna do, Kit? This, the game, it's all I have."

"No, it isn't. You have me, and I already said I'm not going anywhere."

"Thank god." Closing his eyes, he pressed his forehead to hers. "Thanks for not walking out on my sorry ass."

"Never. But try kicking me out again, and I won't be held responsible for what happens."

"Hmm." The corners of his lips lifted and when he opened his eyes, her breath caught in her chest at the wicked gleam in them. "Noted. In the meantime, I owe you for swearing at me. Is that how you talk to your Sir?"

"It is when he's being an idiot."

He laughed, a deep belly laugh that soothed her rattled nerves. "Fair enough. But once I'm healed up a little, I'm going to spend a week reminding you who's in charge."

"As long as you don't ice me out again. Deal?"

"Deal."

CHAPTER 21

AUSTIN

Kit wasn't in bed when he woke the next morning, but he figured it was for the best. The way she'd watched him last night, like she was waiting for him to collapse or have another breakdown, had worn at him, and he wasn't sure he could take a whole day of those pitying glances.

He made it to the bathroom and managed to change into a pair of loose-fitting sweats, but he was sweating bullets by the time he thumped his way to the kitchen.

Stopping in the doorway, he stared at the pile of papers neatly stacked beside the laptop Kit was studying like it held the meaning of life.

"Why aren't you at work?"

He felt a little guilty when she jumped and slapped a hand over her heart. "You scared me! How the hell do you move so quietly on those things?"

"Why aren't you at work?" he repeated, guilt giving away to annoyance at having to repeat himself.

"I'm working remote." She offered up a bright smile, but it

didn't hide the sly triumph in her eyes. "Donna rescheduled my in-person meetings to virtual."

"I don't need you hanging around, playing nurse all day. You have work to do."

"Work I can easily do from right here. And I don't plan on playing nurse, especially since I don't think I'd be very good at it. I can't even watch Grey's Anatomy without feeling sick. Besides, your real nurse should be here around noon."

"What nurse? Coffee," he snapped, cutting off her explanation. "I need coffee, and then we can talk."

"Sit and I'll make you some. You want something to eat? There's not much in the fridge but we have leftovers from last night."

He opened his mouth to tell her to stop, but their conversation from last night kept playing over in his mind. If the situation were reversed, there was no way he'd let her do everything on her own. He'd want to take care of her. So, as much as it grated, he plopped down in the seat she'd pulled out for him. "Just coffee for now, kitten."

The dent to his ego was worth watching her eyes light up. "Yes, sir," she replied without an ounce of sarcasm or sass, which was probably a good thing for her ass at the moment.

Being on crutches wasn't going to keep him from teaching his girl a lesson if she needed it.

To her credit, she didn't pester him with questions while he sipped his coffee. Once she'd placed both their cups on the table, she went back to whatever it was she'd been working on before he'd come in and snapped at her.

Reaching across the table, he laid his hand over hers and gave it a squeeze. "Sorry I'm being an ass right now."

Understanding laced with humor filled those dark eyes he adored. "It's okay. I'd probably be pretty cranky in your shoes."

"Mmhmm. How much is this apology going to cost me?"

"Not much, in the grand scheme of things. You're past flowers, but not quite up to blue box territory."

Laughing, he shook his head and lifted his mug to his lips. "God, I love you."

"What?" Kit's voice was barely a squeak and she was looking at him like he'd just admitted to killing puppies in his spare time.

The enormity of what he'd said slammed into him, and if he hadn't been on crutches, he was pretty sure he would have run from the room and locked himself in the den. But she was a hell of a lot faster than he was at the moment, so there was nothing to do but face it.

Cocking his head to the side, he forced smiled. "Did I stutter, kitten?"

"No. I… did you mean it? What you just said?"

"I don't say things I don't mean, kitten." He hadn't meant to say it, not just then, but that didn't mean it wasn't the truth.

"Okay."

"Okay?" Unease bubbled in his stomach. "All you have to say is just 'okay'?"

"I don't know what you want me to say, Austin. It's not that I don't have feelings for you, it's just… it's too soon, I think."

"Too soon. Right." Of course, it was too soon. They'd barely known each other two months and he was already professing his love.

A loud chime from her computer saved them both from figuring out what to say next and she sent him an apologetic smile. "Sorry. Meeting."

"Don't apologize. You work and I'll…" What? There was no game prep, no practice, nothing for him to *do*. He could watch TV but since he normally spent his time watching sports channels, even that didn't appeal. The last thing he wanted was to watch his own injury play out over and over again while the talking heads discussed when and if he'd be back on the field. "I guess I'll just hang out."

"Hey." Her soft voice pulled his attention back to her. "We'll figure this out. It's not like you have to decide what comes next right this second. Once you go see the orthopedic surgeon and get an idea of how bad it really is, we can talk about what comes next. For now, you just need to focus on resting and healing. Right?"

"Sure. I'll get out of your hair."

He'd managed to make it to the doorway of the kitchen before she called his name. "Yeah?"

"Are we okay?"

Turning back to her, he forced a smile. "Yeah, kitten. We're okay."

"Good. I—that's good."

He waited a heartbeat, then two, to see if she'd say anything else, but her attention had already switched back to her computer. Feeling a hell of a lot less steady than he had when he'd woken up, he went in search of something to occupy his day.

~

Katherine

WHEN THE NURSE came at noon, Kit took the opportunity to slip out of the house for a few minutes. She'd told Austin she had some errands to run, but the truth was she just needed a moment to herself. The car door had barely closed behind her before the panic set in and she was forcing herself to take deep, shuddering breaths to keep it at bay.

He loved her. Austin Barrick had told her he loved her. Like it was just something people said to each other and not an earth-shattering, life-changing admission.

It wasn't even like she was planning to hold him to it. The man had just been through a traumatic event. Everything he knew had been turned on its head, so it only made sense that he was clinging to anything normal, or safe. Which, at the moment, was her. And his supposed love for her.

Her stomach quivered at the memory. What was she supposed to do with that? Just pretend it hadn't happened? Play along until he changed his mind and dumped her?

Because he would, inevitably, change his mind. Maybe he loved her, in his own way, but it couldn't touch this soul-consuming *need* she felt for him. There was no possible way he felt for her a fraction of what she felt for him.

Could she be happy with that? With living the rest of her life knowing she loved him so much more than he could ever love her? Could they really find happiness in such a lopsided partnership?

Of course, *he* could. What man wouldn't want a woman whose entire existence revolved around him? And if they followed love down its natural path to marriage, kids, the house with the fence, and the yappy little dog—because she definitely wanted the dog—then that would be what happened. She knew she couldn't give anything less than all of herself to him, to their theoretical family.

A family she wasn't even sure he wanted. They'd never had a chance to talk about marriage or kids or really anything beyond his next game or their next date. And now he'd gone and told her he loved her.

Maybe she should just pretend it hadn't happened. If she didn't say it back, then he probably wouldn't bring it up again, right? No doubt he was already regretting saying it in the first place, so the polite thing would be to let them both forget the whole conversation.

The nurse was gone by the time she made it back to the

house, and Austin was stretched out on the couch with his injured leg propped up on a pile of pillows.

Stopping by the couch, she leaned over to brush a kiss across his cheek. "Brought you the good drugs."

He held his hand out with a grunt, not taking his eyes off the TV. "Thanks."

"You need anything before my next meeting?"

"No."

Okay, maybe ignoring the elephant in the room wasn't going to work after all. Chewing on her bottom lip, she studied the harsh line of his jaw.

She couldn't give him the words. They gave him too much power. But there was something she could give him, and maybe it would be enough for now.

Walking around to the front of the couch, she knelt in the position he'd taught her before their night at Black Light, her knees spread and her hands facing up, her head dipped down. Somehow, despite the nerves dancing in her stomach, she managed to keep position until he spoke, which felt like an eternity.

"What are you doing?"

"I don't want to fight, sir."

"We're not fighting."

"You're angry with me," she pressed without looking up.

There was another long stretch of silence, and then his heavy sigh. "I'm not angry with you, kitten. Look at me."

Tears sprang to her eyes when she lifted her head and found him watching her with the same well of understanding in his eyes she'd always found there. "Yes, sir?"

"I'm not angry with you. I'm pissed about being laid up, and I'm man enough to admit I'm a little fucking scared on top of it."

That wasn't exactly news to her, but it was the first time

he'd actually said it out loud, so she took the opening. "What are you scared of?"

"Baseball is all I've ever done. What if I'm no good at anything else? What if nothing comes next?"

"Then you can be my houseboy," she said, offering up a cheeky grin in the hopes it would make him laugh. "Make me coffee in the morning, rub my feet when I get home."

Giving her the laugh she'd been after, he cocked an eyebrow at her. "Orgasms on demand?"

"I'm not sure you really understand what a houseboy does, but I'm not going to turn that down."

"And how are we supposed to afford me just hanging around the house all day?"

It clicked then, that he honestly had no idea how good she was at her job. "Are you forgetting that I not only know exactly how much you're worth, but I know how to make that money work for you instead of the other way around? Even if you never made another dime, you could live comfortably for the rest of your life. And it's not like I'm broke, Austin."

"I didn't think you were." But it was clear from the look on his face, he'd never really given her income any thought. Curiosity replaced the fear in his eyes as he studied her. "How much *are* you worth, kitten?"

"Enough." Grinning at his glare, she leaned in and pressed a kiss to his lips. "Look, all I'm saying is, you don't have to rush out tomorrow and find a new career. Right now, you just need to concentrate on your recovery. You're not giving up that easily. And when your inevitable retirement does come, you'll still be able to take a few years to figure out what come next if that's what you need to do."

"You're kinda bossy, you know that?"

"Only when it matters. Sir," she added with a sly grin.

"Brat." Reaching out a hand, he brushed a stray lock of hair away from her face. "Thanks."

"Any time. I have to get back to work. Call if you need me?"

"Sure."

Knowing he probably wouldn't unless it was absolutely necessary, she gave him another kiss and made her way back to the kitchen. She sat in front of the computer, but for a long while she simply stared at the screen, not really seeing what was in front of her.

What if nothing comes next?

He'd been talking about his career, but she couldn't help but wonder how it applied to them. When this was over and he was all healed up, how was she supposed to just walk away? What if nothing came next for them?

A meeting notification popped up on her computer and she pushed aside all the worries and what-ifs. Right now was what mattered, and right now, she had a client.

Ignoring the ache in her chest, she pasted on a bright, happy smile, and started the meeting. "Good afternoon, Mr. Garrison. How was Italy?"

CHAPTER 22

AUSTIN

His kitten was hiding something.

He wasn't sure what, just yet, but she was definitely keeping *something* from him. Every so often, he'd look over and find her watching him. And when he caught her, she'd look away, a guilty blush staining her cheeks.

The question was, what was it? She'd barely left the house for two weeks, other than to run the occasional errand and the trips they'd made together to see the team doctor and the array of specialists the Hawks had arranged for him to see. An affair was out since she spent all her time with him these days.

So, what the hell was going on with her?

Before the injury, he would have just hauled her into the bedroom and tortured the truth out of her. His cock hardened at the thought of her tied to his bed, her ass red and welted from his belt, crying and begging as he forced orgasm after orgasm on her.

But thanks to his knee, that whole scenario was out. Standing for more than a few minutes was excruciating and he was fairly sure what he wanted to do fell under the "rigorous activity" the doctor had warned against at his last checkup.

That didn't necessarily mean he was out of options, though. He let the plan form in his mind as he waited for her to finish for the day. When he heard the telltale *snick* of her laptop closing, he pushed himself up straighter and waited for her to join him in the living room.

"What do you want for dinner? I'm a little tired of—"

"Strip," he ordered, cutting her off. Dinner could wait. He was getting to the bottom of whatever she was hiding from him, tonight.

Her eyes narrowed and for a moment, he just knew she was going to argue with him. But something changed in her and he could swear he saw a flash of guilt in her eyes before she nodded. "Yes, sir."

Fuck. Maybe she was having an affair. Or maybe she was thinking of leaving him now that he couldn't play ball.

Pushing those thoughts to the side, he focused on her as she slowly popped open the buttons on her shirt. It amused him to no end that she insisted on getting dressed, even down to her sexy high heels, when she was working from home.

Not that he was complaining. She favored pencil skirts most days, the kind that hugged her curves in a way that made him want to bend her over the nearest piece of furniture and fuck her senseless.

She was wearing such a skirt today, and his cock strained against the thick material of his gray sweats as she wiggled the material down over her hips.

When she was fully naked, her clothes in a neat pile on the armchair to his left, he waved a hand toward the bedroom. "Go get my play bag."

"Why do you need your bag? Sir," she added hastily when he gave her a hard look.

"Do you need to know why, little girl?"

Her irritation was written all over her face, but she turned on her heel and stomped toward the bedroom. It never failed to amuse him how much she hated being denied an explanation when he gave her an order. The order itself didn't bother her, she just wanted to know *why*. Forcing her to follow through, without providing the reason, was one of his favorite forms of torture.

Returning a few minutes later with the large black duffel he kept ready for nights at the club, she dropped it on the ground in front of him. Though she kept her arms at her side, everything about her stance screamed defiance.

"Legs apart, hands behind your head."

With a small huff, she obeyed, and he leaned down to unzip the bag. When he found what he wanted, he pulled the slender pink tube from the bag and held it out to her. "Turn this on and place it on your clit. But do not come until I tell you."

Excitement sparkled in her eyes as she took the vibrator. No doubt she thought she was being rewarded.

Poor, naive little kitten.

Flipping the vibrator on, she ran it between her already glistening pussy lips. He let her play for awhile, until her breaths grew ragged, and her eyes had drifted closed with pleasure.

"Stop."

The vibrator switched off and her bottom lip pushed out into a pout, but she didn't argue.

"We need to have a talk, kitten."

Her brows drew together in obvious confusion. "A talk, sir?"

"Yes. How do I feel about lying, little girl?"

"You don't like it." The furrow between her brows deepened. "But I haven't lied about anything."

"Turn it back on."

With far more reluctance this time, she switched it on again. She fought it, at first, and fuck if he didn't enjoy the way her jaw clenched with frustration until she finally gave herself over to it.

And just as she did, he cut her off. "Stop."

"Goddammit!" Fist clenched around the device, she turned it off and glared at him. "What do you want?"

"First of all, I want you to remember how to address me when we're playing." The hardness in his tone wasn't all for show. His own temper was rising to match hers, but he did his best to keep a rein on it. The goal was to drive her to lose control, not the opposite.

"Fine," she snapped. "What do you want, *sir*?"

"I want you to tell me what's going on with you."

The expression on her face turned mutinous. "Nothing, sir. I'm fine."

"Bullshit. Turn it on."

"No! I'm not lying to you and I'm not playing this game any more."

For a split second, he was sure she was going to throw the vibrator at him and storm off. But she stayed where she was, still gripping the tube, glaring at him.

This was, he realized, more of a test of her submission than anything he'd put her through before. It was easier to submit when someone held you down or forced you to obey. But knowing you could walk away if you wanted to, and your Dom couldn't physically wrestle you into submission? Damn near impossible.

And yet, there she stood, trembling with some mix of anger and need, knowing she was going to be punished for disobeying. Waiting for her sentence to be handed down.

His own anger faded a bit. *Good girl.*

"I'll give you a choice," he told her, fighting back a grin at the wariness that crept into her eyes.

"A choice, sir?"

"You can take your punishment like a good girl, or you can go stand with your nose pressed to the wall until you're ready to obey."

The little brat had the nerve to actually growl at him. "That's not much of a choice, sir."

"I know. What's it gonna be, kitten?"

"I don't understand why I'm being punished. I haven't lied to you about anything!"

If he'd had any indication that the tears in her eyes were from distress rather than frustration, he might have considered showing her some mercy. But that defiance was still etched into every muscle in her body, so leniency was off the table.

"You are lying to me. Keeping secrets is the same as lying. But that's not why you're being punished."

"It's not?"

"No. This," he gestured at the vibrator she still held in her hand, "wasn't a punishment. I just wanted to get you to open up. You are going to be punished for telling me no."

Some of the color leeched from her cheeks. "Oh."

"Yeah. So, which is it? Are you going to take your punishment or do I have to wait out your stubborn streak?"

Her shoulders hunched forward and for the first time since they'd started their little game, she looked remorseful. "I'm sorry, sir. I was just frustrated."

"Thank you for the apology, kitten. In the bag, there's a small bottle labeled peppermint oil. Find it for me, please."

After a short hesitation, she bent down to search the bag and a moment later, she held up a small bottle of clear liquid.

"Pour some on the vibrator. Enough to coat it, but you don't need to use the whole bottle."

Another beat of hesitation, her mouth turning down into a frown as she considered the request. He could see the wheels turning in her mind and it had to be killing her not to ask *why*, but she silently followed his instructions.

"Turn it back on and start again. But still no coming until I say so."

Still frowning slightly, she returned to her previous position and did as she was instructed. It didn't take more than a few seconds for her eyes to go wide.

"Something wrong, kitten?"

"Sir, it's… it's warm. Too warm."

"Yeah. It's going to burn for awhile. Now, what have you been hiding from me?"

"Nothing, I swear." Desperation filled her voice and her eyes." Sir, it hurts!"

"I know, baby. It's a punishment, remember?"

Bouncing on her toes, she shook her head, her long, dark hair flying wildly around her. "I'll be good, I swear!"

"What are you hiding from me, Katherine? I can do this all night."

"C-can't," she said, panting through the pain. "Can't t-tell you."

Stubborn brat. "Why not?"

"Sir, *please.*"

"As soon as you tell me, you can come, and then we can get some cream for your poor little pussy."

A low whine, filled with distress and need, had him sitting up straighter. The oil shouldn't burn too badly, as he'd tried it on himself when he'd purchased it, but he imagined the burn along with the pain of needing to come was getting the best of her.

Snapping his fingers, he pointed to the ground in front of the couch. "Knees."

She moved quickly, kneeling so her thighs pressed tightly with the hope it would help ease the fire between her legs. "Sir?"

"Knees apart, kitten. You know better," he admonished softly, pleased when she obeyed with nothing more than a groan of protest.

"Good girl." Cupping her cheek with his hand, he held her gaze, searching for any sign of true distress. Thankfully, there wasn't anything beyond what he knew she could handle, so he plowed forward. "Talk to me, kitten. Tell me what's wrong."

"It hurts, sir."

"I know. If you want it to stop, you just have to tell me what's going on in that pretty head of yours."

"Don't want to."

'Don't want to' was a far different being from 'can't', but he wasn't going to point that out. As far as he was concerned, it was progress. "Press the vibrator against your clit. It's barely touching."

"Sir, please, I can't take it."

"Then tell me."

When she didn't move, he reached between them and pressed her hand more firmly against her pussy. She let out a short, high scream and little beads of sweat began popping out along her hairline.

"I love you!" She blurted out. "I love you and I didn't want to tell you, now please just make it stop, please!"

"Why didn't you want to tell me?"

"I'm scared."

Ignoring his own hurt, he pushed more firmly on her hand. "Good girl. Thank you for telling me. Come for me, baby."

With soft words of encouragement, he coaxed her over the edge. Holding her close, he stroked her hair as her body shattered, shaking with the force of the orgasm. When it seemed to run its course, he switched off the vibe and gently pried it from her hands.

Tossing it into the bag with a mental note to wash everything later, he pulled her in so her head was resting on his chest. He waited for her soft whimpers to fade before speaking again.

"Why are you scared?"

Apparently all out of fight, she sighed. "I'm scared that once you're better and you don't need me as much, you'll realize you don't really love me."

"If that's really what you think, you're an idiot."

Jerking away from his hold, she glared up at him. "I am not an idiot. You're just, just…" Trailing off, she waved her hands at him. "You're hurt and you're scared and life as you know it is changing and you need something to cling to. And I'm fine being that thing, but I can't pretend it's ever going to be anything permanent or… more, I guess."

"You think I said I love you because I'm injured and you're taking care of me?"

"Well. Yes."

"You really think I would say those words without meaning it? Goddammit, Kit."

She at least had the grace to look sheepish this time. "I think you think you mean it."

"I swear to God, as soon as my leg heals, I'm going to whip your ass. You won't sit for a week by the time I'm done with you."

"That's not fair!"

"No, what's not fair is you just deciding you know best and that I'm too stupid to even know when I love someone."

"I never said you were stupid."

"No, but you sure as hell implied it." He lifted a hand when she sputtered out a protest, cutting her off. "You want to know how I know I'm in love with you?"

She hesitated, but her curiosity eventually won out. "How?"

"That morning, when you offered to make me coffee? I was going to fight you on it, but then you smiled at me."

"You know you love me because I smiled at you?" Skepticism dripped from her tone.

"I know I love you because I realized that even if I never played another game, it would be worth it if I could just see that smile every day. Baby." Cupping her face with his hands, he brushed his lips over hers. "How could I not be in love with you when my entire fucking world revolves around just seeing you smile?"

"Really?"

"Yeah, kitten. Really."

"Okay." Closing her eyes, she blew out a breath. "You really love me. And I love you. What now?"

"Now we get you some relief for your poor little pussy and figure out what we're eating for dinner. I'm fucking starving."

With a watery laugh, she pushed to her feet. "Well, if you hadn't interrupted me with the Spanish Inquisition, we could have eaten already."

"Didn't expect that, did you?"

With a roll of her eyes, she reached for her clothes, pausing when he cleared his throat. "Am I allowed to get dressed?"

"Nope. Let's order something that can be delivered. I'm not done with you yet."

A sly, purely feminine smile curved her lips upward. "Yes, sir."

CHAPTER 23

KATHERINE

"Sorry, sorry!" Claudia slid into the booth across from Kit, her blonde hair falling haphazardly out of her ponytail. "I thought getting out the door without the kids would be so much faster, but they had other plans. Tony Jr. spilled an entire cup of juice on my shirt as I was walking out the door. So, I'm late. As always."

"You're fine. I just got here myself," Kit assured her, lifting her coffee to her mouth to hide her grin. "You do, ah, appear to have a cartoon dog stuck to your face."

Eyes widening, Claudia slapped a hand to her cheek. "I told Tony a sticker book was a bad idea." Scowling, she peeled the sticker from her skin and wadded it up. "Sorry I'm such a mess."

"You're not a mess. You're a mom." Did Austin want kids? What would their kids be like? Goofy and fun-loving like him? Or more serious, like her? Would they have his eyes?

"Ah, Earth to Kit." Giggling like a teenager, Claudia snapped her fingers in front of Kit's face.

"My turn to apologize. I was daydreaming."

"Oh, was it a sexy daydream?" With a heavy sigh, Claudia propped her chin on her hand. "I miss sexy daydreams."

"Sorry to disappoint you. I was actually thinking about having kids. With Austin."

"Oh! You two would make the prettiest babies! You're so gorgeous and he's got those dreamy eyes."

A familiar unease settled in her chest and Kit shifted uncomfortably in her seat. "I'm not gorgeous, but thank you."

Claudia's mouth dipped down into a frown. "What are you talking about? You're stunning."

"Seriously, you don't have to say things like that just because we're friends."

"Is this because of what those mean girls said at the game?"

"It's because I own a mirror," Kit snapped.

"Well, maybe you need to get your eyes checked, then."

"Look, I don't need pity compliments from the prom queen, so can we just drop it?"

"Pity compliments? Wait, are we fighting?" The look Claudia sent her was so full of bewildered hurt, Kit instantly felt like a complete asshole.

"Sort of. I guess I'm fighting. I just… I know I'm not the kind of woman a guy like Austin normally goes for. You don't have to pretend I am."

"Please. I'd kill for some curves. You have any idea how hard it is to be the skinny girl with no tits in high school? That's probably why it took Tony so damn long to really see me as a girl. Up until our Junior year, I could have walked around topless and nobody would have noticed I wasn't a boy."

"Curves are different than this." Kit waved a hand up and down her torso.

"Whatever. You're drop-dead gorgeous. And Austin isn't blind. It's not like you've tricked him into being attracted to you. So what if you've got some extra cushion for the pushin' as the saying goes."

"He told me he loves me." The confession seemed to just jump out of her mouth. She hadn't meant to tell anyone, not just yet, but suddenly she couldn't hold it back.

"I told you!" A triumphant grin lit her face and Claudia wiggled her butt against her seat. "I told you that man was crazy about you. How did he tell you? Wait, let me go grab a coffee and something sweet and then you're going to tell me the whole story."

She returned to the table with a large mug and a slice of cake nearly as big as her head. "You're going to have to help me eat this. Otherwise I'll gorge myself and get sick and Tony will have my ass."

"Tony doesn't like you eating sweets?"

Pink colored her friend's cheeks. "It's not that. I don't eat them often but when I do, I have a tendency to go overboard. Tony gets all overprotective if I so much as stub my toe. But this isn't about me, tell me about Austin. How did he tell you? Was it super romantic?"

Picking up a fork, Kit cut herself a bite of cake. "I was getting him coffee, the morning after he got hurt, and he laughed at something I said and then he was all 'God, I love you.'"

"He just blurted it out like that? Over coffee?"

"Yup."

"That's so sweet." Claudia's eyes went soft and dreamy. "Like he just couldn't wait another moment to tell you. Did you say it back?"

"Eventually."

"Wait, you didn't say it back?" The dreamy look vanished, quickly replaced by wide-eyed horror. "Why not?"

Shrugging, Kit took another bite of cake. "It was too… big, I guess. And I figured he was only saying it because he was injured and he needed me. I didn't think he really meant it, and I knew if I said it, I would mean it. Possibly too much."

"Did you tell him *that*?"

"Eventually," Kit admitted with a sheepish smile. "He wasn't too thrilled."

"Girl. You do enjoy living dangerously."

"I don't know about that. I was just so freaked out, you know? What I feel for him, it's so impossibly huge and important, it didn't seem possible he could feel the same way about me. It still doesn't, if I'm being honest."

"I get that, actually." At Kit's raised eyebrow, Claudia lifted a shoulder. "Just because Tony and I knew each other forever before we got together didn't make it any less terrifying. But the good things in life are usually scary, right? Because it matters."

"I guess that's true."

"Of course, it's true, I said it." Claudia grinned. "So you said it back, eventually. How did that go down? Was it super romantic?"

Her entire body flushed at the memory of her on her knees, her lady bits on fire as he tortured the confession and a mind-blowing orgasm out of her. "I'm going to need something a hell of a long stronger than coffee for that story."

∼

Austin

"Could you repeat that for me, doc?" Sitting on the examination table, Austin knew he was staring, but he still couldn't quite process what he'd just been told.

"Barring any unforeseen complications, I don't see any reason you can't play next year."

"And no surgery?"

"No surgery. The knee is healing up quite nicely on its own and the physical therapist says you've made a lot of improvement the past few weeks. You're not quite ready to go back to practice, but we're very happy with your progress."

"That's—wow. Holy shit." His face felt like it might split open from smiling. "That's the second-best news I've heard since this happened."

"Happy to be of service. Keep the brace on, even when you're resting. You'll probably need another two months with it on to fully heal, but we'll reevaluate in a couple weeks."

The entire car ride home, he couldn't wipe the grin from his face. He'd kept the appointment a secret from Kit—which had been something of a miracle—so he'd have time to process the news on his own if it had gone the other way. Now, he couldn't wait to get home to her and share the good news with her.

A quick text confirmed she was still out with Claudia, which worked in his favor. He wanted to celebrate, and the beginnings of a plan stirred in his mind.

Remember the dress you wore to Black Light?

Three dots popped up on the screen for several long seconds and he chuckled as he imagined her blushing in the coffee shop, carefully wording her answer before she replied.

The red one? Yes, sir.

That's the one. I want you to go to your place and get ready for dinner. Wear the dress. I'll pick you up around six.

You don't want me to come home?

Not yet.

Why?

He raised an eyebrow before he remembered she couldn't see it. *Do you need to know why, little girl?*

Grrr. I really hate that rule!

I know. See you at six, kitten.

The wait sucked, but he killed a good bit of time getting

himself a shower and shaving for the first time since the accident. By the time the car he'd ordered pulled up in front of her house, his entire body was thrumming with anticipation.

Apparently, the wait had been just as hard on his kitten, since her front door opened before he was even out of the car. She stopped halfway down the front steps, her mouth dropping open when he took a few limping steps toward her.

Her excited squeal disturbed the neighbor's cat, who shot them a glare from where he was napping on their front steps.

"You're off the crutches! Wait, did you go to the doctor today? Why didn't you tell me? What did he say?" Kit peppered him with questions as she hurried toward him as fast as she could without breaking her neck in the needle-thin heels he remembered from their trip to Black Light. They matched the dress perfectly, and without disappointment clouding his judgment, he was able to fully appreciate how off the charts sexy she looked.

"Get in the car and I'll tell you." He propelled her forward with a sharp smack to her ass and she giggled in response as she climbed into the car.

As soon as the door was shut, she pounced again. "Tell me what's going on before I explode!"

Instead of a verbal response, he fisted a hand in her perfectly curled hair and yanked her in for a long, deep kiss. The instant their lips met, she went soft under his touch, sweet and submissive, yielding to him as he demanded.

"Good girl," he murmured, pulling just a breath away. "I really fucking love you."

"I love you back. Please tell me what's going on, sir?"

"Doc says there's a really good chance I can play next season."

With another squeal, she threw her arms around his neck. "I'm so happy for you."

"For us." Gently untangling from her embrace, he shifted

so they were facing each other more fully and lifted each of her hands to his lips in turn. "I couldn't have done this without you, Kit. And you've done so much for me the past month, but I have one more favor."

"Anything."

"Move in with me. We can keep your place and rent it out, or you can sell it, whatever you want. But I want you to move in with me, for real. What do you say, kitten?"

Worrying her bottom lip with her teeth, she pulled back, her eyes searching his face. "I don't know. That's a big step. What if you get tired of me? What if you hate the way I chew my food or the fact that I get up really early or—"

"Stop. You've been there for a month already and I don't hate the way you chew. I'm sure we're going to get on each others' nerves, but there's nobody else I want to growl at in the mornings or fight with over who drank the last of the coffee. You don't have to answer me now, just promise me you'll think about it."

"No." She shook her head, dark curls flying. "No, if I think about it, I'm just going to talk myself out of it. Let's do it. I've been wanting to buy some rental property anyway, so why not start with something I already own?"

"Are you wearing panties?"

"Um, yes?"

"Take them off."

"Why? Never mind." With an exaggerated eye roll, she lifted her hips off the seat and worked the scrap of lace down her legs. "I don't need to know why, right?"

"Such a good girl." Taking the panties from her, he shoved them in his pocket before running his hand up the inside of her thigh. "I think you deserve a reward."

It took an extra three trips around the block once they reached the restaurant, but he managed to give her three screaming rewards before they climbed out of the back seat.

CHAPTER 24

KATHERINE

Humming softly to herself, Kit scanned the display of chicken, carefully selecting a pack and placing it in her cart. Ever since Austin had asked her to officially move in, she'd been walking on air. Everything seemed to be clicking into place. She hadn't started packing up her house, but she told herself she had time.

Maybe the rest of their lives, though neither of them had mentioned marriage yet.

"Slow down, Kit," she quietly lectured herself as she picked out a gallon of milk. "Plenty of time for weddings and babies later."

It was all so normal, making menus together, doing the grocery shopping. Bumping into each other in the bathroom in the mornings while she was getting ready. There were moments she completely forgot he was anything more than just the man she loved, the man who'd asked her to share his home and his life for the foreseeable future.

With her cart full, she maneuvered into line behind a petite woman whose hair made her nearly as tall as Kit herself. Someone to her right snickered and Kit fought the urge to giggle. As ridiculous as the woman looked, it wasn't polite to laugh at strangers.

But the hushed laughter was soon joined by loud whispers and dread settled like a rock in her gut. Risking a glance toward the commotion, she found two teenage girls holding a magazine and staring.

Straight at her.

Whipping her head back around, she tried to ignore the itch between her shoulder blades. Surely, she was imagining things. There was no reason for them to be staring at her.

Desperate for a distraction, she turned her head to scan the selection of magazines beside the register. The usual array of celebrity faces stared out at her, promising youthful skin and Hollywood secrets.

Then her gaze landed on a tabloid well known for nasty rumors which usually turned out to be only partially true or completely made up. But this particular rumor was absolutely true. Because in the corner, surrounded by all the other juicy celebrity gossip, were pictures of her and Austin.

Baseball Star's BIG Secret!

Pictures of her, in jeans and a t-shirt, leaving the physical therapist's office with Austin. The two of them embracing, then kissing on his front porch. And the night they'd gone out to dinner, when he'd asked her to move in with him.

Whoever the photographer was, they'd even managed to snap the few seconds before they got to the restaurant where Austin had slid his hand under her dress, exposing the top of her thigh to the world. She'd slapped at his hand a moment later because he'd refused to return her panties, and she'd been equal parts terrified and exhilarated by the idea that someone might see.

That night had been perfect, from the moment he'd picked her up in a sleek black town car, to the moment they'd fallen into bed together and made love for the first time since his injury.

And a few assholes with cameras had ruined it. Sullied it with their not-at-all-subtle innuendos.

Picking up the tabloid, she tossed it onto the conveyor belt and began stacking the rest of her items behind it. No matter how badly she wanted to break, she would not do it here. She'd be damned if she was going to give her *fans* the satisfaction.

The cashier glanced up when she scanned the tabloid, but if she made the connection, she did an admirable job of hiding it. Ten minutes later, Kit's backseat was filled with groceries and she was backing out of her parking space.

She didn't stop until she was back at Austin's. Parked in the driveway, she opened the tabloid and flipped to the "article".

Nausea bubbled in her stomach. While they never came right out and used the F-word, there were plenty of euphemisms. And the whole thing had a tone of stunned glee, as if they'd caught Austin doing something salacious, something worthy of being printed alongside rumors of adultery and drug use. There was even an entire paragraph dedicated to the theory that Austin had some kind of weird, previously unknown kink. A theory they backed up with pictures of Austin partying with supermodels and a reminder of the brief affair he'd had with Chloe Carlisle, a model who was starting to make a name for herself in Hollywood.

Why, the so-called journalist asked, would he do such a complete one-eighty from his usual type, if it wasn't some cheap thrill he was chasing? Some weird fetish he'd never publicly indulged in before now?

Why, indeed?

Shoving the magazine into her purse, she forced herself to get out of the car and gather up the groceries. God, what if someone was watching her, taking pictures of her struggling with the bags, her arm fat bulging around the plastic straps digging into her arms?

The thought spurred her into action and she raced for the front door. She didn't stop until she was in the kitchen, out of breath, dropping the bags on the table.

"Hey, kitten." Coming up behind her, Austin wrapped his arms around her middle and pressed a kiss to the side of her neck. A move she usually loved, but now all she could feel was how squishy her stomach felt against his muscular arms.

"Hey." Under the pretext of putting away the groceries, she shrugged off his touch and moved to the other side of the table.

"What's for dinner?"

"It's on the menu board," she snapped, snatching up the dry goods to carry them to the giant walk-in pantry.

Moving faster than the brace on his leg should have allowed, he rounded the table and backed her into a corner of the pantry. "Want to try that again, little girl?"

"It's on the menu board, sir," she repeated without dropping any of the attitude.

Bracing one arm on the shelf behind her, he wrapped his free hand around her throat, forcing her head back. "Someone wants to eat dinner standing up. What's gotten into my sweet little kitten?"

"I'm not sweet. And I'm sure as hell not little. Get off me."

The hand around her throat tightened and some dark, desperate part of her wept with relief. *Yes. Punish me. Fuck me. Make me hurt, make me forget.*

"I don't know what's going on with you, but the attitude stops now." There was no questioning the authority in his voice, but it didn't settle her as it usually did. All of her emotions felt wild, untethered, and she didn't know what to do with the chaos tumbling around inside of her.

So she lashed out, praying he'd be able to tame her inner turmoil the way he'd shown her he could. "Whatever."

She shoved at his chest, expecting him to hold his ground. But he stepped back and she stormed past him, even as a part of her screamed for her to stop, to submit. In some distant part of her mind, she recognized the burning desire to have him be in control, but she didn't want to give it to him. Why couldn't he see how desperately she needed him to take it, to take the reins before she spun completely out of control?

"You've got about five seconds to start talking to me before I bend you over this table and whip your ass, little girl. What the hell happened at the store?"

Do it, please, sir. Anything to make it stop.

"You want to know what happened? Fine." Yanking the magazine from her purse, she threw it at him, twin zings of satisfaction and fear running up her spine when it hit him square in the face. "That happened."

Apparently, his curiosity was pressing enough for him to overlook her throwing things at him, because he did nothing more than glare at her before scanning the cover.

The corners of his lips dipped down, but his expression was otherwise carefully guarded when he looked up. "Okay. We're in a tabloid. It happens sometimes."

"Did you read the caption? *Baseball Star's Big Secret?*"

His face crinkled in confusion. "Is that why you're upset? You think I've been keeping you a secret?"

"Read the article."

He frowned again, but flipped open the magazine and scanned the pages. A low, threatening growl filled the kitchen. "This is bullshit. I'm calling my lawyer."

"What are you going to do? Sue them for printing some pictures of us in a magazine?"

"For slander." Slapping the magazine on the table, he

jabbed a finger at the glossy pages. "They can't just say shit like this."

"Slander?" For a moment, she just stared at him before she snorted out a laugh. "You can't sue someone for slander when it's the truth."

"How the fuck do you figure this sorry excuse for journalism is the truth?"

"Because it is, Austin!" Something inside of her snapped and she grabbed two fistfuls of flesh and fat around her stomach. "Newsflash, Mr. Barrick, you're dating the fat girl. Nothing they said in that article is wrong. You used to date supermodels and actresses and now you're dating *this*."

His expression turned thunderous, and those dark, desperate parts of her thrilled. "Call yourself fat again and we're going to have a problem, little girl."

"Why? Because you don't like to hear it? Because if I don't say it, you can still pretend it's not true?" She knew she was pushing too hard, too far, but she couldn't seem to stop herself.

"It's not true!" For the first time in their relationship, he raised his voice at her. But instead of cowering, she stepped forward, going toe to toe with him.

"Reality check, Austin. No matter what pretty words you want to use to get around it, I am fat. I'm a big girl. Not curvy, or voluptuous, or whatever else you tell yourself to avoid admitting the truth. And if you can't accept that, then I guess you can't really accept being with me."

Shocked silence filled the space between them, seemingly pushing them further and further apart even though neither of them moved a muscle. Austin was the first to break it, his words slow and stilted, like he was struggling with each one. "You seriously think I don't want you because I won't let you call yourself fat? Do you even hear yourself right now?"

"Look me in the eye and tell me I'm wrong, Austin. Tell me

I'm not all of those things they said about me." All of a sudden, it was crucial to hear him say it. For him to admit he saw her, really saw her. And for her to know he loved her anyway.

"I'm not going to let you bully me into degrading you."

All of those wounds she'd thought long-since healed ripped open at once. She was almost shocked to realize she wasn't actually bleeding out on the kitchen floor. "How can you be with me if you think being fat is degrading?"

"You're twisting my words."

"Am I?"

"Yes!" Running his hands through his hair, he gave the short locks a sharp pull. "I think you're fucking gorgeous exactly as you are. I wouldn't change a thing about you and that includes *all* of you. Haven't I proven that over and over again? What more do you need me to do, Kit?"

"I don't know! I wish I knew, because then maybe I could stop feeling like this."

The corners of his mouth dipped down and his brow furrowed, like she was some puzzle he couldn't quite figure out. "Like what?"

"Like I'm constantly waiting for the other shoe to drop. For you to wake up one day and realize I'm not all that special after all. I thought I was past it, and then I saw that magazine and I just…" She held up her hands, at a loss for how to explain it to him in a way he might finally understand.

"Oh, kitten." Sighing quietly, he stepped forward, cupping her face in his hands. The playful amusement she was so used to seeing in his eyes had been replaced by an emotion so intense, she couldn't quite put her finger on it. "I wish I had the words to make this better. I want to be able to fix this for you, to make it all go away. But I can't and it's killing me."

"I'm sorry." Tears clogged in her throat, making the words thick and sluggish. "I wish I wasn't like this, too."

"That's not what I meant. I just hate seeing you in pain."

The storm inside of her began to settle, finally. "Really? The giant bag of torture in your closet says otherwise."

"Brat." There was no heat behind the word, and his expression eased into a smirk. "You know what I mean."

"I know." Closing her eyes, she pressed her forehead to his, drinking in his strength and comfort. "Sorry about the blow up. The article just caught me off guard and there were these girls in the store laughing at me and I just freaked out, I guess."

"No apology needed, kitten. It pissed me off, too. Are we good?"

"Yeah. We're good." She drew in a deep breath, and blew it out again slowly. Tilting her head up, she brushed her lips against his, this time offering comfort as well as taking it. "Now get out of here so I can make dinner."

"Want some help?"

"God, no. Get out of my kitchen. Sir," she added with a cheeky smile when he raised an eyebrow.

"I'm going, because I'm starving. But after dinner, you're going to pay for that."

"Yes, Sir."

With another quick kiss, he left, and she gave herself a moment for a few deep breaths before grabbing more groceries to finish putting everything away. But there was an ache in her chest, a pressure she vaguely recognized as a mix of fear and shame. And she wondered if she'd ever truly be free of either.

CHAPTER 25

AUSTIN

Sweat pouring off of him, Austin grunted and groaned his way through the final set of single-leg dips his physical therapist had assigned him. Behind that Barbie-blonde hair and toothy smile beat the heart of a true sadist, one he was certain would send even the most hardcore masochist running for the hills.

"That was great, Mr. Barrick! Don't forget to do those stretches I gave you at home, too. I'll know if you didn't."

Before he'd gotten to know her, he'd brushed comments like that off as good-natured teasing. Now, he recognized them for the threat they were. If she so much as thought he'd been slacking off on his at-home work, she'd make his next session even more tortuous than the last.

"Got it, doc," he managed between panting breaths. "See ya."

It was all he could do not to whimper as he limped his way to the showers. He lingered, letting the heat of the water beat away the stress from his workout, and by the time he was walking out the door he felt almost human again.

He nearly wept with relief when he spotted his driver

waiting for him at the bottom of the steps. Dr. Miller would probably tell him walking was good exercise, but he wasn't sure he could have drummed up the energy to make it the two blocks to the closest parking garage.

Halfway home, his phone rang and he sighed at the sight of his agent's name on the screen. He was tempted to just ignore it, but knowing Mary, she'd just keep calling until she got what she needed.

"Barrick," he answered with a grunt.

"Austin. What the *hell*?"

The urgent, distressed tone had Austin sitting up straighter in his seat. "What? What happened?"

"You just got outed. Goddammit, why didn't you tell me about this so I could be prepared? I can't protect you if I don't know about these things!"

"What are you talking about, Mary? Outed by who? For what?"

"Fucking Chloe Carlisle."

Chloe Carlisle, the model-slash-aspiring actress he'd dated for a few months last year. Ice crept up his spine as his brain played out scenes from their relationship, including the rather epic fight they'd had when he'd finally broken things off. "Shit. What did she say?"

"She did an exclusive interview all about her relationship with you and the kinky shit you're into. Said you forced her to go to some kind of sex club."

"Forced is a bit of an overstatement," he snapped, rubbing at his forehead. "The way I remember it, she fucking begged me to take her."

"Jesus." The line went silent, and if it hadn't been so serious, Austin might have laughed at the idea of Mary Palmer being speechless. "Part of me was sure she was making all this shit up. She's not, is she?"

"Well, since I haven't seen the interview yet, I can't really say. But yes, we did enjoy some kinky sex and yes, I took her to a club. But always with her consent."

"All right. All right," Mary repeated, and Austin could practically hear the wheels turning. "I'll send you the link for the interview. Watch it and then call me back. We need to get in front of this, fast. What about Kit?"

"What about her?" Other than the fact that she was going to lose her shit when she heard about this. He needed to call her, tell her what was going on before she got the news from someone else.

"How's she going to take this? It hasn't even been a week since that damn tabloid article and now this. She going to be okay?"

"I don't know. I need to call her."

"You do that. I'll do what I can for now and then I'll swing by your place in a bit so we can figure out a game plan."

Hanging up with Mary, he dialed Kit's office number, but was routed to the ice queen, as he'd not-so-affectionately dubbed her admin. "Donna, put me through to Katherine. Please."

"Ms. Callahan is in a meeting. May I take a message?"

"This is Austin. I need to talk to her. Now."

"Ms. Callahan is in a meeting," Donna repeated primly, her voice not warming even a fraction of a degree. If anything it seemed to cool even further.

Goddammit. "Fine. Have her call me the second she wraps up."

He jabbed his thumb at the End button and pulled up his texts with Kit.

Call me. I need to talk to you. I love you.

The text would probably freak her out before he even had a chance to talk to her, but it couldn't be helped.

Dropping his head back against the seat of the car, he willed his rioting stomach to calm.

What a fucking mess.

~

Katherine

LEANING BACK IN HER CHAIR, Kit let her head fall back and closed her eyes. It wasn't even two yet and she was ready to walk out the door. Everyone was just so damn needy today, and her calendar already hadn't left much space open as it was.

A brisk knock on the door had her sighing, but she forced herself to sit up straight again and face whatever new problem had cropped up. "Come in."

The door swung open and Donna walked in. If possible, she seemed more stiff and formal than usual. "Your... gentleman friend is in the news again."

"Austin?" Alarm bells rang in her head, and she was instantly alert. "What's wrong? Is he okay?"

"I knew there was something wrong with that man. I never trusted him."

Never trusted him? What the hell? "Donna, what are you talking about?"

Her admin's chin jerked toward the laptop on Kit's desk. "Check your email."

Stomach in knots, Kit spun and opened her email. Seeing the message from Donna, she opened it and clicked the link.

Austin Barrick's ex-Lover Tells All

Oh, god. With trembling fingers, she hit play on the embedded video. Sitting on a couch in what appeared to be a brightly lit television studio was a tearful-looking Chloe Carlisle. Almost in a trance, Kit listened to her talk all about the "depraved" things Austin had subjected her to.

And whenever he was in town, we would... he would make me go to this underground sex club with him. He would parade me around like I was some kind of show pony. It was humiliating, but I didn't know how to make it stop.

One word. All she'd had to do was say one single word and everything would have come screeching to a halt. Kit wanted to scream at the computer screen, but it wouldn't have done any good. The damage was already done.

Unable to listen to another word of Chloe's lies, Kit clicked the button to stop the video.

"I need to go." Her voice sounded hollow, matching how she felt inside. "Reschedule my afternoon calls, and clear my calendar tomorrow. I'll be working from home, but unavailable for calls or meetings."

Donna's eyes widened then narrowed with a censure that made Kit's chest ache. "Katherine! You can't just abandon your clients for that man."

"I'm not." Shame and anger had her cheeks flushing hot as she packed up her computer. "I'm preparing for the inevitable shitstorm when my family, friends, and clients see an interview about my sex life plastered all over the internet."

"Your… you and he… you're not saying…"

"I am." Forcing her gaze to her admin's shocked face, Kit braced herself for the judgement. "Not that it's yours or anyone else's business, but yes. It's all true, except Austin would never force himself on a woman. He would never do anything without explicit consent. Now, please cancel my meetings. I'll call you tomorrow and let you know what the plan is for the rest of the week."

With that, she shoved her laptop into her bag, grabbed her purse, and fled her office as calmly as she could. By the time she reached her car, her hands had started trembling again and each breath was taking more and more effort as she slid into the driver's seat.

She'd barely made it out of the parking lot when her

phone rang. Seeing Austin's name on the display filled her with a mix of relief and fury. The latter of which took the lead when she answered the call. "What the hell is going on, Austin?"

"Fuck. You heard?"

"Yes, I heard. What did you do to Chloe Carlisle?"

A long, heavy pause was followed by his quiet response. "You think this is my fault?"

"You tell me." Despite her bravado with Donna, she couldn't quite help the niggle of doubt in the back of her mind. "Why would she suddenly decide to out you to the entire world? It's not like she's getting anything out of this."

"You don't know Chloe. She fucking thrives on drama. Can you get away early? We need to talk, figure out how we're going to play this. We'll need to make a statement."

A statement. In public. The idea had her trembling all over again. "Austin..."

"I know I'm asking a lot, kitten. But my career is on the line here. I just got cleared to play again, and I'm not losing that because some prima donna with an axe to grind decided to stir the shit pot."

He had a point, as much as she hated to admit it. Pressing her head back against her seat, she closed her eyes, willing her jittery nerves to settled. "All right. I'm already on my way home."

"Drive safe, kitten. I love you."

Words he'd said a dozen times before, but now there was a sense of urgency to them. As if he was using them to reassure her, and maybe even himself, that everything was going to be okay. That love really could conquer all.

And because she needed to, she let herself believe it. "I love you, too."

CHAPTER 26

KATHERINE

"We'll have to do a press conference. Or an interview." Mary Palmer, sports agent extraordinaire, prowled the perimeter of Austin's living room, reminding Kit very much of a lioness pacing her cage at the zoo.

She wasn't what Kit had been expecting. Granted, all of her experience with sports agents came from movies, but where she'd expected sleek and maybe a little slimy, she'd gotten… Mary. Polished, certainly, in her designer suit and perfectly styled hair. But when she'd smiled, there'd been genuine warmth and sympathy in the gesture.

"An interview would be better," she muttered, without waiting for a response. "It will make the two of you seem more human, more approachable than a press conference."

"I'm not giving some rankings hound the chance to pick apart our lives," Austin growled, his grip on Kit's shoulder tightening almost to the point of pain.

"Newsflash, Austin, that's what the entire internet is doing right now. So you can either do an interview and have a chance to set everyone straight or you can let speculation run wild."

"I don't give a flying fuck what the internet thinks about me."

"I do." Two sets of surprised eyes turned on her and she tilted her chin up, prepared to fight as she met Austin's blazing gaze. "Your career isn't the only one on the line, here. Do you have any idea how many clients this could potentially cost me? I can name five, off the top of my head, who I'm expecting an email from tomorrow letting me know they're not comfortable working with me any longer. Five *huge* clients, and losing them will make things extremely tight for my bottomline. I can't afford this kind of negative exposure, Austin."

His expression softened, grief replacing the anger in his eyes. "I know, baby. I'm so fucking sorry. If I'd had any idea she would do something like this, I never would have touched her."

"But you did, and she did, and I'm the one paying for it." Some of the bitterness she'd been trying to hold back crept into her tone.

"So, you want to do the interview?" Austin asked carefully, his eyes searching her face.

"Not really. But I also don't want to do a press conference. I just want this to go away."

"Things like this don't just go away, hon." Mary crouched in front of her, understanding and sympathy etched into her pretty face. "You two could issue statements, say Chloe is full of shit and ask for privacy, but that's not going to stop people from digging. Wouldn't you rather the truth come out on your own terms?"

"No." Kit almost smiled when her eyes widened with surprise. "I don't want any of this to come out, on any terms. But I guess it's too late for that."

"Little bit," Mary said dryly, the corner of her mouth kicking up in a wry smile.

"Fine." She closed her eyes, thinking through their options. "Let's do the press conference. If things don't settle down after that, we can talk about an interview."

"Good enough for now." Pushing to her feet, she held out a hand for Kit to shake. "It was lovely to meet you, Katherine, though I was hoping it would be under better circumstances. I'll let you both know when we get the conference set up."

While Austin walked her out, Kit boxed up their leftovers and stashed the containers in the fridge. Closing the doors, she dropped her forehead to the cool metal and closed her eyes.

Strong, familiar hands settled on her shoulders and she let out a quiet moan when his fingers dug into the tight muscles. "This fucking sucks."

"I know, kitten. But we'll get through it. Come on, let's get you to bed."

"I can't. I need to type something up to send to my clients in the morning."

The hands on her shoulders forced her to turn, cupping her face when she was facing him. "You're exhausted, Kit. Wouldn't it be better to come at it in the morning, after you've had some sleep?"

"Maybe," she admitted reluctantly. The truth was, she wasn't ready to join him in his bed. Everything they'd done there felt... dirty, now. Tainted. "But I'm not sleepy. Movie?"

"Compromise," he said, one corner of his mouth kicking up in a crooked half-grin. "I'll run you a nice hot bath, and if you still don't feel sleepy afterwards, we'll watch a movie."

Because it was so painfully obvious he was trying to comfort her, she smiled up at him. "A bath sounds lovely."

He grinned, and some of the knots in her stomach loosened. "That's my girl. Come on, kitten."

Taking her hand, he led the way to their bathroom, where he filled the giant garden tub with steaming water and sweet-smelling bath salts.

"Is that... lavender?"

"Yup. Helps you relax, or that's what the lady at the store said, anyway."

"When did you buy that?" She hated herself a little for asking, for even feeling like she needed to ask. But there was also a part of her that suddenly wanted to purge the house of anything he'd bought for other women.

"Couple weeks ago. Remember when you first saw this tub, you said how one of your lifelong dreams was to take a bath in a tub where the water covered your knees and tits at the same time?"

She remembered. But the fact that *he* remembered had her blinking back tears. "You bought them for me?"

"Of course, kitten. Who else would I buy them for?"

"I thought maybe they were from... before."

Sliding his arms around her waist, he pulled her close, pressing his forehead to hers. "Nothing that came before you matters, Katherine."

Oh, how she wished it were that simple. But Chloe Carlisle was a stark reminder that their pasts couldn't just be tucked neatly away into a closet somewhere and forgotten. "I've tried not to think too much about the women who came before me, or what you did with them. But now it's being shoved in my face and I can't seem to think about anything else."

"Then we'll make so many of our own memories, you won't have space for anything else in that beautiful brain of yours."

Tears blurring her vision, she tilted her face up, inviting him to kiss her. When he did, it was slow, gentle. A kiss meant to soothe, not to arouse.

And still, she felt the need stirring between her thighs and she sighed into the kiss, melted into him. Pushed aside the worry and the stress and let her mind go blank as he took over.

"So beautiful," he murmured, tugging her blouse up and over her head. "And all mine."

She let her head fall back as he bent to feather kisses down her neck, across her collarbone, down to the swell of her lace-covered breasts. A soft tug and then the lace fell away, exposing her to him. Silently, he worshipped her, using his hands and mouth to inflame every inch of her skin as he undressed her. Except the one place she was already burning with need.

"Sir, please."

"Please, what, kitten? What do you need?"

"You, sir. Inside of me."

Hands on her shoulders, he turned her so she was facing the sink. The sight of them, her completely naked with him still fully clothed behind her was inexplicably erotic. His hands, so dark from his time in the sun, came to rest on her stomach, softly stroking, and she marveled at the contrast of his dark, tanned skin against her own pale, creamy flesh.

They were a study in contradictions. Dark versus light, hard versus soft. On paper, they shouldn't work. But maybe it was those differences that made them fit together like puzzle pieces.

"Are you wet for me, kitten?" His quiet question jolted her out of her contemplation.

"Yes, sir." Always. It only seemed to take a look or a single touch to have her wanting him.

"Show me."

Her eyes snapped up to meet his in the mirror. "Sir?"

"Put your fingers inside of your pussy and show me how wet you are for me."

Her clit throbbed at the hard edge to his tone. It was an

order, meant to be obeyed. For a fraction of a second, she wondered what the penalty would be for disobeying him or arguing, but she dismissed it just as quickly as it came. Tonight, she didn't want to fight. She wanted to submit, to not have to make any of the decisions.

To forget, even if it was only for a little while, what waited for them out in the real world.

Eyes still locked on his, she slipped a hand between her thighs, gasping softly at the zing of pure electric need when her fingers pressed against her clit. Desire that matched her own flared in Austin's eyes as she pushed two fingers between her folds.

"Good girl. Now, show me."

With a whimper of distress at having her pleasure delayed, she pulled her hand away and lifted her glistening fingers for his approval.

"Soaked, as usual. But now you're all messy. Clean yourself up, like a good little kitty."

Embarrassment washed over her, and she watched with fascination as pink crept over her skin. In the mirror, she watched her reflection bring its hand up to its mouth, watched as its tongue darted out to brush over one of its fingers. At the same time, the smell of her own musk filled her nostrils and the sweet, sharp flavor of her juices washed over her tongue.

"That's my good girl. Make sure you get all of it."

His voice was thick with need and she could feel the hard length of him pressing against her bottom. Hunger burned in his eyes as he watched her lick her fingers clean.

"Elbows on the sink, feet apart," he growled, placing a hand between her shoulder blades to guide her into position. Her arousal spiraled higher as he shoved his grey sweatpants to the floor and drove into her.

Crying out at the sudden sensation of being filled, she

closed her eyes, her head dropping as pleasure overwhelmed her. A sharp, stinging swat to her hip had her head snapping up again, her eyes flying open to glare at his reflection.

"Eyes open, kitten. I want you to watch us."

"Yes, sir."

And watch, she did. She watched her breasts sway each time he thrust inside of her. She watched his hands grip her hips as his movements became more frenzied. She watched her own eyes go glassy, her pupils widening when he moved one hand to her clit. And she watched as they came together, his cock jerking inside of her as her pussy clamped down on him and wave after wave of pleasure swamped her.

By the time he maneuvered both of them into the tub, he had to let out half the cooled water and refill it with hot water. But she didn't care. Her muscles were practically liquid and her mind was blessedly blank as they soaked together.

"I love you, Katherine." A soft kiss brushed against her temple. "I'm going to make this right, I promise."

God, if it were only that easy. In the bedroom, she could simply sit back and let him lead, knowing he would never let anything bad happen to her. Why couldn't the rest of their lives be so simple? "You can't promise that, Austin."

"Yes, I can. You'll see, kitten."

Since she didn't want to think about it, she let it drop. But despite his promises, she couldn't help but wonder if anything would ever be right again.

CHAPTER 27

KATHERINE

Sitting on the edge of their bed, staring down at her phone, Kit willed herself to turn off the "Do Not Disturb" feature. Austin had insisted they both turn it on before bed, so they could get some sleep without being jolted out of sleep every ten minutes with a text or a phone call.

But now, she was out of excuses and it was time to face reality. Taking a deep breath, she swiped the screen down and hit the button to turn it off.

There were a few texts from Claudia and her dad, but she wasn't exactly looking forward to discussing the interview with either of them — especially her father — so she ignored them.

Social media was a different story. Dozens of messages from so-called friends she hadn't spoken to in years, asking her what was going on. Tags in posts and comments offering support faker than Chloe Carlisle's perfect nose.

The tabloid, despite shaking her to her core, had barely been a blip on everyone's radar. But Chloe's interview had gone fucking viral and now everyone knew who Austin

Barrick was dating and the awful things that had been said about both of them.

With her stomach rolling, she clicked on one of the news articles and scrolled the comments.

Well, that explains why Austin is with that fatty. She probably lets him do all kinds of weird, kinky shit. How else would she get a man?

I don't care how good she is in bed, I wouldn't touch her if you paid me a million dollars LOL. Do better, Barrick.

And on and on and on. Whore. Slut. Cow. Bitch. Gold-digger. The words crowded together, ricocheting around her brain until she wanted to scream.

This was only the beginning. After the press conference, the speculation would become even wilder. More people watching her, judging her and finding her lacking.

"I can't do this," she whispered to the empty room. Clutching her phone in her hand, she threw on a pair of leggings and a t-shirt and hurried to the living room where she'd left her bags the night before.

"Kit? What's wrong?"

The concern in Austin's voice just pushed the burgeoning tears closer to the surface. Worried she might break if she spoke, she shook her head and grabbed her bags, hauling them up over her shoulder.

"Where are you going? I thought you were working from home today." His hand wrapped around her upper arm, forcing her to stop moving. "What happened? Talk to me, baby."

"Can't."

"Okay. We don't have to talk but you're not going anywhere when you're this upset. Sit down and I'll make you some coffee."

"No." The panic she was trying so hard to keep at bay

settled in her chest, making each breath a chore. "I need to go."

"You're not going anywhere like this." His tone was still gentle, but there was steel beneath it that told her he wasn't going to back down.

"I can't do this, Austin."

"Do what, baby? What happened?"

"I can't —" Her voice seemed to desert her, so she waved her hand at him. "Do *this*. You. Me. Us. It's too much."

"I know it's a lot right now, but we'll get through it. Look, let me talk to Mary and we can postpone the press conference until you're feeling better."

A harsh, bitter laugh escaped, scraping her throat raw on the way out. "You know what would make me feel better, Austin?"

"What? Tell me, kitten, and I'll make it happen."

She finally forced herself to look up, to meet his confused, concerned gaze. "Not having my life picked apart by assholes on the internet. Not being forced to listen as people wonder what exactly you see in me. Not being called crude, horrible names for daring to be fat in public. All of that would make me happy. So unless you plan on postponing indefinitely, you should just go ahead and do the press conference."

"I'm not putting you through that when you're this upset."

"You won't be." Hiking the straps for her bags up higher onto her shoulders, she let her gaze drop to the floor. Her heart was breaking enough as it was. She wasn't sure she could handle looking him in the eye as she broke his as well. "I'm going home, Austin."

"This is your home, Katherine."

"No, it's not. I'm sorry." Without giving him a chance to stop her, she turned and fled.

∼

GONE. She was gone.

He had no idea how long he stood in the middle of his living room, trying to process what had just happened. Trying to figure out how everything had gone so fucking wrong so quickly.

Last night, he'd been sure everything would work out. Sure, she'd been upset and jittery, but he'd thought he'd done a decent job of settling her down and assuring her that everything would be fine.

Obviously not.

The sound of the doorbell jolted him back to reality and his only thought was that she'd changed her mind.

"Baby, whatever happened this morning, we can —" He cut off when he opened the door and found two vaguely familiar men standing on his front porch.

Not Kit. She's really gone. And his heart shattered all over again.

"Who the fuck are you?"

The taller of the pair cocked an eyebrow. "Mr. Barrick?"

"Yes. Who are you?" They didn't look like reporters, but if they were, he was going to have their asses arrested for trespassing faster than they could scream "First Amendment".

"Jaxson Davidson." The taller, darker man brushed his fingertips across the blonde's shoulder in a gesture that spoke of the kind of intimacy built over years. "My husband and I wanted to discuss some things with you before your press conference this afternoon."

Oh, shit. Feeling slightly dazed, Austin shook each of their hands in turn. "Ah, come in, I guess."

Jaxson brushed past him without a word, but Chase hung back, surprising Austin with an exaggerated roll of his eyes.

"You'll have to excuse Jaxson. We had a long night and he's cranky this morning. Thank you for inviting us in."

"Cranky?" There was a note in Jaxson's voice Austin recognized immediately and he nearly grinned when Chase tilted his chin up just like Kit probably would have done in the same situation.

"Yes, you're cranky. I know we're in the middle of a shit show, but you don't have to be rude."

Austin's stomach pitched as the pieces began to fit together in his mind. "You're here about the interview Chloe did."

"Yes," Jaxson confirmed, his tone clipped as though he were holding back his temper. "She was your guest at Black Light on three separate occasions, correct?"

"Yeah. Should I have a lawyer?"

Despite the sudden heaviness between them, Chase's lips twitched. "You're not being arrested, Austin. Can I call you Austin?"

"What? Sure." Narrowing his eyes at Jaxson, Austin folded his arms over his chest. "You may not be arresting me but that doesn't mean you're above suing me. I repeat — Do I need a lawyer?"

"That depends," Jaxson said.

"No it doesn't, Jaxson. Would you stop trying to intimidate the man?" With a scowl for his husband, Chase stepped between them. "He's the victim here, too. He's the one who got outed as a kinky freak, remember?"

To Austin's surprise, Jaxson sighed and rubbed a hand over his face. "I'm sorry. I'm short on sleep and patience at the moment. No, you don't need a lawyer right now, but I would strongly suggest you get in touch with one. Our names have already been linked to this fiasco and we're doing as much damage control as we can and I'd hate to see you and Ms. Callahan caught in the crossfire."

"We'd like to speak with her, as well." Chase's expression smoothed out into a sympathetic smile. "I know Emma would be beside herself if something like this happened to us."

"She's not here." The words were like twisting the knife in his still-bleeding heart. "She left."

Chase frowned. "Like, left to go to work or…?"

"Left as in, she left me. I don't even know what happened. Everything was fine last night and then this morning she just had a total meltdown and she left." He wasn't even sure why he was telling them all of this, other than they were there and he needed to talk to *someone* before he had his own meltdown.

Jaxson and Chase shared a meaningful look. Stepping forward, Chase laid a hand on Austin's arm. "Did she get online at all this morning?"

"I don't know. I made her turn her phone off last night but… shit."

Chase winced. "We've been following this story closely to make sure Black Light hasn't actually been identified by the public and there are some, well, some downright shitty things being said about your woman."

"Goddammit. Why didn't she just talk to me?"

"Normally I would suggest tracking her down and making her talk, but unfortunately we're up against the wall here, Austin." Glancing down at his watch, Jaxson grimaced. "We need to talk strategy before your press conference. We'll be there, of course, in case one of those vultures has managed to dig up anything about Black Light."

As much as he wanted to do exactly as Jaxson had said and drive straight over to Kit's house to force her to talk to him, damage control was the more pressing need.

"All right. What do you need from me?"

CHAPTER 28

KATHERINE

She didn't go home. Couldn't bring herself to sit on the couch where Austin had first spanked her, sleep in the bed where they'd first made love.

The front door of her childhood home opened before she'd even parked her car, which meant he'd been waiting for her. And the second his arms wrapped around her, she broke.

Without a word, her dad ushered her inside to the living room where he gently nudged her into her chair. "I'll be right back, pumpkin."

A few moments later, a wad of tissues was pressed into her hand and his arm was around her shoulder again. They sat in silence, with him rocking her gently side to side until her sobs quieted. Kit let out a deep, shuddering breath and blew her nose loudly before looking up at him. "Sorry. I didn't mean to fall apart like that."

"Figure you needed it. When Austin called last night, I —"

"Austin called you?" she interrupted, guilt making her stomach churn all over again. She should have called, should have been the one to talk to her dad, but she'd been too busy wallowing in her own feelings to even consider it.

"Yeah. He wanted to give me a heads up about the interview."

"Oh, god." Groaning, she dropped her head into her hands. "This couldn't possibly get any worse."

"Sure it could. They coulda caught you two in the act."

"Dad!" A laugh burst out of her, surprising her. Maybe it was dramatic, but it seemed wrong to be laughing when her entire life was falling apart.

"I'm just saying. Gossip will eventually go away but pictures are forever."

"You're being surprisingly cool about this. Shouldn't you be threatening to string Austin up by his balls or something?"

"Got that out of my system last night." His mouth twisted up in a pained grimace, as though the conversation had left a bad taste in his mouth. "Can't say I was excited to learn so much about your, uh, personal life but that's between you and him. As long as you're happy, I'm happy. And that's really as much as I want to say about it."

"I *was* happy." The tears started over again and she pressed her face against his side.

"This will all blow over soon, pumpkin. And then everything will get back to normal."

"No, it won't. I broke up with Austin."

"Well why would you go and do a thing like that?"

"Because I can't do this, dad. I'm not strong enough."

"Well that's a load of bullshit."

The ferocity of his tone surprised her and she pulled away enough to glare up at him. "You didn't read the things people are saying about me."

"People are always gonna say shit, pumpkin. You really gonna let that steal your happiness?"

Sighing, she scrubbed a hand over her face. "It's not that simple. Can I stay here for a few days, until this starts to blow over? I don't want to go back to my place just yet."

For a moment, she thought he might argue or push her to go back to Austin's. But his expression softened and he ran a hand over her hair. "Of course you can, pumpkin. Whatever you need."

"Thanks, dad."

A loud buzz cut off their conversation. Scowling, he dug a hand into the pocket of his jeans and pulled out his phone. The grim smile on his face told her who it might be before he even answered the phone. "Gonna guess you're looking for my daughter. Yup, she's right here. Hang on."

Kit shook her head when he tried to hand her the phone, but he gave her a look she hadn't seen since she was a teenager, the one that said she had better take the damn phone or else. With a scowl of her own, she snatched the phone from him and stalked to the kitchen. Lowering herself into a chair at the table, she took a deep breath and pressed the phone to her ear. "Hey."

"Hey, kitten."

"What do you want, Austin?" She hadn't meant to be so blunt, but god, all she wanted was to go lie down and pretend the past twenty-four hours had never happened.

"When are you coming home?"

"I'm not." The finality of it had tears welling in her eyes again. How had she not cried herself out already? Surely the human body could only create so many tears before they simply dried up.

"Why not? I don't understand what I did and if you'd just talk to me, I can fix it."

The frustration was clear in his voice and her stomach churned with guilt. "You didn't do anything. This is about me."

"Then come home so we can talk about it."

"I can't."

"Why the hell not? I'm trying to be patient, Kit, but you're making it really fucking hard."

"I know. And I'm sorry. It's just… I don't know how to explain it."

"Try, baby. Please?"

She paused, searching for the right words to help him understand. "What's the most embarrassing thing that's ever happened to you?"

"What does that have to do with you coming home?"

"Just humor me, please?" At the last minute, she stopped herself from tacking on a "Sir" to the end of her plea, but it felt manipulative to use the dynamic they no longer shared to get what she wanted from him.

"Fine. I guess it was in middle school when I asked Jenny O'Neil to the eighth-grade dance and she told me no and laughed at me in front of the whole cafeteria."

"And how did you feel when that happened?"

"Like shit. What's your point, Katherine?"

Wincing at the use of her full name, she forged ahead. "That shitty, 'everyone is looking at me and laughing at me' feeling you had? Imagine feeling like that every day. That's how I felt for a really long time. How I still feel sometimes."

There was a long, weighty silence before he replied. "Why?"

"Because there was a time when I couldn't even go to school without someone commenting on my weight or making animal noises in my direction. Telling their friends they'd get me to sit on them as a punishment for something they did. Boys daring each other to ask me out as a prank. You have, what, a handful of humiliating experiences? I have years and years of them."

"Oh, baby." Pity filled his voice, making her stomach do a long, slow, nauseating roll. Of everything she'd wanted from him, pity had never been on the list. "I—fuck, I'm sorry. You didn't deserve that."

"No, I didn't. And I don't deserve it now. I don't deserve people wondering if I'm just some weird fetish for you. Maybe it makes me a coward, but I can't open myself back up to that kind of constant shame and judgment. I have a good life, a good business. I can't and won't give up the self-respect I've worked damn hard for, not even for you."

"I'd never ask you to. But running and hiding isn't the answer, either. You do that and they win."

"I know. I just don't know that I have it in me to fight them, Austin. I've been fighting my whole fucking life. I'm tired, and eventually you'll get tired of it, too."

"I'll fight the whole world every second of every day if it means I get to spend those days with you."

Ugh. Why couldn't he just be an asshole? All of this would be so much easier if he could be a little less understanding. "I'm sorry, Austin. I'm not interested in being some side-show freak for the enjoyment of the masses."

"Yeah, I get that. But I'm not giving up on us, kitten."

"You should. You'll be much happier in the long run."

"Impossible."

In spite of it all, she couldn't help but smile. "You sound so sure of yourself."

"Because I am. Listen, I gotta go. Just… promise you won't give up on us completely."

"Goodbye, Austin." Pulling the phone from her ear, she tapped the button to end the call. For a moment, she sat and stared at the blank screen, trying to summon the strength to move. But the enormity of what she'd done overcame her, rooting her to the chair. Giving in to it, she curled into herself and wept. For herself, for Austin. And for the life they'd only started building together, that now lay in ashes at her feet.

CHAPTER 29

AUSTIN

"Austin? Yo, Earth to Barrick."

A pair of fingers snapping in front of his face had Austin jerking his gaze up from the phone he'd been scowling at. "What?" he snarled at Mary, who was studying him through narrowed eyes.

"Did you hear a word we just said?"

"Ah, yeah. Sure I did." Lies. He'd been thinking about the conversation he'd had with Kit that morning. The way she'd said goodbye had felt like her slamming the door on their relationship and locking it for good. And it had shaken him to his core.

"Right. Just stick to the damn script, okay?"

"Yeah, okay."

Mary shoved him towards the side of the stage to wait for his cue. A moment later, his jaw nearly hit the floor when Jaxson and Chase flanked him.

"What the hell are you doing here?"

To his right, Jaxson snorted and adjusted his tie. "You didn't really think we were going to let you go out there on your own, did you?"

"Yeah, I did. Look, this is my mess, I can clean it up myself."

"Well, sure you can." Grinning, Chase clapped him on the shoulder. "But it's more fun this way."

"I can't ask you guys to stick your neck out for me like this."

"We aren't. We're protecting our own names and our assets." Jaxson slid a sideways glance his way and the corner of his lip twitched ever so slightly. "Besides, it's always fun to tweak the press."

Austin shot him a grin, the knots in his stomach loosening for the first time since Kit had walked out on him that morning. "It sure is. All right, boys. Let's do this."

They stepped through the curtains, Austin heading straight for the podium with Jaxson and Chase standing behind him, silent sentries. A hush fell over the crowd of reporters for a moment, and then the room exploded with noise as questions were hurled at them.

Why are the Davidson-Cartwrights with you?

How long have you been engaging in these deviant sex acts?

Where is Katherine Callahan? Are you two still together?

Is there any truth to Chloe Carlisle's accusations?

He waited for the roar to dull to a loud hum before pointing to one of his favorite reporters. Lacey Reynolds was as sharp as she was pretty and she'd always been fair with him. She stood, her face set in a serious expression. "Did you force Chloe Carlisle to perform sexual acts with you without her consent?"

Leave it to Lacey to cut right to the heart of the matter. "No, I did not. I won't comment on the nature of our private relationship, but I can honestly say that everything between us was consensual and Chloe was always a willing and enthusiastic participant."

With that out of the way, he selected another reporter, one he didn't recognize. "You, with the goofy tie."

Laughter rolled through the crowd as a scowling man with a glaringly bright orange tie pushed to his feed. "What about the secret sex club Ms. Carlisle mentioned? Is there any truth to that?"

He didn't need Jaxson practically vibrating with furious energy behind him to know how to answer that question. Summoning some of his famous Barrick charm, he gave the crowd an easy, cocky grin. "Well, it wouldn't be much of a secret if I went and told everyone about it, now would it?"

Goofy Tie's scowl deepened at that, but Austin ignored it and picked on another reporter, a knockout blonde in a tight red dress. The curve of her smile told Austin he'd made a mistake even before she opened her mouth.

"Natalie O'Hara, with *Silhouette* magazine. Did you break up with Chloe Carlisle so you could date Katherine Callahan?"

"No." At least it was an easy question. "Chloe and I broke up several months before I even met Katherine."

He looked around, searching for someone else to call on, but Natalie spoke up again before he could choose another reporter. "There has been some speculation that your... attraction to Katherine Callahan is based in some kind of kink. Is *that* true?"

"No." Another easy question, though he let his tone harden. "That is absolutely not true."

"Then how do you explain your relationship with her?" Natalie pressed. "You have to admit, it seems odd to move from a woman like Chloe to a woman, well, so *different* from Chloe."

The crowd went silent, as though they were all holding a collective breath, waiting to see how he'd respond to such a bold question. Red colored his vision and he had to take a deep breath before he felt in control enough to answer.

"Katherine Callahan is the most beautiful woman I've ever known, inside and out." Meeting Natalie's wide-eyed stare, he held her gaze as he continued. "She is smart, and kind, and sexy as hell. I love everything about her, with absolutely no exceptions or qualifications." He let some of the fury he was feeling seep into his tone. "My attraction to her isn't strange. It isn't a fetish. It simply is. And if you don't understand that, well, the problem is with you. Not me. No further questions."

Turning on his heel, he marched toward the side of the stage. But a single question rose over the din, stopping in his tracks. "Why are Jaxson Davidson and Chase Cartwright here with you? Are they into the same kinky things as you?"

Oh, fuck.

Spinning back around, he scanned the audience, his brain racing to think of a response. Before he had a chance to come up with anything, Jaxson stepped up to the podium. "Allow me to answer that, Austin."

Looking out at the crowd, he smiled, sophisticated charm rolling off of him in waves. "Chase and I have been friends with Austin for years and we wanted to come out to support him. As for the second part of your question, well." His smile turned smug as Chase stepped up beside him, snuggling up under his arm. "I'm married to two of the sexiest people on the planet. Did you think we were all living as monks or something?"

The room exploded again, but the pair simply walked away, ushering a shell-shocked Austin off stage with them. A pair of bulky bodyguards rushed them through a hallway, out a back door, and all but shoved the three of them into the back of a limo.

"So." Leaning back in the seat across from Austin, Chase shot him a boyish grin as Jaxson whipped out his phone and began tapping away at the screen. "Wanna go play with the lawyers?"

"Will Chloe be there?"

Chase's grin widened. "Yup."

Something primal rose up in him, and he matched Chase's grin with a wide, wolfish one of his own. "Then what are we waiting for?"

∽

IT WAS worth showing up to the meeting with the lawyers just to watch Chloe's eyes go wide and her face lose all of its color when he walked through the doors.

"What the hell is he doing here?" Her voice was several octaves higher than the smooth, sexy tones she used for interviews. He recognized it as her "I'm about to lose my shit" voice and he couldn't help but smile down at her.

An older gentleman to her right patted her arm in an almost fatherly fashion before turning a stern glare on the pair of suited men sitting across from them. "We weren't made aware Mr. Barrick would be attending this meeting."

"Mr. Barrick was a last minute addition to our party." One of the suits, a man Austin vaguely recognized from the club, smiled at Chloe's lawyer, but there was no warmth in the gesture. "And since this is merely a deposition, I'm sure you know we aren't obligated to inform you of who, exactly, will be sitting in."

The other man sighed, but didn't argue. "Very well. But if his presence unduly upsets my client, we reserve the right to call a halt to these proceedings."

Austin opened his mouth to remind everyone that *he* was the one who'd been accused of being an abusive monster, and since it was a hundred percent *not true,* Chloe didn't have any right to be 'upset' by his presence. But Jaxson laid a hand on his arm and silenced his diatribe before it could begin with a subtle shake of his head.

Clamping his mouth shut so tightly it made his teeth ache, Austin dropped into a chair beside the other lawyer. He did a double take when he recognized him as the Daddy Dom they'd run into at the club. Park, Austin thought his name was.

Good. Maybe since he knew Kit personally, he'd have even more of a reason to take the bitch down.

Once everyone was settled into their seats, the fun started. At least, he assumed the lawyers were having fun by the glint in their eyes each time one of them landed some kind of barb.

Then it was Chloe's turn. It didn't escape his notice that she glanced his way and tugged at her necklace when the Cartwright-Davidson's lawyers addressed her. The necklace thing was her tell that she was nervous as hell. He'd seen it a few times when they'd been dating, usually when he'd caught her in a lie of some kind.

That was what had ultimately broken them up — her inability to be honest on a consistent basis. He'd take Kit's sweet if sometimes brutal honesty over Chloe's lies and manipulation any day. Honestly, in that moment, he was wondering what he'd ever seen in Chloe. Everything about her paled in comparison to Kit.

"Miss Carlisle, have you ever attended a club named Black Light?" Mr. Park kicked off Chloe's questioning once the introductions and legal bullshit was out of the way.

"Yes." Head bobbing, Chloe twisted the chain of her necklace around one finger.

"As you know, Black Light is a very exclusive club. It's not the kind of place you can simply stumble into. How did you learn about Black Light?"

Austin sat up straighter in his chair, glancing from Park to Chloe, anxious to hear her version of events.

"Austin told me about it, while we were dating."

That much was true.

"And at that point, did he ask you to accompany him to the club?"

"Yes."

Not true. A growl rumbled in his chest, but at a sharp look from the other lawyer who'd been introduced as Alexander Reed, he swallowed it back.

Park continued, in the same cool, level tone. "What did Mr. Barrick say, exactly?"

Chloe rolled her eyes. "That was like a year ago. How am I supposed to remember?"

Park's smile was understanding, but not quite sympathetic. "To the best of your memory, Ms. Carlisle."

"I don't know. It was something like 'We should go sometime', probably."

"Interesting." Reed picked up the thread, pulling a piece of paper from a folder. "In your interview, you claimed 'he would make me go to this underground sex club with him'. So, which is it, Ms. Carlisle? Did he merely suggest that you accompany him, or did he force you?"

The delicate chain around her neck twisted so tightly Austin thought it might break. "Well, at first it was just a suggestion, then he kept pushing it so I just eventually gave in."

Reed made a soft humming sound in his throat as he jotted down notes. "Did you ever feel threatened by Mr. Barrick?"

Smug triumph flashed in her eyes, but her bottom lip wobbled, perfectly on cue. Maybe she'd have a shot at the acting career she'd been chasing after all. "Several times. He had so many rules, and he would punish me for any little infraction."

"Specifically with regards to Black Light, Ms. Carlisle. Did you feel, at any time, that Mr. Barrick would cause you harm if you refused to accompany him to the club?"

There was something in Reed's tone that set Austin's teeth on edge. Did they really think, for one second, that he'd forced her to go with him? Never in his life had he abused a submissive in his care or forced them to do something that truly terrified them. He wasn't goddamn Ethen O'Dowell.

Chloe hesitated, long enough for Park to prop his elbows on the table and lean in. "Ms. Carlisle, I'd like to remind you that you are under oath and the consequences for perjury are rather steep."

Across the table, Chloe shifted in her chair. If she had a submissive bone in her body, it had to be quaking at the moment, facing off with five dominant men. He might have felt sorry for her, if she hadn't been trying to ruin his life with her lies.

"Ummm. Well, I wasn't sure how he'd react if I said no, so I just went along with it."

"Ms. Carlisle, what is your safe word?"

"Red," she replied automatically, her face flushing as soon as the word left her mouth. She narrowed her eyes at Reed, obviously annoyed at being caught so off guard. "What does that matter?"

"Have you ever used it?" Reed pressed.

"What is the relevance of these questions?" Chloe's lawyer broke in before she had a chance to respond.

"They are relevant to determining Ms. Carlisle's understanding of consent with regards to her and Mr. Barrick's relationship," Reed answered easily, as if he'd been waiting for the objection.

Chloe's lawyer leaned over and the two shared a brief, heated discussion before Chloe turned back to face them, her chin tilted high. "Yes. I had to use my safe word twice with Austin."

"And when you called 'Red', did he stop what he was doing?"

The air in Austin's lungs seemed to thicken, making it impossible for him to exhale while he waited for her to answer. He remembered each moment vividly, just as he remembered halting the scene to comfort her both times. But if she lied, if she claimed he'd kept going despite her calling her safe word, then not only would he face losing his career, he'd be blacklisted from any halfway decent BDSM club in the country. Not to mention what the public would do to him.

Chloe darted a glance over to her lawyer, then Austin, before settling on the table in front of her before she answered. "I don't remember."

Reed and Park shared a look before Reed pushed. "You don't remember what, exactly? Either he stopped or he didn't, Ms. Carlisle. Please answer the question. *Truthfully.*"

"Yes, he stopped," she finally forced out through clenched teeth.

Park pulled a second sheet of paper from the folder in front of him and scanned the contents, though Austin had a feeling he already knew every word by heart. "So, when you said you 'didn't know how to make him stop', that wasn't exactly true, was it? Mr. Barrick had already proven to be the type of man who would abide by a safe word in private, so you had no reason to believe he wouldn't abide by one in public where everyone could hear you."

Red was creeping up her neck, a sure sign her temper was going to explode all over them at any second. *Keep pushing*, Austin silently willed.

As if he'd heard the silent plea, Reed pulled another sheet of paper from his folder and slid it across the table toward Chloe. "Is this your signature, Ms. Carlisle?"

Chloe glanced down, then nodded sharply.

"Verbally, please, Ms. Carlisle."

"Yes, it's my signature," she snapped, glaring daggers at the two men currently tearing her story to shreds.

Reaching across the table, Reed tapped the paper. "Please read the highlighted section."

If looks could kill, every one of them would have died on the spot before she lowered her gaze to the paper and forced herself to read out loud. "I am here of my own free will and have not been threatened, bribed, blackmailed, or otherwise coerced to participate in any activities of any nature during my time at Black Light."

"So according to this legal document, signed by you, Mr. Barrick did not force you."

"Fine!" Just as Austin had predicted, Chloe jumped to her feet, her voice rising to a shriek. "He didn't force me. Are you fucking happy now?"

It was, technically, all they needed, but Park leaned in, his expression hard and serious. "Then why lie about it, Ms. Carlisle?"

"Because he fucking *humiliated* me!" Chloe turned her murderous glare on Austin. "Did you really think I wouldn't know what you were doing, Austin? Parading that fat cow around, right after you dumped me? I refuse to sit by and let you make a fucking joke out of me!"

Stunned silence filled the room. Keeping his gaze locked with Chloe's, Austin pushed to his feet. "I can promise you two things, Chloe. One, you were the absolute last person on my mind when I started dating Katherine. I haven't thought of you once since the moment I laid eyes on her."

Chloe's lower lip wobbled for just a moment before she sneered. "Sure. Keep telling yourself that, Barrick."

"And two," he continued, ignoring her. "I couldn't possibly turn you into a bigger fucking joke than you already are."

Pushing away from the table, he strode from the room, a grin spreading across his face when he heard Reed's cool, firm voice behind him. "Sit down, Ms. Carlisle. We haven't even gotten to the NDA, yet."

CHAPTER 30

KATHERINE

Curled up on her couch in her favorite pineapple pajamas, Kit reread the same page for about the hundredth time. With a frustrated sigh, she slammed the book shut and tossed it on the cushion. She eyed her phone, debating whether or not to pick it up. Ever since she'd watched Austin's press conference from a few days ago (on repeat, probably a hundred times) she'd been tempted to call him, to tell him she wanted to come home.

In the end, she opted for a trip to the kitchen. There was still half a pint of fudge brownie ice cream in the freezer she hadn't polished off yet.

She'd just shoved a spoonful of gooey, chocolatey goodness into her mouth when the doorbell rang. If those fucking reporters were back, she was going back to her dad's. Being a big girl and getting over Austin could wait until she wasn't being hounded by the press.

But when she opened the door, her mouth fell open and the spoon she'd been half-prepared to throw at someone's head clattered to the floor. "Holy shit," she whispered, staring in shock at the woman on her front steps.

"Hello. You must be Katherine." Emma Cartwright-Davidson, looking the absolute picture of perfection in curve-hugging jeans and a flowy, off-the-shoulder top, smiled warmly at her. "I hope you don't mind the intrusion. May I come in?"

"Umm." Kit winced internally when she glanced around at the disaster her house had become. "Sure. I mean, yes, of course. Just... don't mind the mess."

"Oh, honey, if I'd just been put through the wringer the way you have this past week, I wouldn't feel like cleaning, either." Emma patted Kit's shoulder as she stepped inside. "Your home is so charming, Katherine."

"Thank you. Ah, you can call me Kit."

Eyes sparkling with mischief, Emma grinned. "I'm Emma. Now that we're friends...I don't suppose there's more where that ice cream came from?"

Still in a daze, Kit looked down at the container she'd completely forgotten she was holding. "Oh. Yes. I have a few different flavors in the freezer. What would you like?"

"I'm not picky."

Picking up the spoon she'd dropped, Kit made her way back to the kitchen. She tossed the dirty spoon in the sink, grabbed two clean ones, and blindly snatched the first pint of ice cream she saw from the freezer.

"What are you doing here?" she blurted out when she turned back to Emma.

"I was wondering when you were going to ask that." Humor colored her tone as she peeled the lid back and dug in. "Mmm. To paraphrase Ben Franklin, I'm fully convinced ice cream is proof that God loves us and wants us to be happy."

"He never actually said that, you know. It was an internet prank and pretty much every idiot with internet access fell for it. Oh, god." Kit slapped a hand over her mouth, nearly stabbing herself in the eye with her spoon. "I'm sorry. That was so rude of me."

"Rude?" Tossing her head back, Emma let out a long, loud laugh. "Honey, I live in California. You haven't even seen rude."

"I tell politicians what to do with their money on a regular basis," Kit returned dryly. "Trust me, I've seen my fair share."

Emma laughed again and scooped up another mouthful of ice cream. "I like you. I had a feeling I would, just from what I've heard about you, but you can never really tell until you meet someone face to face, you know?"

"You've heard of me?" With every passing minute, this entire situation just seemed to get increasingly more bizarre.

"Well, you know, when one of our members is publicly outed, we sort of have to do our research."

"Oh, god. I need to sit down." Back pressed to the fridge, Kit slid to the floor and closed her eyes as if she could just block out the misery and humiliation of the past week. "Is that why you're here?"

"Not exactly. My men are handling the legal bits and when I talked to them a couple nights ago, I realized Austin had someone to lean on through all of this, but you might not. So... here I am."

"You flew all the way across the country to check on a woman you've never met?"

"When you put it that way, it sounds a little crazy."

"Maybe that's because it *is* crazy."

"Maybe it is. But I just..." Emma trailed off, for the first time since she'd arrived sounding unsure of herself and Kit opened her eyes to look up at her.

"You just what?" Kit prompted.

"I just wanted to be able to tell you that it does get better. I promise."

Tears blurring her vision, Kit shook her head. "You can't know that."

"Yes, I can. I've been there. And it's hard and it hurts, but it does get better."

Kit barked out a bitter laugh. "Yeah, sure. Beautiful, confident Emma Cartwright-Davidson with her two gorgeous husbands and her two perfect kids knows *exactly* how I feel right now."

It was Emma's turn to laugh as she joined Kit on the floor. "Trust me, that was *not* me when I met my husbands. And honestly, it's not how I feel half the time, even now."

"How did you get past it?" Kit asked softly, poking at her slowly melting ice cream.

"Jaxson and Chase, mostly." Emma's smile turned dreamy, the love she felt for her men written all over her face. "Whenever I feel like I'm not good enough, or thin enough, or pretty enough for them, they're right there to remind me that I'm the one they want and that they love me exactly as I am."

"That's lovely."

"Austin doesn't do that for you?" There was something in Emma's voice that implied he'd be answering to her if the answer wasn't to her liking.

"No, he does. Did," Kit corrected herself quietly.

"Did?" The ball must have dropped because a moment later, Emma let out a pained groan. "Tell me you didn't do what I think you did."

"What choice did I have? I can't stand the idea of being put on display for everyone to laugh at on a regular basis. And as long as Austin is playing ball, that's exactly what I'm going to be. A permanent punchline."

"Can I ask you a personal question?"

Kit snorted and rolled her eyes. "I think that ship has sailed."

"True. Do you love him?"

"That's not the point."

Emma cocked an eyebrow at her, and Kit wondered if it was a gesture she'd picked up from her husbands since it so perfectly mimicked the expression she'd seen from Austin whenever she'd pushed him a little too far. "And that's not an answer."

"Of course I love him. But sometimes love isn't enough."

"I get that. And I get that this is really fucking hard. But if you back down, if you break things off with Austin and go into hiding, then those keyboard commandos win." Righteous fury flashed in Emma's eyes. "Every single person who has ever bullied you, or made you feel like you're somehow less of a person because you're not a size two, wins. And the women like us, the women who have spent our entire lives fighting that uphill battle against a culture that wants us to feel ashamed for just daring to exist — we lose."

Guilt and shame coated Kit's stomach. "That's not fair," she whispered, shaking her head. "It's not fair to put all of that on me."

"I know. More so than most, *I know*. I've felt every ounce of that burden from the moment Jaxson and Chase and I made our relationship public." The corners of her lips tilted up in a sad smile. "It would be nice to have someone to share it with."

"I don't know if I'm strong enough for all of that, Emma."

"You don't have to be. If you let him, Austin will give you strength when yours fails. I saw his press conference; there's no doubt that man worships you. He'll do whatever it takes to keep you safe and happy. And I'll be just a phone call away."

"Really?"

"Of course." Grinning, Emma bumped her shoulder against Kit's. "Us big girls have to stick together. And rumor has it you're exceptionally good at your job. I fully plan to take advantage of our newfound friendship and pick your brain about some of our investments that aren't performing as well as I'd like."

"Oh, god. Please take advantage. I've been lusting over the Cartwright-Davidson empire pretty much my entire career. I would do immoral and possibly illegal things for a peek behind the curtain."

Laying her hand over Kit's, Emma squeezed. "I'd settle for a promise that you won't let the assholes win."

"How about a promise to think about it?" Kit conceded after a lengthy pause.

"Good enough."

∽

EMMA HAD ONLY BEEN GONE a few minutes when there was another knock on the door. Annoyed at the idea of yet another interruption, Kit yanked the door open, prepared to give whoever it was a piece of her mind.

But as soon as she did, a kid who barely looked old enough to drive shoved a long white box at her. "Mr. Barrick covered the tip, ma'am. Have a good day."

And with that, he turned on his heel and hurried back down the front steps to where his still-running car was parked in her visitor's spot. Shaking her head, Kit shut the door and carried the box to her bedroom.

Should she even open it? There was no card, but the delivery kid had already confirmed it was from Austin.

Of course, it was from Austin. Who the hell else would it be from?

Placing the box on the bed, she crossed her arms and glared down at it. From the wrapping, it was most likely from the same place he'd gotten her corset. But that didn't automatically mean it was lingerie. The store could sell perfectly normal clothes as well.

Yeah, right.

Giving in to temptation, she tugged on the silk ribbon and pulled the top off the box. Nestled on top of the tissue paper was a small envelope. She opened it, butterflies dancing in her stomach as she read the note.

Meet me at our spot at 9:00pm sharp. Wear the outfit. If you still want to call it quits after tonight, I'll let you go. Just give me one more night, kitten.

Their spot. Was he talking about the club?

Shifting the tissue paper aside, she stared down at the contents.

He *definitely* meant Black Light.

Instead of a corset, he'd sent a bodysuit made entirely of black lace. Attached to each leg hole were two straps with clips at the end, which were obviously meant to hold up the black thigh high stockings he'd included.

Don't let the assholes win.

Emma's words had a lump forming in her throat. Was she strong enough for this? Maybe not, but she wasn't going to find out if she kept hiding herself away from the world. She owed it to herself and Austin to give their love another chance.

Even if, in the end, she could only give him tonight, she had to at least try.

CHAPTER 31

AUSTIN

"Are you sure she's coming?" Bouncing lightly on his toes, Chase seemed more nervous about whether Kit was going to show than Austin was.

Ignoring the doubt churning in his stomach, Austin gave a sharp nod. "She's coming."

Maybe.

A small hand landed on his arm and Austin looked down into Emma's wide, warm eyes. "She'll be here. She's stronger than you give her credit for."

"I think she's strong as hell," he snapped, inwardly sighing when her men stiffened and glared at him. "Sorry. I'm just feeling a little antsy."

Antsy didn't even begin to describe it. At nearly half past nine, he was just about to give up all hope when the bell above the door of the psychic shop jingled. His heart stuttered to a stop in his chest when she stepped through the door, twin flags of red coloring riding high on her cheeks.

Despite the sultry warmth of the summer evening, she was wearing a long coat, and what was visible of her legs was sheathed in the sheer black stockings he'd sent her. Pride welled in his chest as he watched her cross the lobby of the shop to him, her eyes downcast.

When she was standing in front of him, he gripped her chin and gently nudged her face up to look at him. She'd done some kind of women's magic with her eyes, making them look wider, with flecks of gold reflected in the dark depths.

"You're late, kitten," he admonished softly.

"I'm sorry, sir." She hesitated, seemingly weighing her next words. "I kept changing my mind about coming."

"You made the right choice." His grip on her chin tightened and he deliberately lowered his voice. "But you're still going to be punished."

Her lips parted on a sharp intake of breath. "Yes, sir. I'm sorry."

"There's my good girl. Let's go."

But as soon as he turned, Emma brushed past him and threw her arms around Kit's neck. "I'm so proud of you!"

To his surprise, Kit returned the embrace. "Thank you. I don't know if I would have come tonight if it hadn't been for you."

He glanced over at Jaxson and Chase, both of whom gave a resigned shrug as if to say they didn't have any control over what Emma did. Austin didn't buy their innocent act for a minute, but if it had helped to get Kit to the club, he certainly wasn't going to hold any meddling they may have done against them.

"Come on, kitten. We have a spot reserved and I have plans for you."

Kit gave Emma a quick, hard squeeze before pulling away and smiling up at him. There was worry in her eyes he hated seeing, but hopefully what he had planned would help to alleviate it. Slipping an arm around her waist, he led her through the back entrance, down the steps and long tunnel under the alley. When it came time to hand over her coat in the locker room entrance, she hesitated, giving him a pleading look.

He took the decision out of her hands by reaching over and sliding the buttons through their holes and pushing the coat from her shoulders. With a small whimper, she let her arms relax and he was able to pull it all the way off.

"Holy fuck, kitten. You look amazing."

The bodysuit was better than he'd imagined. Black lace criss-crossed over her breasts, her already hard nipples clearly visible through the sheer fabric. Coupled with the stockings and the vibrant red heels she'd added on her own, it was enough to make a man want to drop to his knees and thank every god in existence for her.

"Thank you, sir."

Chuckling, he pulled her close to him again and nuzzled her neck. "That thanks might sound more sincere if you weren't looking like you might bolt at any second."

"I liked the corset better."

"Bet you won't fight me so hard the next time I ask you to wear it, will you?"

"You seem awfully sure there will be a next time, Mr. Barrick."

Stopping in front of the lockers, they both waited for one to pop open to place their phones and her purse inside. When they closed the door again, he wrapped an arm around her back, forcing her to bend forward as he peppered her barely covered ass with swats hard enough to make her squeal.

When he released her, she straightened, pushing at her hair as she glared at him. "What was that for?"

She asked the question like she hadn't been deliberately baiting him, and he had to bite the inside of his cheek to keep from grinning. "How are you supposed to address me when we're playing, kitten?"

Her bottom lip pushed out into a pout, but her eyes were dancing with mischief. "Sorry, sir."

"God it's good to hear that word from your lips again. Come on, baby. Let's go find a spot to sit."

Picking up his bag, he placed a hand on her back as they wound their way through the club. They stopped in front of the giant stage, where a long-legged brunette wrapped in an intricate pattern of ropes and knots was currently being suspended from the ceiling. Despite the crowd, they were lucky enough to find an empty spot. Settling himself on the couch, he pointed to the ground in front of him.

Kit didn't even hesitate before slowly lowering to her knees in front of him. No doubt she figured less people would notice her if she was on her knees. He was willing to let her keep that sense of security for now. Once he had her up on the stage, there wouldn't be any hiding from him, or their audience.

Reaching into his pocket, he pulled out a thin strip of leather and held it out for her inspection. "Do you know what this is, kitten?"

"A collar, sir?"

"Good girl. You're going to wear it for me tonight. To let everyone in this club know you belong to me."

A short hesitation was followed by her quiet, "Yes, sir."

Fuck. He was going to embarrass himself if she kept speaking in that low, husky voice. "Turn around and lift your hair for me, kitten."

She obeyed without argument, raising the mass of curls to expose the gentle slope of her neck. When the collar locked into place, he leaned down to nip at her earlobe. "Mine."

"For tonight, sir."

Winding a hand through her hair, he pulled her head back, far enough for him to see the muscles of her throat working as she audibly swallowed. "Forever, Katherine. I know you don't believe me, but that's okay. I'm a patient man."

He wasn't, not by nature. But for her, he could be. Would be, if that was what it took to keep her by his side for the rest of their lives.

Before she could protest, he used his hold on her hair to direct her attention to the stage. "What do you see, kitten?"

A soft huff told him she was annoyed, but she answered anyway. "I see a woman tied up in a bunch of ropes, hanging from the ceiling. Is that safe?"

"Very." Slipping his hands around to her front, he cupped her heavy breasts and rolled the pert nipples between his fingers. "What do you notice about the woman?"

Her breath caught at his touch. "She's very pretty."

"What else?"

"Ah. I don't know."

He gave each nipple a hard pinch in response. "Focus, kitten."

"Yes, sir," was delivered through clenched teeth. "She looks peaceful. Happy."

"Anything else?"

"Um. I like the ropes, sir. The way they make a pattern."

"Interesting."

Because he was watching her profile, he saw the corner of her mouth dip down. "What's interesting, sir?"

"When you look at her, you just see a woman. You don't seem to be picking apart her body or cataloging her flaws. So why, kitten, is that all you do when you look in the mirror?"

"That's different."

"Why?"

Another soft huff, and this time she tried to move away, but a quick twist of his fingers settled her back into position. "I don't know. It's just different. Aren't you more critical of yourself than others, especially on the field?"

"Yeah. But I also know that when the fans are watching me, most of them aren't critiquing every second of my performance. Even on my worst days, I know I'm putting on a good show. And I'm damn proud of it."

"I don't want to be putting on a show." Her eyes fluttered closed and she leaned back, leaned into him. "I just want to be allowed to exist, as I am, without needing to justify myself."

The sadness in her voice nearly broke him. "You don't have to justify yourself to me. Fuck everybody else."

"I wish it were that easy."

On stage, the brunette was gently lowered to the ground, where her Dom promptly wrapped her in a blanket and ushered her down the steps on the side. At the edge of his vision, one of the DMs caught his attention and waved him up.

"Come on, kitten. It's our turn."

∼

Katherine

It's our turn.

Kit's eyes flew open and she tilted her head further back to look up at him. "Our turn? What do you mean 'our turn'?"

"You're forgetting yourself, kitten." He tapped her lightly on the nose. "How do you address me?"

Really? That was what he expected her to focus on? "What do you mean it's our turn, sir?" she managed to force out, though the words lacked anything even in the neighborhood of respect.

"Our scene. On your feet."

"Why?"

A strong hand wrapped around her throat as he smiled down at her. "Do you need to know why?"

A dozen arguments danced on her tongue, but she held them back and shook her head as much as his hold on her allowed. When he released her, she placed her hand in his, allowing him to pull her to her feet. She wobbled a bit, between the heels and the fuzzy feeling in her legs from having been on her knees. But Austin caught her, held her in place until she gave him an equally wobbly smile.

"I'm fine, sir."

With a quick nod of acknowledgement, he took her hand and led her up those same steps to the stage. She froze when they reached the middle of the stage, painfully aware of the people sprawled across the couches in front of the stage, watching as they took their places.

"Hey. Eyes on me, kitten."

Shifting her attention to him, the hammering of her heart dulled to a quiet knocking. "Sir?"

"Do you trust me?"

Since that was the only thing keeping her from running out the door, she nodded. "Yes. Completely, sir."

"Then eyes on me. We're the only ones who matter, yeah?"

"Yes, sir."

"Good girl. Now, strip."

The edges of her vision went dark, and she couldn't quite keep herself from whimpering. "Sir?"

"Is there something you don't understand about my instructions?"

"No, I understand." And as he'd just reminded her, his instructions were all that mattered in this moment. Not the why, or what came next. Pleasing him, obeying him, was all she was meant to be focused on.

The coils of fear and panic wrapped around her chest eased and she drew in her first easy breath since he'd ordered her up here. Her mind began to clear as she put all of her attention into doing as he'd asked.

By the time she was naked, with her clothes neatly folded at the edge of the stage, a sense of calm had completely enveloped her. And when she glanced out at the audience again, when she found their attention completely riveted on her, she felt only that surge of power she remembered from their first scene at the club.

On its heels was a relief so powerful, it made her want to weep. After the story had run, after she'd walked out on him, she'd grieved for this rush, this feeling, thinking she'd never have it again.

See me now, assholes? You can't take this from me. I won't allow it.

Emboldened, she returned to her place beside Austin and silently waited for his next instruction.

"Arms up."

Without argument, she lifted her arms. Soft rope wound its way around her wrists and forearms, binding them together. Austin worked in silence, for once not explaining each step as he took it, giving her no indication of what came next.

A quiet whirr caught her attention and a moment later, she felt a tug on the rope, forcing her to her toes.

"Feet apart."

Again, she obeyed, a blush creeping up her neck as she considered how fully and obscenely on display she was in this position.

"How are the ropes? Too tight?"

"No, sir. They're good."

"Use your safe word if they start to hurt too much or if your shoulders feel like they're stretching too far. Understood?"

"Yes, sir."

"Good girl." Moving into her line of vision, he cupped her face in his hands, his expression serious. "You know I'll never push you past what you can take, right?"

For the first time that night, true fear settled in her stomach and she trembled. "Y-yes?"

"I want you to know this isn't a punishment. It's a lesson. Do you understand the difference?"

Oh, shit. What the hell had she gotten herself into? "Not really, sir."

"A punishment is meant to correct your behavior. This isn't about correcting you, since you didn't do anything wrong. This is just a lesson I want to help you learn, so that maybe you can start to see yourself the way I see you. Does that make sense?"

"I think so, sir." Lesson or punishment, something told her it was still going to be painful.

"Good. Here we go, kitten."

And with that, he was gone. Because of the way he'd strung her up, she couldn't turn or twist to see him, and the soft sounds of him searching his play bag didn't give her any indication of what he was planning. Closing her eyes, she tried to block out everything but him.

Obeying him.

Pleasing him.

Trusting him.

"Do you know what I love about you, kitten?"

Keeping her eyes closed, she shook her head. "No, sir."

"Yeah, I figured as much. That's why I'm going to tell you."

Warm, familiar hands cupped her breasts, rolling the nipples to hard, painful points. "Let's start with the obvious. I really fucking love your tits."

A laugh burst out of her, even as he drew one of the taut peaks in his mouth and heat pooled low in her belly. "I've never doubted that, sir."

"Like I said. Starting with the obvious. But you know what I love more than your tits?"

"No, sir."

Something soft and wet pressed against her skin, and he dragged it along her chest, up to her collarbone, then back down. Opening her eyes, she glanced down, and everything in her went soft when she saw what he'd drawn.

"Your heart. You love so hard, baby. And as much as you try not to, you wear this heart on your sleeve and I hope you never stop." Lowering his head, he pressed a kiss to the center of the heart he'd drawn, right over the one that was threatening to beat right out of her chest.

Emotion robbed her of the ability to speak, so she simply nodded. Apparently satisfied with her response, he moved to the side, running his hand from her wrist to her shoulder, the gentle touch settling her system again with a sigh.

"I love having your arms wrapped around me as we make love." The marker she now saw in his hand pressed against the inside of her arm, and she watched as he spelled out the word *STRONG* in capital letters. "But more importantly, I love your strength. When I was injured, you became my rock. You gave me the strength to push forward, to believe I could heal enough to walk out on that field again next year. I don't know if I could have done it without you, baby."

Guilt was a knife to the gut. How could he consider her strong when she'd walked out on him the second things had gotten hard? She'd run, without a second thought, because she was weak.

Shifting to the opposite side, he repeated the process, caressing her, making her tremble with need and emotion before he set ink to skin. "At the same time, I love how tender you can be when it's needed. As much as you were my rock, you were also my safe place to land."

Tears blurred her vision when she turned her head and found *HOME* carefully printed on her flesh. "Sir," she whispered, but he cut her off with a kiss.

"No talking unless you're asked a question, okay baby?"

"Yes, sir," she agreed with a reluctant sigh.

"Such a good girl. Which brings me to my next point." Kneeling in front of her, he pressed a trail of kisses from her left knee up to her hip. Need coiled inside of her and she let out a quiet groan when he pulled away instead of continuing the path to where she burned for him.

"These gorgeous legs. I don't think I've ever really told you, but I love them. I love how thick they are, I love how tightly they wrap around me when I'm fucking you. And I love the way you look when you're kneeling in front of me, giving me all of you, even when you don't really want to."

The next word was significantly longer, and she had to strain to see it.

SUBMISSION.

"And I know you hate the way your thighs rub together when you walk. So what if they do? You wanna know what I see when I watch you walk, baby?"

"Yes, sir."

GRACE.

Nobody—nobody—had ever called her graceful. It was part of her secret shame, that she'd never have the effortless elegance she so craved. Something inside of her shifted and she was suddenly, intimately aware of how clearly he saw her. Pressure built in her chest, turning her breaths to shallow pants as he rose and circled her.

"Do you know what those people watching you see, kitten?" he asked as he took his place behind her, lightly trailing his fingers down her spine.

"No, sir."

"They see what I see. A beautiful, brave woman. Giving her man the greatest treasure a dominant could ever ask for. Not just her submission, but her trust. You don't know how incredible you are, Katherine."

A shiver raced through her when the marker pressed against her spine. "You're the bravest person I know. Even when you're scared out of your fucking mind, even when you're certain you're going to make a fool of yourself, you still trust me. And I'm sorry I let you down, I'm sorry I couldn't protect you, baby. It won't happen again."

The pressure in her chest tightened. "It wasn't your fault, sir."

"Maybe. But the fact is, you trusted me, and I let you get hurt. Forgive me?"

"There's nothing to forgive, sir."

"Maybe," he repeated, and her heart broke at the pain in his voice. "Courage," he announced quietly, tapping a finger at the small of her back. "A spine of damn steel. You even take me on when it's needed, and I respect the hell out of that."

Returning to his place in front of her, he once again took her face in his hands. "And this face. God, I love this face. I don't know if I can live without waking up every day and seeing it."

She nearly shattered. As it was, she felt like she was made of glass, like a single word or a touch would splinter her into a million pieces. And she knew if it happened, she'd never be the same. Those pieces would never fit together exactly the way they had before.

Was that his intention? To break her?

And if he succeeded, would he be the one to put her back together? Would he even be able to?

Desperation filled her and she opened her mouth, her safe word trembling on her lips. She couldn't do this. Letting him punish her and pleasure her in front of a crowd was one thing. But this was stripping her down, baring not just her body but her soul. It was too much. How dare he expect this of her, after everything?

"Let me down. Please, sir, it's too much."

"It's not. I promised you a lesson, baby, and lessons are often hard and uncomfortable. And I'm afraid this one is about to get harder."

Again, he stepped away and disappeared behind her. Something long and thin tapped against her ass and she froze. "Sir?"

"I want this lesson to stick. Six of the best, kitten. You'll remember this lesson every time you sit for the next few days. And if I have to repeat it every time the welts fade, then that's what I'll do until you believe every word of it in your very bones."

It was all the warning he gave before a line of pure agony exploded across her skin. Deep, piercing pain took her breath away, robbing her of even the release of being able to scream.

"Oh, I forgot to mention how much I love your ass. I love the way it looks in those prim business suits you like to wear."

Another line of fire, just below the first. She managed a whimper this time, but the pressure in her chest was still unbearably tight.

"I love the way it dances under my palm when I'm spanking it."

Number three finally loosed a scream. "Sir! Please!"

"I really love the way it looks right now, so perfectly striped."

At number four she let out a quiet sob and he stepped forward to run the tips of his fingers lightly over the welts. "Are you starting to believe me, kitten? About how amazing you are?"

"Please stop. Please."

"No. I promised you six and that's what you'll get. Because when I tell you I'm going to do something, I damn well do it. You need to know that. You need to believe that."

There was something in his voice, an undertone that

bordered on desperate. But a fifth stripe tore her attention away from him, back to the pain that seemed to consume her.

"One more, kitten. You're taking this so well, baby. I'm so fucking proud of you."

And with number six, she shattered, just as she'd feared. The pressure in her chest exploded on a sob and in an instant he was there, stroking her, murmuring words of comfort she couldn't hear, but just the sound of his voice centered her, grounded her.

That quiet whirr filled her ears again, and she was slowly lowered to the ground. Gentle hands held her as another set, unfamiliar but just as gentle, tugged at the ropes encircling her wrists.

She nearly collapsed when she was freed, but her Sir caught her, steadied her as someone else draped a blanket around her shoulders. She whined when the soft fabric brushed against her ass, earning her a quiet chuckle.

"Let's get you to a cool down room and I'll rub some ointment on those welts. Come on, kitten."

Wordlessly, she let him escort her off the stage. Everything felt fuzzy, almost surreal as she was guided into a small room and gently lowered onto a soft leather couch. She was dimly aware of him talking to someone before she closed her eyes and surrendered to the darkness pulling at her.

CHAPTER 32

KATHERINE

When she opened her eyes again, she was cradled against him, her damp cheek pressed against his warm, bare chest. With a quiet sigh, she shifted, burrowing into his warmth.

"Hey there, sleepyhead. How are you feeling?"

Words felt beyond her at that moment, so she settled for shrugging a shoulder.

"Let's get some food and water into you, and then we can talk. Can you sit up for me, baby?"

She didn't want to, but she instinctively knew it wasn't really a request, so she pushed herself up, wincing when her welted ass pressed into the cushion. "Sore," she managed to mumble before he pressed an open bottle of water to her lips.

"Yeah, I bet you are. Here." Handing her the water, he shifted her to the side and went to work kneading the stiff muscles of her neck and shoulders. "Better?"

"Yes, sir."

"Good. There's a chocolate bar too, on the table there. You need to eat."

"Not hungry."

"Eat." There was a hint of warning in his voice, prompting her to lean over and grab the candy.

"Good girl," he murmured when she unwrapped it and took a bite.

Bit by bit, her system settled, and by the time the candy and water were gone, she felt slightly more human. The soreness in her arms and ass lingered, but nothing alarming, which she told him when he asked.

"Good." He placed a hand over the heart he'd drawn. "What about here?"

"Fine."

Liar.

"You do not want to lie to me right now, little girl."

Again, that warning note, sending a not entirely unpleasant shiver down her spine. "Sorry, sir."

"Tell me how you're feeling."

"Do I have to?"

"Yes. It's important."

Picking at the wrapper on the water bottle, she searched for the right words. "I feel...raw. And kind of empty. You know how when you carve a pumpkin, you scoop everything out and you have to scrape at the inside parts to make sure you got all the gross stuff?"

His chest vibrated with laughter. "Yeah."

"Like that."

"Good. That's what I was going for."

Tears sprang to her eyes and as much as she wanted to hate him just then, she found herself leaning into him for comfort. "So, what now?"

"I guess that depends on you."

"On me? How so?"

"I told you that if I couldn't change your mind tonight, I'd walk away for good. So, what's the verdict, kitten?"

Nestled against him, she considered her options. Was she

willing to put herself out there, risk further public ridicule, just to be with him? Was she strong enough for that?

Before she'd walked into Black Light earlier that night, she hadn't been sure. But then he'd broken her down, stripped her of all her defenses, her excuses. Still, she felt herself hesitating, holding back. "What about Chloe?"

"What about her?"

Twisting her head around, she looked up at him. "She basically told the entire world you were a monster. What if she doesn't go away? What if she just keeps coming after you?"

"Ah." A fierce smile curved his lips. "She won't be a problem. The Cartwright-Davidsons' lawyers are ruthless. Between them and the Hawk's lawyers, I don't think we'll have to worry about her bothering us ever again."

"Oh. Good." She hesitated a moment before blurting out what she really wanted to say. "I saw your press conference."

"Yeah?" For once, it was Austin's turn to sound unsure of himself. "What did you think?"

"Did you mean all those things you said about me?"

Lifting a hand to her cheek, he stroked the pad of his thumb over her cheekbone. "Every last word, baby. And if you come home, I swear I will spend every second of my life making sure you never doubt it again."

"Okay," she whispered breathlessly.

"Okay, what, Katherine?"

"I'd like to come home, sir. With you."

The blue of his eyes lit with happiness as he grinned down at her. "Really?"

"Yes. Even if that means being in the spotlight from time to time, I'll handle it. I shouldn't have to run and hide just because some morons with a computer don't think I'm skinny enough to fuck a baseball player."

"That's my girl. Come here, kitten."

Shifting to straddle him, she brushed a kiss over his lips. "Make love to me, sir. Please?"

Those strong, calloused hands ran up her sides to cup her breasts, rolling her nipples into hardened points until she whimpered with need.

"My beautiful kitten," he murmured, pinching the peaks just hard enough to send a zing of pleasure directly to her clit. "My beautiful, smart, strong girl. I love you."

"I love you, too, sir."

"On your back, kitten. I want to taste you."

Desperate for him, she scrambled off his lap, stretching out on the couch, completely exposed to his hungry gaze.

"You were such a good girl for me tonight." Shifting to kneel between her thighs, he pressed a kiss to her stomach. "Would you like your reward?"

"Yes, sir."

"Come as often as you want. You don't have to wait for permission."

"Yes, sir," she answered again with a grin.

He took his time with her, using his tongue and those clever fingers to push her straight over the edge of the first orgasm before she could blink. And when the shockwaves of pleasure had slowed, when he normally would have stopped and pulled away, he took her clit in his mouth and sucked hard enough to have her arching up off the cushions.

"Sir!"

"Again, kitten."

As usual, he got his way, ignoring her pleas for him to stop until they turned into demands for him to continue. Again, she shattered, everything in her turning liquid and molten as she collapsed under him.

And still, he didn't stop. Pleasure so sharp it bordered on pain lanced through her when he speared her with his fingers, stroking that sensitive spot inside of her as he continued to work her clit.

"Sir, please. I can't. It hurts!"

But her pleas fell on deaf ears. Fleetingly, she wondered if he meant to break her again, just as he had on stage. He was doing a damn good job of it, if that was his intent.

By the time he finished with her, every breath was a sob of desperation, and her throat was raw from screaming his name with each climax. And then he braced himself above her, entering her so slowly that she felt each torturous inch moving inside her swollen, abused pussy.

"Sir." The word was a sigh, torn from her lips as she arched under him, welcoming him.

Leaning down, he pressed a kiss to her right bicep, where *HOME* was still printed in his neat, bold lettering. His lips met hers, and they moved together until he reached his own peak, emptying himself into her.

She didn't know how long they lay there, wrapped in each other, but eventually a quiet knock interrupted their reverie.

"Hey guys," a male voice she couldn't quite place called out. "Sorry to interrupt, but we'll need the room soon."

"Five minutes," Austin called back.

"Fine. But not a second more," the voice shot back with obvious amusement.

"Wait here." Rolling off the couch, Austin bent and picked something up off the floor before returning to her.

"What are you doing?" she asked as he popped the top off the marker and dragged the cold, wet tip across her belly.

"You'll see."

The felt tickled her skin, which already felt impossibly sensitive, and she giggled. "Stop, it tickles!"

"Almost there, kitten."

Two more letters, from what she could tell, and he was done. "What does it say?"

Instead of answering, he climbed off the couch and pulled her to her feet, then placed her neat pile of clothes in her arms. "Go get cleaned up and meet me by the lockers. But no shower, you can do that at home."

"You want me to walk through the club naked?"

"Yes."

Could a person's whole body blush? Because if it could, she was certain hers was doing exactly that. "Can't I get dressed in here, sir?"

"You could. But is that what I asked you to do?"

"No, sir."

He dropped a kiss on her forehead, then turned her and sent her hurrying toward the side door with a sharp swat to her aching bottom. With one quick glare over her shoulder, she scooted out the door and made a beeline for the bathroom.

A wall of mirrors caught her attention when she burst through the doors and she slowed, curiosity edging out over the need to cover herself. Setting the clothes aside, she faced the mirrors and stared at her reflection.

Another round of tears filled her eyes, slipping silently down her cheeks as she lifted a hand and gently followed the outline of each letter with the tip of a trembling finger. The sound of the door swinging open jolted her out of her trance just as she finished the last letter. Snatching up her clothes, she ran for a stall and hurried into the body suit and heels, too impatient to fiddle with the stockings.

When she was done, she left out the side door and found her Sir waiting for her, with the Cartwright-Davidsons by his side. Ignoring them, she walked straight to him, wrapped a hand around the back of his neck, and yanked him to her for a hot, desperate kiss.

"Thank you," she said when they broke apart, pressing a hand to her stomach.

"I didn't say anything that wasn't true, kitten."

The sound of someone clearing their throat drew her attention to the trio beside him. Jaxson's smile was indulgent as he stepped forward and placed his hands on her shoulders. "That was a stunning scene, Ms. Callahan. It was a pleasure to watch."

"Ah, thank you, sir." Pleasure and embarrassment had heat rising to her cheeks at the compliment.

"You're welcome. If either of you need anything from us, please don't hesitate to call."

"Oh, I'm sure that won't be necessary, sir. But thank you."

Chase nudged his husband aside, openly ignoring the dangerous narrowing of Jaxson's eyes. "Look, sweetheart, you'll actually be doing us a favor. Dragging Jaxson away from work for more than five minutes pretty much takes an act of Congress these days, and we don't spend nearly enough time on the East Coast. So, help Emma and me out and call, okay?"

Laughing, she nodded. "Okay, okay. We'll call."

"My turn!" Emma pushed forward, throwing her arms around Kit's neck. "You were amazing! That caning looked like it hurt. How's your butt look?"

"I haven't checked yet but it hurts like hell."

With a loud, happy laugh, Emma pulled away, beaming. "I bet. You took it like a champ, though. Now," running her hands down Kit's arms, she grabbed her hands and squeezed. "You better listen to my men and call me whenever. And don't forget to have your admin set up a meeting to talk about those investments."

Without giving Kit a chance to agree or argue, she turned to Austin and drilled a finger into his chest. "And you, mister. You better treat my friend right, or you'll have me to answer to. And I have the means to make your life miserable, if I want to."

"Emma!" Jaxson's censure was somewhat ruined by the twitching of his lips.

"Sorry, sir." She didn't look remotely sorry, which made Kit giggle, earning her a mock-glare from her own sexy, dominant man.

"Your ass obviously doesn't hurt enough," Austin growled, pulling her into him. "Don't forget I still owe you for being late tonight, kitten."

"Yes, sir," she said, grinning up at him.

"Well." Jaxson clapped a hand on each of his spouses' necks, their eyes widening with excitement. "I'd like to get to the scene I have planned for my own naughty little subs. Apparently, I've been neglecting them. Austin, Kit. It was wonderful meeting you both."

As he led his stammering submissives away, Austin held out Kit's coat and helped her into it. "Ready to go home, kitten?"

"Hell, yes, sir."

Slipping her arm through his, she followed him out through the back entrance to the psychic shop. She didn't care that her hair was a disaster, her makeup ruined. Or that the summer breeze was playing with the hem of her coat, flashing bits of skin with each gust. Because nothing could strip her of who and what she was.

WORTHY.

∾

THANK you so much for reading **Black Light: Worthy**. We hope you enjoyed Austin and Kit's story, and would be eternally grateful if you would take a few minutes to leave a review.

The next Black Light book is **Black Light: Saved** by Raisa Greywood. Check out this juicy excerpt from her follow-up story to last year's roulette story!

Kacy

"So, Kentucky?" Jafari asked.

"Yeah."

Valentine Roulette seemed like a faded fantasy in the brassy light of early morning, yet her body reminded her of every moment, every scene. Tiny pulses of pain warmed her, both from the needle play on her abdomen and breasts, and the branded design on her thigh. The cane marks on her butt throbbed and would keep their scenes firmly in mind for miles.

Runway West disappeared in the side mirror of the Mercedes SUV she'd been unceremoniously dumped in, tied, and gagged like a prisoner. Kacy had expected to be taken straight to jail, and she'd more than earned a stint in a cell for trying to steal money from him. Instead, he was coming with her.

"And what shall we do when we get there?"

"Drink bourbon and kick some asses," she muttered, only half-kidding. The bottles wouldn't be stamped with a tax seal, but there was plenty of bourbon and rye to be had.

Jafari had a point about refusing to let her drive her own car. The ancient Ford probably wouldn't make it to Arizona, much less Kentucky. Aside from being loaded with all her worldly possessions, it leaked oil and she had to dump a bottle of transmission fluid into it at least twice a month. Worse, she still owed money on it.

Then again, it would fit perfectly in the sprawling metropolis of Boone Ridge, population eighty-one. The plush vehicle he was driving was worth easily three times the value of the singlewide trailer she'd grown up in. Probably closer to four. She closed her eyes, unwilling to think about it. How the hell was she supposed to introduce a man like Jafari to a place like that?

The thought of Jafari seeing her hometown made her want

to be sick, but she was too worried about Gran to protest. The only way Uncle Gerald could have gotten his filthy hands on Kacy's cousin Macie was if something had happened to her, but Kacy didn't dare call the lawyer back where Jafari could hear. She'd have to tell him everything eventually though.

"Bourbon?" He arched a brow, keeping his attention on the road. "I confess, I'm not much for spirits. Is there no wine?"

"Mad Dog 20/20 if you're feeling fancy." She straightened and laid a hand on his knee. "Look, I appreciate you wanting to help, but I'm just not sure it's going to work."

"I don't know what that is."

"What?"

"The Mad Dog you mentioned. What is it?"

"It's wine. Kind of."

"Kind of? It is or it isn't."

"It comes in a screw top bottle and people usually drink it from a brown paper bag." Knowing they were getting off topic, she said, "Look, if you're willing to loan me a few hundred dollars, I can take a Greyhound. You don't have to drive me all that way."

"There are some surprisingly decent wines that come in boxes. Perhaps I'll try it." He glanced at her out of the corner of his eye and winked. "Are you hungry? We have pastries in the back seat."

"Didn't you hear me? I asked—"

"I heard you. You needn't worry about money, but you are not taking a bus at all, much less for a trip of two thousand miles. You can either stop arguing, or you can enjoy this lovely road trip with a very sore bottom."

"Jafari, I…" Kacy shut her mouth, then looked out the window again. She had no doubt he'd pull over and spank her butt until she obeyed, and she didn't want to do it during Monday morning rush hour on a Los Angeles expressway. Thankfully, he probably didn't have another e-stim plug.

Then again... She pushed away the thought. Now was not the time to think about how amazing those electrical shocks on her most sensitive tissues had felt.

He took her hand, rubbing her knuckles gently. "What worries you so, little rabbit?"

"I... yellow."

"Very well." He drove in silence for several seconds, then said, "Kacy, I'm a patient man, but won't allow you to shut me out again. I'm willing to wait until we know each other better and you're more comfortable with me, but please do not use a safe word to avoid a conversation."

Shoulders hunching, she looked down at her hands, feeling like a heel. His disappointment hurt more than anything physical he might have done to her. "You're right, and I'm sorry, sir. I won't do it again."

Safe words weren't meant to be used so frivolously, but she didn't know how to tell him they were going to the literal armpit of Kentucky, so deep in the hills that daylight had to be imported. Worse, Kacy had no idea what she'd do about Macie when she could barely take care of herself.

"Don't make promises you can't keep," he replied, chuckling softly. "But I will give you until we stop for the night before I ask again."

"Yes, sir." She clenched her hands in her lap, trying not to think about it.

"Neither of us got breakfast, so let's find out what Jaxson organized for us."

"Is this his car?" she asked, stretching to reach the back seat. Her fingers brushed the box and she pulled it closer before managing to get her hand under it.

"Yes. I traded him a case of wine for it."

Setting the box in her lap, she opened it, revealing an assortment of fresh pastries. She gave them a doubtful look, then said, "Maybe we should stop somewhere to eat. I don't want to make a mess in his car. What if he—"

"I'll have it cleaned before I return it." He reached into the box and grabbed a pastry without looking, somehow managing to eat it without scattering crumbs everywhere, then touched his lips with the napkin she gave him.

Kacy wasn't very hungry, but maybe the small cherry Danish would settle her stomach. Trying her best to keep the mess contained, she finished it and wiped her hands.

"Do you want another?" she asked.

"No, thank you." He took a sip of his coffee, one hand lazily on the bottom of the steering wheel. "Tell me about yourself, little rabbit. I want to know everything you're willing to share with me."

Closing the box, she put it in the back seat, then drank her coffee. "Well, you already know I'm homeless. I'm not sure—"

"We'll discuss that later." He reached over the console and squeezed her hand. "That is a topic for when I have time to spank you for not asking for help."

"Hey! I was doing fine."

He turned his head to peer at her, his lips set in a frown. "Really?"

Even irritated, Jafari Laurent was the most beautiful man she'd ever seen. The short, grizzled stubble on his face was a bit thicker and longer than it had been last night, and he was impeccably dressed in a casual sweater and a pair of jeans. The only imperfection she could find was a single twisted loc that insisted on falling over his forehead, but it just made him sexier.

She looked like she was still doing the walk of shame in her consignment store dress and shoes. Her hair was a tangled halo around her head, sticking out in all directions because she hadn't taken the time to deal with it. Her makeup was gone and she wasn't even wearing panties or a bra under her short dress.

"Yes, I really was doing fine." She returned his glare with interest. "I had a car. I had friends who helped as much as they could, and I usually had enough to eat. Maybe I wasn't living in some palatial estate in Napa, but it could have been a lot worse."

"Very well. I will concede the point to you. However, you will allow me to help you find somewhere more suitable when we get home. Understood?"

For a moment, she considered unloading on him, but the dumbass idea went away before she could act on it. He was a dominant and could no more change his authoritative character than she could erase her tattoos.

∼

GRAB your copy of **Black Light: Saved** by Raisa Greywood. And make sure you are signed up on the Black Collar Press new release newsletter so you don't miss any Black Light releases!

ABOUT THE AUTHOR

Stella is a USA Today Bestselling author of romance featuring irresistibly sassy heroines and the strict, dominant men who try to tame them. Her favorite place to write is on her deck, with a glass of wine, enjoying her fabulous view of the countryside. Aside from reading and writing, Stella's favorite hobby is shopping. She is a fierce advocate for teaching women to love themselves, both in her writing and in the real world!

Keep up with Stella and stay up to date on new releases through the following social media links and Stella would love you to join her Facebook Group, Stella's Sassy Minxes:

https://www.facebook.com/groups/StellasSassyMinxes/

ALSO BY STELLA MOORE

Standalones

Cassandra's Curse

Daddy's Captive

Shape of Love Series

Daddy's Perfect Princess

Daddy's Way Series

Daddy's Way

Holidays at Rawhide Ranch

Hayleigh's Little Halloween

Missing Pieces Series

Finding Evie

Finding Forever

Smoky Mountain Series

Healing Hurts

Healing Divides

Healing Fears

GET A FREE BLACK LIGHT BOOK

Enjoy your trip to Black Light? There's a lot more sexy fun to be had. All of the books in the series can be read as standalone stories and can also be enjoyed in any reading order.

Get started with a FREE copy of **Black Light: Rocked** today. Your fun doesn't need to end yet!

BLACK COLLAR PRESS

Black Collar Press is a small publishing house started by authors Livia Grant and Jennifer Bene in late 2016. The purpose was simple - to create a place where the erotic, kinky, and exciting worlds they love to explore could thrive and be joined by other like-minded authors.

If this is something that interests you, please go to the Black Collar Press website and read through the FAQs. If your questions are not answered there, please contact us directly at: blackcollarpress@gmail.com

WHERE TO FIND BLACK COLLAR PRESS:

- Newsletter: http://bit.ly/2JY23Wi
- Website: http://www.blackcollarpress.com/
- Facebook: https://www.facebook.com/blackcollarpress/
- Twitter: https://twitter.com/BlackCollarPres
- Black Light East and West may be fictitious, but you can now join our very real Facebook Group for Black Light Fans - Black Light Central

BLACK LIGHT SERIES

Did you enjoy your visit to Black Light? Have you read the other books in the series? They can all be enjoyed as stand-alone books read in any order.

Season One

Infamous Love, A Black Light Prequel by Livia Grant
Black Light: Rocked by Livia Grant
Black Light: Exposed by Jennifer Bene
Black Light: Valentine Roulette by Various Authors
Black Light: Suspended by Maggie Ryan
Black Light: Cuffed by Measha Stone
Black Light: Rescued by Livia Grant

Season Two

Black Light: Roulette Redux by Various Authors
Complicated Love, A Black Light Novel by Livia Grant
Black Light: Suspicion by Measha Stone
Black Light: Obsessed by Dani René

Black Light: Fearless by Maren Smith
Black Light: Possession by LK Shaw

Season Three
Black Light: Celebrity Roulette by Various Authors
Black Light: Purged by Livia Grant
Black Light: Defended by Golden Angel
Black Light: Scandalized by Livia Grant
Black Light: Charmed by Jennifer Bene

Season Four
Black Light: Roulette War by Various Authors
Black Light: Brave by Maren Smith
Black Light: Unbound by Jennifer Bene and Lesley Clark
Black Light: Branded by Kay Elle Parker

Season Five
Black Light: Roulette Rematch by Various Authors
Black Light: Bred by Shane Starrett
Black Light: Wanted by Maren Smith
Black Light: Worthy by Stella Moore
Black Light: Saved by Raisa Greywood

Season Six
Black Light: The Menagerie by Maren Smith
Infamous Trio Boxed Set by Livia Grant
Black Light: Cured by Vivian Murdoch
Black Light: Disciplined by Livia Grant (Fall 2022)
Black Light: Protocol by Shane Starrett (Fall 2022)
Black Light: Secret by Samantha A. Cole (Fall 2022)
And many more planned!

Season Seven

Black Light: Gamble by Livia Grant (Early 2023)
Black Light: Roulette Finale by Various Authors (Coming Feb. 2023)